Best Wishes from
Sylvia!

ORPHA

CW00386449

DCI Forbes Thriller - 1

The heart of Derbyshire, England, connects four traumatised girls, a series of late night murders and an old mausoleum of a house – a house with a grim secret.

For Derbyshire Detective DCI Michael Forbes, these are the bones of a case which refuses to go away.

***

Notes

While the criminals and victims are the protagonists of many of my novels, I hope readers of the series will gradually come to know and love my dedicated team of detectives.

Leaburn, where my officers are based, is a small market town existing only in my imagination, located approximately fifteen miles from Buxton, Bakewell, Matlock and Ashbourne, close to the Staffordshire border in the southern quarter of the Peak District. Its nearest neighbour, to its north-west, is the small, picturesque village of Hartington, a real place known best for its production of stilton cheese.

***

This novel is entirely a work of fiction.

The names, characters, incidents, events or localities portrayed in this publication, other than those clearly in the public domain, are fictitious and are the work of the author's imagination. Any resemblance to actual persons, living or dead is entirely coincidental.

***

Dedicated to Kim and Herman – yesterday's shadows –
always missed.

***

Books in the same series by the same author

SERENE VALLEY KILL

MINE TO KILL

KILL FOR LUCK

Follow me on Facebook for news of my books at

fb.me/sylviamarsdenbooks

***

Sylvia Marsden was born in Mansfield, Nottinghamshire. She grew up in the Peak District of Derbyshire and always thinks of that area as home. She now spends much of the summer in a campervan touring Derbyshire with her husband and rescue greyhound – and of course her laptop.

*

Her novels are available in paperback from several Derbyshire bookshops and as e-books on Amazon kindle and kindle unlimited.

*

From the first disturbing paragraph through to the thrilling conclusion I was hooked. The characters are all very believable; the story gathers pace and is full of unseen plot twists.

Goodreads reviewer

*

Chapter 1

Prologue

'A woman's frailness belies her capacity to survive so much.'

The words were still ringing in her ears as she stepped from the shadows onto the glistening, Chesterfield pavement.

She'd timed her exit to perfection.

"Trade is slow tonight, don't you think? This weather must be keeping our punters indoors." She smiled at the startled, young, heavily made-up face. "I really admire your top. I wouldn't mind one like that. Where did you buy it from?"

She always used an open question. It never failed to draw them in.

"Do I know you?" Startled girl enquired.

"Probably not," she reached into her handbag and with an exaggerated flourish pulled out a small bunch of keys. "I move around quite a lot. I have a little van parked on the next street, with some big, comfy cushions in it. Do you fancy sharing a joint with me? I could do with a sit down and some female company."

She linked arms, partly to assist skinny girl on her ridiculously high heels, and partly to experience that first hit of cool flesh against her own.

She didn't have to be here. It would have been simple to have broken the chain, to have driven on into the night, to have left the only person she had any kind of feelings for – and all without ever looking back.

But then why should she when she'd come to appreciate the art of inflicting suffering on others?

It really was quite addictive.

Chapter 2

Verona and Anna

Verona eased herself along the edge of her only furniture, a double bed, following the last vestiges of warmth from the fading, afternoon sun before cold crept once more into her young bones. Four angry flies hammered against her window – the same four since early that morning.

There was to be no flight to freedom – not for any of them.

Finally, the smallest of the insects accepted the inevitable and began buzzing and tumbling its way towards the dirt floor to begin its slow, dusty, circles of death. She stood, walked to the window, picked up a damp, palm-sized pebble and ended its misery.

Even such brief moments of exertion were an effort these days. She rubbed the flat of her hands against her thighs in an attempt to ease the tiredness clawing at her limbs, and when that failed went on to grind her knuckles against her sore eyelids.

The days and months had long since run into each other and her memories were becoming sketchy.

"Am I fifteen yet, do you think?" she whispered to the three remaining insects.

The flies ignored her, but then, they always did.

She peered through the six, black-painted, metal bars, the cracked and dirt-streaked window, and across open grassland to where a line of red and golden trees signalled the beginning of her second winter of imprisonment.

Her window faced directly south, soaking up and magnifying the heat of the day but offering little protection from the cold after sunset. Throughout what seemed like the longest summer of her life, the stronger the sun had shone, the greater the number of flies she'd counted and the louder their buzzing had been. She'd learned to close her eyes, to allow the noise to fill her brain until it drove out all other thoughts, and to experience a strange floating sensation. It never lasted, but it did allow her a few precious moments of escape from her sore body.

Ignoring the burning in her leg muscles she forced herself upwards onto her toes, rested the bones of her pelvis against the concrete windowsill and watched the sun sink behind glowing trees. Her damp skin tingled against the cooling t-shirt and her stomach rumbled.

When her legs would take no more, she returned to the bed and perched on its edge, flinching at the all-too-familiar screech of metal from the rusty frame. She lay back, took a deep breath, pulled the rough, grey blanket around her shivering body and drew her knees up to her chest.

There was nothing to do now except wait.

A familiar flame of fear shot through her. She took a moment to compose herself and then opened her eyes and tried to swallow. Her mouth was too dry.

She didn't move. There was never any in point resisting. She'd quickly learned that lesson. The man looking down at her now, the one with the spider tattoos, had been to her room many times before, and although he wasn't one of the most brutal, he was probably the oldest and most definitely the heaviest.

She took a deep breath and forced a smile.

When he'd finished, after he'd patted the top of her head as if she'd been his favourite pet dog, he left the room without as much as a backward glance.

This was to be her life now until she too was ground into the dirt.

"You're an object to be used. Get used to it," she'd been ordered by more than one of the men.

Alone once more, every inch of her body prickled with mingled sweat. The damp blanket clung to her skin as she wrapped her arms around her knees and surrendered to the muscular spasms that she knew would last until, hopefully, she managed to fall asleep.

She'd learned to shut down some of her senses. She could even close out many of the things happening around her and inside her, almost pretending none of it was real, that is until she looked across at the cracked, stained toilet and the bucket of cold water in the corner, and at the frayed towel and bar of slimy soap.

Over those first degrading weeks she'd scrubbed her skin raw. She'd wondered what would happen if she stopped keeping herself clean, but knowing that it wouldn't be good, each time she'd forced her thoughts onto something else.

Sleep hadn't come when she heard the scrape of a key and the familiar rattle of plastic plates and plastic cutlery on a plastic tray. This was her second, and final, meal of the day. The food was rarely a surprise – they brought her biscuits and fruit each morning, and sandwiches and salad, or cold potatoes and vegetables with a little meat or fish, each night. It was the one thing that was a marginal improvement on her life back home.

And, she'd noticed, the meals were always brought in by one of the two slightly friendlier people.

Verona feigned sleep whenever it was the turn of the stooped, grey-haired woman. This lady would quietly talk to her, but only if she kept her eyes tightly closed. It didn't matter that she couldn't understand every single word – she was learning some English, repeating words and phrases out loud over and over again when alone. She also tried hard to remember the few phrases she'd learned from the older girls from her village back home, the ones whose parents had been wealthy enough to send them to the school, and who had sometimes spoken in English. She wished now she'd paid more attention.

Home, as she remembered it, had been a one-roomed mud and timber house with a cracked window that the winter winds had howled through. The floor, oddly similar to the one she had now, had consisted of dirt and rocks, complemented by the occasional luxury of an armful of damp and prickly straw that she'd used for stuffing underneath the goat pelt that had been her bed. She hadn't forgotten having hardly any food for days on end while her father had lain in a stupor in the corner. He'd worked in the vineyards, or in the winery, often away for days at a time and bringing full cartons and bottles home with him. Nor had she forgotten the two occasions when a tiny baby had appeared in her mother's bed. Both babies had cried, after which she'd been sent out for water only to return to see her mother crying alone in bed and her father with another full bottle in his hand.

The two women who'd come to her village that final, hot day had told of rich women in the towns who were looking for young girls to train as nannies. Together with her friend, Svetlana, she'd clambered into the back of a huge white van, giggling with excitement at the idea of setting off on an actual adventure. She hadn't realised the significance until much later, but her last memory of her father had been of him grinning wildly and holding a larger than normal wooden box in his dirt-ingrained arms.

She opened her eyes just enough to see the shaven-headed man bringing in her food – the man who always slammed the door shut behind him with his oversized left boot. He set the tray down and as always she felt his warm, sour breath on her face. She didn't flinch. Instead, she watched as he hobbled across her room to gaze for a minute through her window. She sometimes wondered if he might be a prisoner here too.

The food smelled good, cold sausage and chips, her favourite, but she stayed still and watched him moving away from the window and back to the door.

"I don't really like little girls." He was telling her yet again in the strange voice that didn't seem to fit his broad, male body. "It's such a shame you're not a little boy. They haven't brought me a little boy for absolutely ages. We could have had such fun together."

Then the door slammed shut, the room fell silent, and she reached down for the tray.

The last piece of meat rolled around her mouth when familiar footsteps echoed past her locked door. It wouldn't be long before she heard them returning. With the remaining few chips wedged inside her hollow cheeks, she stood up. Not eating everything or failing to place the tray beside her door would only mean another beating.

Gathering up the blanket, draping it over her head and shoulders and around her body, she crossed over to the window to squeeze her fingers between the bars and clear a circular hole in the condensation. The flies had all found somewhere else to spend the night but a cloudless, moonlit sky meant she might see rabbits skipping through the long grass.

The creatures, the closest things she had to friends, were oblivious to her, of course.

She gently rested her forehead against cold bars.

Had Svetlana also ended up in a room like this? A year younger and far less mature, it would be so much worse for her, assuming she was even still alive.

She brushed a trickle of icy moisture from her cheek. What would once have been a hot tear was now merely condensation.

She'd marked her first days, on the wall with a sharp stone, until there had become too many to count and then marked each full moon, remembering something her mother had told her about the thirteen moons of the year in her cosmic calendar. Eleven lines marked the soft stone, behind the mould and mildew, a few inches above the floor. Tonight she would mark the twelfth. She bent down and reached for the flat stone she'd hidden in some soft soil beneath her bed, but before her fingers could wrap around its sharp edges she heard the heavy footsteps.

*

Through two closed doors, inside the clean and brightly lit Hannage Brook Medical Centre in Wirksworth, Anna Jenkins could clearly hear every word her mother was yelling at the unfortunate doctor. Everyone in the waiting room could hear. Wedged into a plastic chair, between a teenage youth who jabbed at her ribs with his elbow every time he scratched at his stomach, and an old man whose breathing sounded as she imagined an orchestra would while in the process of tuning up, she was holding as still as she possibly could. One of the two smelled strongly of pee and she was afraid that, if she moved, so might they, and that then the stench might overpower everyone inside the centre.

It was a big responsibility – the others ought to be thanking her.

Moving only her eyes, she scanned the waiting room.

A couple of her fellow plastic chair occupants exchanged uncomfortable looks. Another, a braver one, looked in her direction and she mentally challenged him to hold her gaze for longer than a second. He failed. It was obvious they all believed it to be her fault – all the anguish they were hearing through the closed doors – all the torment that her mother was suffering. And who could blame them after everything they'd been forced to listen to over the previous minutes.

She smiled sweetly back at the elderly woman in the corner, and then at the young couple sitting by the door. Her mind was a puzzle for them for them to read... if they dared.

"But I've reached the point of complete... absolute... bloody exhaustion," her mother screeched out the words for the fourth time in as many minutes.

Anna smiled, but to herself this time. The louder her mother yelled the more chance she seemed to believe she had of convincing the doctor of the desperation of her plight. Each visit to The Centre had become only a slight variation on the previous one. It was all so boringly predictable.

Another few seconds of silence... Presumably the doctor was managing to squeeze in a few words.

Anna dropped her smile and began grating her teeth together.

"And I'm telling you, for the umpteenth time," her mother was back in full flow, "that you've still got the diagnosis of my daughter's mental illness completely wrong."

Anna couldn't help smiling at that one. 'Attention Deficit Hyperactivity Disorder' was the latest label they'd pinned onto her. From her view point, it was neither better nor worse than any of the others she'd been given, apart from the fact that the doctors had banned her from eating ice-cream, sugar, cheese, chocolate, frozen pizzas, chips, all fast foods, and of all things, swordfish. They'd also banned her from drinking fruit juice, coffee and pop. With a useless mother who never cooked anything from scratch, it was nothing short of a miracle that she was still alive. It had also meant different packets of little coloured tablets, but she'd become extremely adept at hiding them behind her back teeth, so that when asked, she could obligingly show anyone an empty mouth.

"She needs someone who actually knows what they're doing." The yelling had become a loud, ugly, sobbing sound. "Someone who can give us a correct diagnosis... and the right kind of help... please... you people are still... still not listening to me... we both need help."

Another minute of silence... apart from the musical man on her right...

Anna knew this latest doctor. He was a fairly young, softly-spoken man who looked as if he ought to be intimidated by her mother. Fortunately, he wasn't.

The surgery door swung open and her red-faced mother viewed the packed, but silent, waiting room. "But these latest drugs haven't helped at all. Look at her – she's still so bloody unpredictable. You should try living with her... "

Everyone in the immediate vicinity of Anna found a sudden need to examine the floor around their feet.

"Ms Jenkins... Rose... I told you only last week that there are no miracle cures." The doctor was calmly and skilfully shepherding her mother through the waiting room towards the swing-doors. "You have to give these new medications time to work. I'm quite sure that you'll see an improvement in her behaviour over the next few weeks, and if you don't, then I'll refer you both back to the consultant."

"An improvement... " Her mother screeched again.

Anna pursed her lips and began swinging her feet back and forth over her own little patch of tiled floor. She could so easily have mimed the words of the following few sentences.

"The only improvement I've seen in the three months I've been coming here is in your salaries. My daughter's violence is becoming progressively worse, and if you aren't prepared to act, then I hope you're at least prepared to live with the consequences!" With one last dramatic wave of her arms, Rose Jenkins slammed through the double doors and marched off towards the car park.

Anna knew her mother would be waiting there, glaring back at the buildings as if they were somehow to blame for all her woes. She could picture the pasty-faced woman, hands on hips and unimpressive breasts heaving in defiance at the injustice of it all.

She slowly counted to ten, as taught by one of the social workers as a way of controlling her temper. In actual fact, she'd found it a very useful tool for winding up her mother even more. She rose very slowly, smiled sweetly at the receptionist, who didn't look at all sure whether or not she ought to smile back, and then strolled out with her head held high and her chest pushed out. Let them look, she thought, defiantly.

Her mother's lips were moving, but at least she'd ceased that infuriating screeching. It promised to be a tense walk home, up the hill to the two-bedroomed flat on Malthouse Close, on the outskirts of Wirksworth, that they'd been moved to after residents on the Hurst Farm Estate in Matlock had complained once too often.

"You were such an affectionate baby," her mother reverted to her 'poor me' voice.

"Blah... blah... blah... I've heard it all before, but do carry on, mother dearest."

"Whatever did I do that was so wrong? Why me? Why should I have to contend with all of this? Why...? "

"It's nobody's fault," Anna shrugged, knowing her body language would infuriate her mother even more. "It's just who I am – take it or leave it."

"How can I, you stupid, stupid girl? Before you were eighteen months old you were causing chaos every time I took you out. How many toddlers do you think have ever been banned from three supermarkets? None of our neighbours had ever heard of such a thing. And that was only the beginning. How can I possibly take it or leave it? You're my daughter and that means that I'm stuck with you."

"Charming..." Anna pouted but turned her head away, determined not to let her mother see how her last remark had stung.

"Mrs Jones, our old neighbour, used to tell me how her daughter was almost as bad until she was nearly three. I don't think so! And the doctors faithfully promised me that you'd grow out of it. They were wrong! Not one of them has had to live through the shame of having their only child expelled from two primary schools before the age of nine, have they? No!"

"I keep trying to tell you that they don't understand me. I can't help feeling different to the other kids."

"Different... different...?" both volume and pitch were on the rise again, "that's some understatement, girl! Have you any idea of how it feels to have the neighbours shun you in the street? And stop swinging your arms about like some demented gorilla. Why couldn't you be a normal girl – a daughter I could be proud of?"

That was a question Anna had frequently asked herself. After much deliberation, she'd decided it had to be something her mother had caused. After all, she kept on reminding everyone of what a perfect baby her little Anna had been, so something must have happened to change that, something that nobody knew about. Maybe... just maybe... her mother had tried to poison her, or smother her, or perhaps she'd dropped her on her head and not taken her to a hospital.

And after all, her mother must have been a really irresponsible slut to have had a child at the age of thirteen with absolutely no idea of who the father might have been. And to top it all, with the numbers of men her mother had brought into their house over the years, what right did she have to tell her daughter to behave properly?

It couldn't possibly be Anna's own fault that she felt so angry and worthless, and so out of control sometimes. She was simply a traumatised, misunderstood, fifteen year old girl.

Chapter 3

Verona gripped the cover to her chin, tucked her bony elbows into her ribs and brought her knees up to her chest. As a defensive action it was pointless, but still she held the position for as long as she was able. The blanket jerked from her grasp and she opened her eyes to see one of her original captors. She straightened her legs but kept them pressed tightly together.

"Wash," fingers dug into the bones of her arm and she felt herself pulled from the bed and on to her feet in one easy movement. "Dirty little whore, wash…," he repeated, dragging the stained cover from her bed with his free hand.

The woman who sometimes brought in the food stood behind him clutching a large, battered, cardboard box, discomfort coming off her in waves. Verona was reminded of how her mother had looked when her father was drunk, her head always at that same low angle, avoiding eye contact and nervously glancing around.

Knowing she had no choice, she crossed to the bucket and allowed the pink nightdress to slide from her shoulders onto the floor. In her previous life, she'd only seen pictures of the things she had to wear now, and she'd imagined owning them, thinking how pretty they were. Next she tugged off the bed socks, a luxury she'd been allowed only after the windows had been covered with ice for several nights over the previous winter. Nudity meant nothing now. She soaped up the flannel and began scrubbing at her goose-pimpled arms and legs.

Instinctively she imitated the woman, holding her head at the same low angle and glancing across at the clean blankets. They meant only one thing. She glanced the opposite way, towards the dark-haired man leaning against her window sill, for barely a second. That was a mistake. His smile chilled her insides as his gaze moved slowly down her naked body towards the nightdress on the floor. In a moment of panic she bent to retrieve the garment, but with just four of his long strides he was standing up against her, smirking down at her pimpled breasts.

Her leg muscles shook. She squeezed the fabric against her stomach and concentrated on controlling her bladder. Then just as quickly, he laughed, took the nightdress from her and strode across the room to check on the progress of the bed. The clean blankets and the two children's books obviously met with his approval because, as usual after the bed had been changed, he delivered a well-aimed kick sending both woman and box through the open door together. Then he followed them out.

She pulled the bed socks back on before padding across the narrow strip of lino. She wouldn't be alone for long. The lemon coloured, perfumed nightdress told her that. And although the books were musty, she always welcomed them. They brought with them a smell from the outside world, and often they'd be left with her for several days.

The next visitor was going to be 'her special papa'. At least that's what he'd always called himself. Clean blankets and one or two books always arrived in advance of his visit. His 'special' way meant treating her like a child – an even younger child than she really was. He read to her, and tucked the blankets around her, before slowly removing his suit, and his shirt and tie and then climbing into her bed. Sometimes he even sang to her.

At least she had something to distract her mind while she waited.

The stooped woman had once told her they were in a country that she'd only ever heard of, and because of that, the books had given her a glimmer of hope. They were helping her learn more of the English language and, if she was ever to escape, that knowledge could be vital to her survival.

Great Britain is a good place, she remembered someone from her village telling her. *If you ever get the opportunity to go there, you must take it,* they'd said.

She'd studied her captors. The woman was usually unaccompanied, and the man with the withered foot and the sing-song voice always came alone. Those two appeared the weakest, but even if she got past either of them, she had no idea of what lay beyond the dark corridor.

Before breakfast, the man with the strange voice always came in saying the exact same thing. "Vitamin pills – take them now – they will keep you healthy." Then he'd hold out the pills and a large glass of watery juice.

The pills had increased from two to three, six moons ago, on the week that she'd begun bleeding. Her stomach had hurt so much that she'd cried until her ribs had ached, and for days she'd tried to prepare herself for the fact that she'd never see the outside world again. That was when the leaflet with the long words and the pictures of men and women had been pushed under her door. She still had it hidden away, in the driest area of soil beneath her bed.

With each fading moon she'd been growing weaker. What was there left to lose? If the tablets really were keeping her healthy, then why not just stop taking them, she'd reasoned. Trying to fool her captors wasn't much of a plan, but it was better than none.

They tasted terrible – she hadn't realised just how terrible until she'd begun putting her plan into action, holding the pills under her tongue until she was alone and then spitting them out and washing her mouth out with water from the bucket. If they really were keeping her healthy, then maybe not taking them would make her sick. Surely then, they might take her to see a doctor. They'd bought and paid for her after all, she was certain of that. She was their property and they wouldn't want to lose their investment... would they?

It felt scarily exciting, and it had to be worth a try. Loose dirt underneath her bed hid the evidence, and if she were to never get out alive then this would be her final act of defiance.

But maybe it was actually working – something was definitely happening to her. It was two moons since she'd last had a bleed and she felt overwhelmingly tired. And each morning of the previous week, her breakfast had come back up. But she couldn't let them see that she was being sick – not yet.

She rinsed the remains of her breakfast from her mouth. A day and a night had passed and the books were still with her. She opened the top one. "Little Red Riding Hood...," facing the window, reading the first page aloud slowly and deliberately, she let her mind drift to where she was standing among sweet-smelling pine trees.

Startled, she looked up and turned. At the foot of her bed, staring at her and smiling, was her 'special' customer.

Her heart thumped loudly – he must surely hear it.

Neither moved... had he become one of those ghosts her father had told her about when he'd been trying to frighten her?

But he was stepping towards her. He was real, and he looked different somehow. He wore different clothes – the suit replaced by jeans and a dirty-looking jumper. She barely stopped herself vomiting onto his polished, brown shoes.

She flinched as he stroked her hair, brushed her cheek with the back of his hand, and then kissed her on her forehead. The first two were a normal part of his ritual but he'd never kissed her there before. He looked almost tearful.

"My beautiful baby girl, let's read one last story together," he crooned. "Whatever shall I do without you?"

She blinked at him. Had she understood correctly?

Please God, let it be true, she wanted to blurt out but daren't. Either he's going away somewhere, or please... please... please... let it mean that I'm getting out of here.

The words on the pages rolled into each other as he read them, and when he closed the book she saw the faintest of smiles on his sad face.

Despite her revulsion, she let the corners of her mouth twitch upwards for a second.

Only then did she look past him and see the coil of blue rope beside her door.

*

"Anna Jenkins, fifteen years on this earth and still behaving like a spoilt two-year old, how do you ever expect anyone to treat you normally, let alone love you when you behave like this?"

Anna's crime today was her refusal to eat her dinner. Tuesday was usually the day for beans on toast, but for once her mother had actually cooked something, and it smelt decidedly funny. She was determined not to leave the table until she'd been given something straight out of a tin – even if it was classed as the forbidden 'fast food'.

A row had simmered along since their last visit to the doctors four days earlier, and Anna was now more convinced than ever that the blame for her troubles lay squarely with her toxic mother.

"You do realise I could have you committed," her mother rambled on. "The doctor explained to me that it was always an option. Then without me, where would you be?"

It seemed a really stupid question. She'd no idea where the nearest loony bin was. And what's more, she'd no intentions of finding out. "Really...?" Anna laid on the sarcasm. "Well how should I know, and how much worse could it be than this? What kind of a mother would feed her only child with this muck?" She couldn't stop herself pushing the plate of food across the table with such force it crashed to the floor. Then she reached for the glass of tepid water. That flew across the room with an unaccustomed, deadly accuracy. "I hate you!"

Anna watched in fascination as her mother reeled backwards against the kitchen door, both hands clutching her face and blood seeping between her fingers. She wasn't feeling sorry – not in the least. "Poor Rose Jenkins," she spat. "I can just hear them all saying – she has such a troublesome daughter – it must be so awful for her. Oh yes mother, I've heard the mutterings. But one day I'll show them. You wait and see, mother dearest. You see if I don't. I'll show them all what it's like to be me."

"You need help..." Her mother reached for a tee-towel and Anna smiled as she realised the glass had been a direct hit on the bridge of her nose.

"You think...?"

"Please, just try to calm down."

But Anna's fury wasn't ready to subside. "If you hadn't been such a slapper," this was one of her favourites, "I'd be more like the other girls, with a real father I could have gone to live with instead of being stuck here in this dump with you. Whoever he is, he couldn't possibly be worse at parenting than you."

Using her non-existent father to wind her mother up was a regular occurrence, but she felt his absence as keenly as if he'd been a part of her life and only recently walked out. That's what her school friend Donna's dad had done, and two years on, Donna still hadn't got over her loss.

"Your father used me – you know that. I was very young. I was a teenage victim. He didn't give me his real name, and for all I know your mental problems are all inherited from his family."

Knowing those facts only made Anna feel worse. "Well maybe my father was also sick, and maybe we could have helped each other." Maybe… maybe… she stared down at the broken glass. "Oh, what's the point?" The mist was clearing. She turned to go to her room, leaving her mother to clean up.

It was half-term, but none of her classmates from Anthony Gell School had invited her round to any of their houses. She got up from her bed, walked to her bedroom door and opened it.

The small estate in Wirksworth was nothing like the larger one they'd been moved from in Matlock. The people were the same, most of them looking down their noses at her, but with less than a minute's walking she could be on the High Peak Trail and out of the sight of any of them.

She stepped through the gap in the wall and decided to turn left, not fancying the alternative walk to the right today, up the steep incline. Fifty yards on, she came to the Steeple Grange Railway, an eighteen inch narrow gauge railway which had been reopened by local railway enthusiasts a few years earlier and which she had yet to experience. She'd spoken to the staff and volunteers who ran it, and been intrigued to learn that the reopened section had been laid on part of the trackbed named Killers' Branch.

Her intrigue hadn't lasted long – apparently in days gone by the Hopton Wood and Middleton stone quarries, which were served by this particular line, were owned by the Killer brothers who had paid for this branch to be built off the main Cromford and High Peak Railway.

Mid-week, no one was about, either on the railway or the trail. Happy to be anywhere other than home, she strolled along the metalled track. To her left were fields containing a couple of miserable-looking horses, and to her right were fenced-in back gardens with bushes and trees which absorbed the mechanical rumbling sounds of the cars and lorries.

When she reached the bridge over the main road she peered over the stone wall. Behind her the hill tipped down into Wirksworth, and in front of her was the steep descent into Cromford, where she assumed the residents must live in constant fear of one of the hundreds of stone-laden lorries from the quarries ploughing into their properties. A crash barrier could only stop so much, she would have thought.

She wandered on without meeting anyone, but stopped short of the Black Rocks Car Park, turned and began very slowly walking home.

The smell of freshly cooked fish and chips, one of her forbidden foods, met her as she walked through the door. It was her mother's normal way of breaking the deadlock after a major row, and it always worked.

Rose Jenkins gestured towards the sofa and Anna looked at the pine coffee table. It was crammed full. Grease seeped through the steaming paper parcel, and at the centre of the table were slices of white bread and butter, a plastic salt pot and a bottle of vinegar, and Anna's favourite accompaniment, sliced, sweetened, pickled beetroot. On the shelf below she saw a supermarket, 'reduced to clear' chocolate cake, and two small plates.

Next she looked at her mother's lined face and the plaster on her nose. "Thank you... I'm really sorry...."

Her mother looked at her for a moment with serious blue eyes, then forced a smile and sat down in the armchair opposite the television.

Neither of them could ever have been described as overweight. One portion of fish and chips between them was all they could usually afford, and she was looking forward to her half of the chocolate cake once the chip papers had been cleared away. She wasn't intending to leave as much as a crumb.

"I'll clear the table, mum, and take out the rubbish. And if you wash up, I'll dry." It wasn't much of a gesture; there were only two forks, two knives and three plates, but nevertheless she felt obliged to make it. It was so long since she'd tasted chocolate cake, and it looked so tempting, she could hardly wait to savour it.

Rose Jenkins placed the dry cutlery into the drawer before she remembered the cake. She almost wrapped her fingers around the wooden handle of her sharpest knife.

It was only one moment of hesitation, but Anna had noticed. Their eyes locked for a second and Anna watched her mother deliberately select a different knife.

They returned to the living room together in an awkward silence.

The television program had changed. She heard laughter, lots of it, saw tear-stained faces, and grown-ups with youngsters all accepting hugs and kisses from long lost family members. She'd no idea what the background music might have been, but it had obviously deliberately been chosen to stir the emotions of the viewers.

Anna wasn't sure what happened next. Someone had screamed — it may even have been her. She remembered sitting on the floor and looking around. Cushions were shredded and the sofa bore a gaping hole. She saw metal springs and masses of yellow foam. But the chocolate cake tasted so good. It was only good manners to offer some to the doctor and the two nice police women, but they all declined, and her mother certainly didn't look as if she wanted to share. She cut herself another slice.

"I warned you, didn't I?" Her mother was sobbing to the doctor. "She's totally out of control. I warned you that something like this was bound to happen. I really thought she was going to kill me. Well I won't be terrorised in my own home any longer, and I refuse to be bullied by those social workers... this time I'm never taking her back... never... !"

Anna broke off a large chunk of the chocolate icing and stuffed the whole piece into her mouth. She wasn't normally allowed chocolate.

"Look at her," her mother was screeching again. "She's underage and unstable; totally unstable! The state will have to take care of her. God knows, I've tried my best, but I can't do it any longer... I really can't."

*

After the hospital had stitched and dressed her cuts, and she'd been assured that her daughter would not be released in the foreseeable future, Rose Jenkins caught a bus home.

As the light faded and a soft autumn rain dusted the living room windows, Rose returned her vacuum cleaner to its home underneath the stairs, threw an old duvet over what was left of her sofa, and settled into her armchair with a mug of strong tea. Her overpowering sense of relief didn't feel even remotely wrong. There was no more fear, no anguish, and no sorrow left inside her. It had all been released in those few crazy, terrifying minutes that afternoon. No more wedging a chair against her bedroom door at night, or leaving the bedroom window unlatched; just in case. Only the smell of chocolate remained. Tea didn't seem appropriate somehow. The corner shop would still be open, and for the first time in years she wouldn't have to sneak her alcohol into the house. To hell with what the neighbours were saying, she was going to sit here alone, watch whatever rubbish came onto her television screen, and then fall asleep in her chair with an empty bottle at her side and a glass in her hand.

Chapter 4
Maisie and Carol

The raven-haired social worker leaned across the duty nurse's desk and whispered. "Those two have given the phrase *'double trouble'* a whole new meaning to me this afternoon. I've finally got them quietened down but they're both still wide awake. It's been one hell of a long day!"

"You know that it isn't their fault," the nurse snapped back, "and if their foster parents, Mr and Mrs Stevens, hadn't been away on holiday then the twins would have gone straight to their house, whatever the hour. The girls feel safe there, but in the middle of the night where else could they have gone? You'd play up a bit if you'd had to cope with the kind of family life that they've had. They're sweet girls underneath." She wondered if perhaps she'd been a little over-sensitive, but she'd known the family for an awful lot longer than this woman had. "They're teenagers, and you only see them at their worst," she added with a forced smile. "Just give them a chance to settle and you'll be surprised at the change in them."

"I'm sure you're right," the smile was grudgingly returned. "My motherly instinct is at an all-time low after the day I've had. I'll go and say goodnight to them and be back in the morning to see how they are. Hopefully by then we'll have found out when Mr and Mrs Stevens are expected home."

Maisie and Carol Evans were separated by just ten minutes, Maisie being the eldest and the most confident. They were identical in every external detail, and had realised early on just how much trouble their similarity could cause to the adults who were frequently called upon to take care of them.

Their mother, Sophie Evans, had struggled. She'd done her level best to stay away from the hard liquor while she'd been pregnant, and a ten week stay in hospital had undoubtedly saved them, but since their difficult birth it had been a downward spiral for Sophie.

They'd been frail two year old toddlers when first brought to the attention of social services and placed into temporary foster care.

"They're like two little china dolls," Mrs Stevens had exclaimed when she'd first been introduced to them. "Of course we'll take care of them, we'd be honoured."

Since then they'd been allocated their own bedrooms in the foster house, rooms permanently aired and filled with games and books, and ready for use at a moment's notice.

Their foster carers, Craig and Josie Stevens, owned one of the Victorian, sandstone, three-bedroomed cottages on the edge of the market town of Bakewell. They had a five-year old, black and white cocker spaniel called Judy, and until they'd decided to try fostering, dogs had been a substitute for the family they'd failed to conceive.

When Craig's redundancy had forced them to reconsider their lifestyle, fostering had seemed a natural progression and the twins had been welcomed into their home. At whatever time their phone rang, Craig and Josie would jump into their car on another rescue mission.

But on this occasion the couple were on a well-earned holiday, so in the middle of the night the girls had found themselves dumped into a hospital ward which was designed for small children, with just two other occupied beds.

"Promise me," Carol whispered across to the adjacent bed, "that neither of us will ever become as fat as that social worker." They giggled as they looked through the frosted glass partitions at the silhouette swaying back down the corridor.

"You don't eat enough to ever get fat. Besides, we made a solemn pact – remember – we're going to be nothing like our mother, and always look out for each other. We're going to be slim, sexy, and above all, sober. And no one is ever going to come between us."

"We did do the right thing, didn't we, phoning for help this afternoon?" Carol whispered.

"What choice did our mother give us? She wouldn't get up off the kitchen floor, and if old Mrs nosey-parker Sheridan had looked in through the kitchen window like she sometimes does, she'd have called the police again. And the last time that happened we spent three hours in the police station."

"I suppose so. And they won't keep mum in hospital for long, will they? They never do."

"They kept her in a lot longer the last time, remember? And she still looked awful when she came out. Her skin was all yellow and she kept on being sick," Maisie whispered. "She's in the best place now, everyone said so."

It was all very well Maisie taking charge and phoning for the ambulance, but Carol had seen her sister stealing the vodka from the corner shop on their way home from school the previous afternoon. And Maisie was unaware that Carol had seen her placing the bottle under the sink where she knew their mother would easily find it. But she hadn't said anything because she understood why her twin had done that. When she was really, really bad, their mum would beg in the streets for alcohol. It was so embarrassing.

Carol closed her eyes but couldn't sleep. "I think this is the same ward as last time," she whispered into the shadows.

"My pneumonia was worse than yours. I don't really remember much."

"You must do. That's the same nurse. She lives on the next block from us and she's friends with mum. I heard them talking only last week. She was telling mum about liver disease and it sounded really gruesome stuff. I don't think I'd like to become a nurse."

Maisie swung her legs out, tip toed over to her sister's bed and pulled the sheets back. "Budge up," she whispered; forcing her sister to wriggle across and then folding the sheets back over them both. "Mum's proper poorly this time. I'm scared we won't see her again."

"I know. I'm scared too. I wonder whether Craig and Josie will take us in permanently. I really, really wish I hadn't broken that vase the last time we were there. It belonged to Josie's gran and Craig was furious with me. I didn't mean to do it. I just caught it with my sleeve when I was dusting."

"Shut up you two!" A gruff, but definitely female voice came from the mound of covers opposite.

The twins raised their heads and peered into the darkness. Nothing looked to be moving.

"We'd better get some sleep," Carol whispered. She turned her back on Maisie and felt a cool, slim arm being wrapped around her waist. It was a long time since they'd slept together this way.

"So... how come you two arrived in the middle of the night, waking everyone up?"

The twins blinked their eyes open. A tangled mass of mouse-coloured curls framed the freckled young face barely six inches from theirs.

"Come on," the mop-headed girl insisted, "I do love a good story. Did someone creep into your house and attack your parents while they were asleep? I heard you last night, saying that your mum might be dying." She wriggled on the bed, a few inches from Maisie's face, pinning Maisie between her and Carol. "Tell Aunty Anna everything before the nurse comes in."

"Don't be so horrible," Maisie inched herself up the bed to put some slight distance between her and the piercing eyes. Then she shifted onto one elbow and peered down at Carol. Her twin's face looked red and puffy. "Our mum's sick and there was nowhere else for us to go at that time of night. We've got regular foster carers. They're on holiday but they'll come for us just as soon as they know what's happening."

"So... what about your dad – has he been murdered?"

"Stop it.... You're being mean. He left mum when we were three months old. We've no idea where he is."

"That's a bit of an anti-climax. I do love a good murder story. I haven't got a clue about my dad, and my mum's a proper head-case. I think she's been trying to slowly poison me. She tells everyone that I'm a fruit-loop and that's why I'm in here now; for an assessment, but I know it's her fault because I always get better when I'm away from her. I wish she'd get properly sick and die and then I know that I'd get treated better. Everyone feels sorry for an orphan, don't they?"

Carol wiped her eyes on the sheets and stared at the tousled mess. "I like your curls." It was the only thing she could think of at that moment. "How long have you been in here?"

"Nearly a week because my slapper of a mother says she's too frightened to ever let me back into the house. And with the lies she spins to the social, no foster carers would ever dare to take me on. I don't think they know what to do with me because I keep telling them that *'mother dearest'* is the one who needs the psychiatric help, not me." She grinned at them.

"Is your mum a junkie?" Maisie was beginning to like this forthright girl.

"No, worse luck; it's me who has to keep taking the tablets. Actually, they all think I take them but I manage to spit most of them out when they're not looking. My mother sometimes does drugs, but she drinks vodka every day. She hides the bottles and thinks I don't know. Is yours a junkie?"

"No, an alcoholic, and she was even before we were born. The doctors all said we were lucky not to have been damaged inside her. I think we must have been responsible for the only time she'd been sober for longer than one day since she'd been in her teens."

"Don't talk about her in the past tense," Carol wriggled herself up the bed.

"Sorry… but you know what I mean." Maisie touched her twin's hand.

"It's all right… she's going to be fine… I just know it."

Carol took her first full look into the piercing eyes. "So what's your name and how old are you?"

"Anna Jenkins aged fifteen, pleased to meet you and forever at your service. You see," she laughed, "I can be quite charming when I set my mind to it. And you are obviously twins, so what, pretty maidens, are your names? And how the bloody hell does anyone tell you apart?"

"Maisie Evans aged fifteen."

"Carol Evans aged fifteen. We're charmed to meet you, Anna Jenkins." They all laughed and the twins noticed the covers on the forth bed move slightly.

"Who's that?"

"What's wrong with her?"

"I dunno," Anna stuck her head forward and peered at the mound. "She came into this ward yesterday but the nurses won't tell me anything. She's been here longer than me, but in the side ward with loads of coppers milling around her. I thought she must be a murderer at the very least, but they wouldn't put her in here with me if she was... would they?"

"Well... you did say they didn't know what to do with you," Maisie giggled. "It could be one way of quietly getting rid of you."

"Yeah... yeah... very funny, but there's no way I'm ever going quietly." Anna sat up straight. "And if you think I'm a bit strange, just wait till you see her. I haven't heard her speak much but she's definitely foreign. She just keeps on being sick. It's gross. It can't be anything contagious or they wouldn't have placed her in here with... hmm... perhaps you're right after all." She smirked at the twins. "But if I catch it, I'll make sure you both go down with the bug as well. Now watch this."

Anna's hard-soled slippers clonked over to the corner bed and she leaned over the mound, just as she'd done with the twins.

"Weirdo," Maisie mouthed to her twin.

"I like her," Carol mouthed back.

"Hey, missy...," Anna addressed the pillow end of the small mound. "What are you doing here? Don't you have a name? Wake up, we've got guests." Nothing moved. Anna straightened up, turned to the twins and smiled, then held out her index finger. One sharp prod of the covers rewarded her with an immediate response. A young girl in a whirl of blue fabric leapt from underneath the covers, stumbled against the wall, and then ran to the bathroom.

The cotton garment hung like an oversized tent over what they could see of her skeletal frame.

"See what I mean," Anna shrugged her shoulders and walked back to the twins. "She doesn't speak. She can, but she doesn't. Now… wait for it… any second now."

As if on cue, the noises from the bathroom were unmistakable.

"Gross," Maisie agreed.

The three sat in silence for a full five minutes, watching the bathroom door. The twins flinched when they saw the swollen and reddened eyes of the girl's grey face, lips devoid of any colour and the bones of her jaws and cheeks looking as if they might poke out through her skin at any moment. The apparition climbed back into bed, pulled the covers over her bony legs and reached for a glass of water, all without looking up.

Anna was unimpressed. "I've seen people like you in the crazy ward. What's happened to you? Aren't you going to tell us who are you?"

The girl finished her water and, still without looking up, whispered, "I called Verona. No other name. Your people ask me, but I never have one."

Anna beckoned the twins to follow her. It was the first response that she'd had from the girl and she had to have a closer look.

"You must have," Anna insisted as she plonked herself onto Verona's bed. "Have you got amnesia? You must have a mother, at least. What's her name?"

"Mother and father in Moldova… have older brother… mother had babies… I don't know… they sold me… I think, how you say… maybe? Police, they ask again and again, I don't know. Have you been sold also?"

"See… I told you so," Anna exclaimed to the twins, "she's loopier than I am!"

The girl's eyes widened even more. "What is loopier?" She looked past Anna to the twins.

"It's all right," Maisie reached out and touched the girl's shoulder. "She means strange, silly, and a bit odd, but it's fine to be a bit odd in this place." She gave Anna a wink. "So how come you're in here and why have the police been hanging around? What have you done?"

By the time Verona was half way through telling her story, in her own limited words, her audience of three had all reached for the tissues.

"You must have thought they were going to finish you off," Anna reached for the girl's hand. It felt cold.

"Yes, I know them going to kill me. Man and woman tied me. Put me in back of van and drive. I roll about, very scared, not to move and not to make noise, the woman say. I don't know how long. I had felt poorly for many days, many weeks. I wanted doctor but I know that they not taking me there. The man who reads stories and the food lady, they in front of van and no one else I can see. Stop van and man lifts me out. Trees, like at home, very big trees and no paths. He carries me a long way, keep falling, keep dropping me, put me on ground, take hammer out of coat and hit me on head." She pointed to the dressing over her right eye.

"Why aren't you dead?" Carol gasped.

"I know... I think dead... must be. I look into man's eyes before he hit me and he not like that. When he hit down he close his eyes. Hammer hurt, but not dead. I close eyes and in my head I ask my mama to help me. I think him to hit me again, but he did not. I hear him walk away and woman comes to look at me. I try to look dead but I too scared to not shake. I hear man shout, 'Is she dead?' Then woman look at me and shout to him. 'Yes, she is dead.' She put little knife into my hand, push me so I roll down bank, and she walk away. I hear van go and open little knife. Ropes very hard to cut, took long time and fingers hurt and bleed but I do it."

None of them heard the nurse coming in.

"Come along now girls, back to your beds, this isn't a social club. Verona, how are you this morning, are you still being sick?"

"Yes... miss... " her voice trembled.

"I'll bring you something for that in a moment. Now you three don't badger the poor girl. She needs rest."

"Everyone is being so kind. No one has ever been kind like this to me. I had friend..." her voice faded to a whisper. "Svetlana is her name and we both sold together. We both in England, I think, but then she go somewhere else. I do not know. I have not seen her since before the room. She is younger than me, one year, and I am frightened she is dead. She is very, very nice girl, and best friend. Police, they say they look for her, but I do not know."

The twins, back to sharing one bed, watched Anna who had refused to budge and was still sitting on the edge of the strange girl's bed.

"The police in this country are very good." Maisie tried to sound convincing. "She may still be alive, and if she is then they'll find her. So tell us, how did you get from the woods to here? You must have been terrified."

"I walked and I walked, one day and one night. I only have socks, no shoes, and feet cut. It is so cold at night. I keep trying to walk to keep warm. I only have nightdress so I find big leaves to put over me when I stop. One time I find ants, I have bites. Not frightened of animals, very frightened of people, but I was so hungry and when it is light, I hear voices. I hear ladies voices so I lie down and dog runs to me, friendly dog, and black and white with big fluffy tail. Then I hear shouts, "Kim... Kim... where is Kim?" and dog runs away. I cry and cry and then dog come back and lie down with me and lick my face. Then two women find me. I try to run away, but I fall. They wrap me in coat and carry me to car, wrap dog blanket around me also and take me to your police. Everyone is so kind now. Everyone listens to my story and everyone cries. I stop crying now. I feel safe, but still sick sometimes."

Chapter 5
Twenty-nine years earlier.
Mark and Katy.

Mark's wife, Katy, stifled a scream. Another tree branch clattered across the car's windscreen, but by some miracle, the glass held. Mark, a roofer by trade, by virtue of the hurricane-force winds had been confined to their cottage in Pilsbury with his new wife for the past week and food had been running low. When the weather looked as if it might be easing slightly, they'd grabbed their coats and set off to do the weekly shop. On reaching the A515, the main Buxton to Ashbourne road, because of a traffic incident to their north, Bakewell had been the nearest town in which to restock their empty fridge.

Two hours later, with the boot of their Ford Mondeo crammed full with boxes of food, and after passing through the narrow streets of the limestone village of Youlgreave, the storm had suddenly picked up its violent pace once more.

Mark fought with the steering wheel to avoid one fallen branch after another.

Their only option was to keep moving forward, along the tree-lined road which passed the calcite mines of Long Rake and back across the A515.

Katy's hands gripped her seatbelt while her blue eyes, wide with fear, stared upwards at swaying branches. "How is it possible," she shouted over the roar of the wind, "for trees to bend that far without breaking off or blowing over?"

"It must be one of those freak tornadoes," Mark yelled back. "We've got caught in the wrong place at the wrong time. With any luck it won't last much longer... hold on!"

Katy's head jolted forwards and then smartly back. She felt pains shooting through her shoulder as the seatbelt bit into it.

"Are you all right?" Mark yelled. "I saw it falling and thought we could get past, but I bottled it."

"I'm not hurt, but the road's blocked and we can't turn here, the road's far too narrow and that grass verge will be soft after so much rain. We can't risk getting stuck here."

"I'll back up. That last passing place might be wide enough to make a turn." The Mondeo was in reverse before he'd finished speaking and its tyres screamed back at the trees.

Katy instinctively raised her arms as another branch bounced off the car bonnet. She felt an overload of adrenalin transforming fear into claustrophobia. Her body screamed to get out and run for her life, but she had to trust in Mark's skill as a driver. "There's a house to the left, I caught a glimpse of it through the trees. It might be in a clearing."

"It looks like our only option," Mark yelled, forcing their battered car further back over the rough carpet of leaves and branches.

The sign was partly obscured by another fallen branch, but as they drew level with it Katy read out loud, "Woodbine Cottage... I think that's what it's called."

The narrow driveway appeared almost as impassable as the road. All around them huge trees were being uprooted, the noise of them crashing to the ground masked by the roar of the wind. As fast as he dared, Mark forced the Mondeo over shattered brown limbs until finally the desperately-needed clearing opened up in front of them. He relaxed his grip on the steering wheel very slightly.

Katy hadn't pictured a country cottage with shutters on the windows and a well-tended rose garden, but neither had she expected to see something that would have looked perfectly at home in an old black and white horror movie.

The car was undoubtedly dented, they were in the middle of the most terrifying storm of their lives and now they were facing this austere-looking building. How much worse was this day going to get?

A feeble light flickered in one of the ground floor windows, suggesting the property's electricity had been taken down by falling trees. Instead of a welcoming refuge, the place felt almost institutional with its dark windows, and even the front door, all painted black. The huge property had been built out of dark gritstone with even the roof covered in black slates. The windows looked out of proportion, far too small, yet each further divided into square panes, giving the overall impression of the building actually being an enormous cage. In fact everything about it looked intimidating, and totally out of place, on the edge of Middleton Moor, little more than a mile from the famous Arbor Low Neolithic and Bronze Age Henge, in an area dotted by limestone farms and cottages. Then she saw what she thought must have subconsciously added to her foreboding. The windows along the top floor were all behind black bars.

Over the roar of the wind came repetitive, metallic-sounding crashes from corrugated iron sheets flapping against the timbers of dilapidated sheds.

Mark steered their car into the centre of a gravelled courtyard. "As long as none of those roof sheets blow off, this looks like the safest place to be. I'll park here where the owners of the cottage can see us." Mark released the steering wheel and flexed his fingers. "We don't want to alarm these people."

Katy stared at him. If anyone was alarmed right now, it was her, and not the people safely tucked up in this monstrous place. It must have been a farm at some time, she thought, the sheds and barns being too large and too numerous for any ordinary domestic dwelling. Nothing about it appeared right in any way shape or form. "This isn't what I would have called a cottage," she said. "It looks more like a mausoleum."

"We'll sit tight and hope for the best," Mark was being forced to raise his voice again. "If we try to open the doors now the wind will rip them off their hinges. If it is a tornado it should soon move away. Is there any chocolate left in the glove box?"

"Shouldn't we save it for later?" Katy fingered the remaining half of the large bar of choc mint chip. She didn't feel much like eating and didn't know why Mark could think of food at such a time.

"What… ration it? I don't plan on sitting here that long, sweetheart. Even if both roads out of here are blocked, we can walk out just as soon as this wind dies down, and come back for the car later."

"I never realised this place was so huge," Katy's attention was back on the building. "We've used this road before, and I knew someone lived here, I've seen the dustbins, but I never expected this."

"It looks as though the storm's knocked out their power supply. I hope they're all right."

They stared at each other and both realised he'd stopped shouting. The trees shuddered, and then were still. Katy grabbed his hand and they sat, both holding their breath, both now looking straight ahead, bracing themselves, but there was only silence.

"Either we're in the eye of a tornado, or the storm's passed over. I'd better go over to make sure everyone in the house is safe. It might be one old lady living here alone."

"In a house this size…?" Kate didn't think that was very likely. "I'll come with you." Curiosity was tempering her trepidation. Those bars may have been for the nursery, keeping generations of infants safe – it could have been a lovely family home at some time, probably built before the trees were even planted. Maybe the whole place would be look welcoming on a calm summer's day.

Katy smiled, more at herself than at the ordinary, middle-aged couple standing in the open doorway. He was storing several years' worth of food around his middle and was practically bald, and she was taller than him and quite shapely, with auburn, dyed hair escaping from a black ribbon on the top of her head. They both seemed welcoming enough.

Mark opened his mouth but the man raised his hand.

"No need to explain," the man gestured them into the huge, dark hallway. "Please, come inside."

Katy followed Mark in and then turned. The heavy door had slammed shut behind them and she shuddered.

"We could see your predicament," the man was saying, "and I said to Lizzy, 'I'll bet there's trees down across the road', didn't I love? I'm Ian Chester, and my wife here is Elizabeth. What a storm! You both look frozen. Come on through and get yourselves warmed up."

"Thank you, I'm Mark Brundell and this is my wife, Katy. We're sorry to intrude like this, but if we could just use your phone we can let Katy's family know where we are. Then if we can walk out of the woods, hopefully they'll be able to come and pick us up."

"I'm afraid both the phone line and the electricity line went down within seconds of the storm hitting us. For the moment we've no idea what's happening beyond what we can see from these windows."

"Then we'll have to walk out of the woods and hope for the best. Would it be all right to leave the car where it is?"

"Nonsense, there's no need for you to go anywhere for a while. We don't get many visitors and always have a kettle on the old log burner. It's one of the advantages of living here, a plentiful supply of free firewood, and there'll be plenty more of that after this storm. Nature has a way of looking after us, I always say. Would you prefer tea or coffee?"

"We'd love a tea please, if you're sure it's no trouble." Mark took a step deeper into the hallway.

Katy hated it when he answered for both of them. She stiffened and took two steps forward, sensing rather than feeling the lightest touch of the man's hand on the small of her back.

"Oh my dears," the woman was leading them all deeper into the house, "you both look chilled to the bone. This old place is so draughty. Come on through into the kitchen. It's the only warm room in the house when it gets really breezy out there."

They were being guided into a huge, candle-lit room. Warmth from the stove wrapped around her and until the woman spoke Katy hadn't realised how much she'd been shivering.

A large black wood burner filled the chimney alcove. She would have described it as more of a range than a stove, and it was a source of light as well as heat in the un-modernised kitchen. The glass fronted firebox had an oven to one side of it, and a huge silver kettle and a large saucepan simmering on its flat surface. She felt warm moist air being drawn into her lungs, bringing with it the smell of vegetable soup. One tea light flickered in each of the four corners of the room, but for what light they were contributing they may as well not have been there. Flickering black shadows and dark corners were everywhere and she half expected a green-eyed black cat to emerge from one of them.

"Take a seat in the old armchair, my dear. Make yourself comfortable while I make us a brew." Elizabeth pointed to a large low chair with several flat cushions stacked on it, all of which could have been almost any colour except white.

It provoked an unexpected memory of her late grandfather who had loved his tatty old armchair at the side of his coal fire in the living room. Caring and funny, he'd been her idol for many years while she'd been growing up. She'd loved hearing him talking about his own, long dead parents, and his stories of the things they'd had to do to survive post-war rationing. And they'd gone through all his old photos together so many times that she wasn't sure now whether her very early recollections of her great-grandparents were real or false memories. "My old mom spent most of her time in that kitchen," he'd told her, fondly. "She could make a meal out of practically anything. I sometimes thought that was where all my old odd socks had disappeared to," they'd laughed together at that one more than once.

The pictures embedded in her head were of a tiny room in comparison to this one, but the range looked oddly familiar.

It didn't feel right to be here – not with these strangers.

The chair moulded to her slight frame and it was obvious Mark was getting comfortable on one of the eight wooden chairs at the long table. Her eyesight was adjusting and she glared at him, but he was deliberately ignoring her. There were times when his obliging nature towards complete strangers made her want to scream at him. And this was definitely one of those occasions. Mark could be too charming and too generous for his own good when the mood took him. Her mother had welcomed him into the family with such enthusiasm that anyone could have been forgiven for thinking that all her previous boyfriends had been from the planet Zog. Even her father, who had always maintained that no one would ever be good enough for his only daughter, was wholeheartedly patting his potential son-in-law on the back and offering to share his best malt whisky, after just a couple of meetings.

And to top it all, Mark was a self-employed general builder. She cringed whenever he let that snippet of information leave his lips, because without exception, wherever they were, the conversation would instantly turn to construction, or renovation, or building regulations. She hadn't heard exactly what Ian Chester had said to Mark but she had heard the fateful word, 'woodworm'. Whatever it was, it was obviously enough for Mark to offer to take a look. And it wasn't as if he didn't know how she felt. Katy pressed her lips together and watched the two men disappearing back into the dark hallway, with Mr Chester holding a large torch in front of them.

She scanned the room, taking in small details that had eluded her earlier. The woman was quietly watching her, she could feel it – but her mouth felt too dry to speak. Once the footsteps and voices had faded away completely, the simmering pan and her own breathing were all she could hear.

She reached for her tea, but neither the liquid nor the warmth from the rose-patterned mug made her feel any less uncomfortable. The core of her body was still trembling. It must be the shock, she thought. That's it – I'm still in shock from the near miss with that huge tree, and from the complete helplessness of being caught in that storm. Anyone would be in shock after an experience like that. She looked at the woman and forced a smile.

"Would you care for something a little stronger, my dear?" The woman spoke softly, as if to a child. "We don't keep spirits in the house – not the liquid kind anyway," she added, without any outward signs of joking. "But we do keep a selection of homemade wines. The elderflower is ready, and it's particularly fine this year. It packs quite a punch, mind you."

Katy opened her mouth to refuse.

"...not that either of you will be driving anywhere for a while."

"That's very kind of you," her instincts screamed at her to humour this woman. "But I'm on a strict diet. I need to lose a few pounds."

"Oh my dear... of course... let me guess... you're newlyweds aren't you? I thought as much when I first saw you together. You need to keep in shape for your new husband. How long have the two of you been as one?"

What a quaint way of phrasing it, Katy thought. Mark would be in stitches when she told him. "Only a couple of months," she replied, at the same time wondering why she was discussing a private matter with this dour woman.

"But you must at least let me get you a biscuit to enjoy with your tea. You must keep your energy levels up. You really look quite peaky and sugar is very good for shock." As she spoke, and before Katy could refuse, the woman was disappearing with one of the candles down stone steps into the darkness of what Katy guessed must be an old fashioned larder or a cellar. Possibly it was the type her grandfather had described, with stone slabs on the floor, and more thick slabs for shelving, all situated on the north-facing side of the property and all designed to maintain the freshness of the family's food in the days before refrigeration.

She blinked. Was her mind drifting? She didn't want a biscuit, and in this light how could the woman possibly tell whether she looked peaky or not? The house was too quiet. If Mark would just come back downstairs, she'd grab his hand

and drag him out of this place. They could get clear of the woods before the light started to fade, and there might even be people out there beginning to clear the roads by now. She was considering getting up and going in search of him when she heard the woman's footsteps.

"Just one of my homemade biscuits will make you feel so much better. I'll be truly offended if you don't at least try one." She held the blue and white biscuit barrel inches from Katy's face.

"Thank you, I'll just have one. They do smell delicious." She saw the first flicker of a smile.

"Life holds such pitfalls for a beautiful girl of your tender age, don't you think?"

"What do...?" Katy stiffened.

"You're so vulnerable, my dear... surely you must realise that. You're open to attack... at the mercy of any evil-doer out there... and such a beautiful girl."

Katy stared at the pattern on the biscuit barrel. It had been moved away slightly but was still too close to her face. Everything else in the room was fading, something was very wrong. She wanted to stand, to move towards the table – but she couldn't lean forward and her legs wouldn't respond. She could only stare.

There were noises now, coming from somewhere above her head. Or were they in her head? She felt sure she heard a shout, a thud, another thud, and then silence. They weren't in her head. It sounded distant, muffled, but it was definitely Mark's voice she'd heard. Where was he when she needed him?

"Too tired to eat another one of my special biscuits, are you my dear?" The woman was still staring at her. "That's one of those pitfalls I was trying to warn you about. Keeping a new husband satisfied can be so tiring. Why don't we get you off to bed?"

"I don't want..." Hot breath brushed the back of her neck. Why hadn't she heard anyone coming into the room? Everything was so distorted. A man's arms scooped her from the chair, but they didn't smell right. Mark had his new aftershave on when they'd left home. She'd teased him about it. These arms smelled of sweat and wood smoke. She must wriggle free, she had to twist and turn until she forced him to drop her. But she couldn't. She felt his movements jerk. Stairs... they were climbing stairs. Perhaps she was being taken to Mark.

Oh God... what's happened to Mark?

Chapter 6
Present Day

Anna Jenkins wrinkled her brow and fixed her stare on the social worker's expression. It was hard to read, but it didn't look good. She felt relieved that it wasn't her bed that misery was approaching.

She watched and listened to the woman quietly asking the twins to accompany her out of the ward. "Leave your things here for now. We need to have a talk in private."

It definitely didn't sound good, either.

Anna scooped up the last spoonful of her sticky porridge, watched the three of them disappearing through the swing doors, and then turned her attention to Verona who had just returned from the showers. Once the girl had stopped throwing up, and had a bit of colour in her cheeks, she was really quite decent-looking. Anna felt she was watching a transformation. The girl had almost black, perfectly straight hair down to her shoulders, a slightly olive complexion with full pink lips, and large deep brown eyes; soulful eyes which were almost continually focused on Anna.

She wasn't about to allow this weird foreign girl to wallow in self-pity because she knew exactly how that felt. She moved across to Verona's bed and sat down. This girl needed a friend, and besides, she was intrigued. "Verona, are you pregnant?" There… she'd said it! She'd asked the question the three of them had been whispering and wondering about since she'd first prodded the girl out of her bed.

"The doctors tell me that is why I am being so sick. I did not know until I came to this hospital. I believed I was poorly only because I did not take vitamin pills. The nice nurses – they explain. I am going to have a little baby in less than twenty more weeks they think. It is too late to stop baby, they tell me."

"Aren't you scared?"

"They tell me I will be OK if I eat well, but yes, I am scared. Mum had babies but... I don't know where... I don't want a baby, but I don't want it to die. I want all of this to go away."

"Have you ever thought your mum's babies might have been murdered; smothered by your dad because he couldn't afford to feed them? I've heard about things like that."

"Yes," Verona's eyes filled with tears, "and I also should be dead."

"Hell... I'm sorry! I didn't mean to upset you." She placed an arm around the girl's shoulders. It was an act she couldn't remember ever doing before and it felt strange. Here was someone in a far worse predicament than herself, and that didn't happen too often. "I was only messing. I'm sure that isn't what really happened. Could you and I be best friends?"

An hour later, the twins still hadn't returned and Anna was sitting on her new best friend's bed with an unopened bottle of juice in one hand and a magazine in the other. She felt she was showing the whole world to this girl. Verona showed so much interest in everything Anna was telling her that it was lunch time before either of them mentioned the twins.

"I'm sure they'll soon be back," she reassured Verona. "They won't want to miss lunch."

But the plates and cutlery were being cleared away, and Anna was back on Verona's bed before Maisie and Carol returned, their faces red and puffy.

The social worker eventually left them and Anna could wait no longer. "Your mum's not gone and died, has she?" She'd never met anyone who had only just lost a parent. She felt Verona squeeze her left hand and they got up and walked across together.

The four sat together on Maisie's bed.

"Mum died at six o'clock this morning," Carol mumbled.

"Last night they told us not to worry," Maisie sobbed. "They said she'd be all right. We never even got to say goodbye."

"They should have warned us, and then we could have seen her before she got too sick."

"She began having seizures in the night and after a while they just couldn't stop them. They said they didn't want us to see her like that. Then her heart stopped and they tried but they couldn't restart it."

"We don't know what's going to happen to us now. No one knows. We've no grandparents or anyone like that to take care of us."

Anna placed a hand on each of the twins. "I'm real sorry for what I said this morning about being an orphan. I was only messing. Where's your dad?"

"He could be dead for all we know," Carol blew her nose, hard. "Mum refused to talk about him. They were never actually an item and our birth certificates named him as John Smith. What would you think were the chances of finding him, even if that is his real name? We've been through all this just now with the social workers."

"But you said you really liked your foster carers, so won't they take you in? They sound like good people, and good people are scarce."

"Oooo...." Carol leaned back onto the bed and buried her damp face into the pillow.

"What...?" Anna and Verona spoke in unison.

"Social workers phoned them last night," Maisie mumbled. "We knew they were in Cornwall. They were driving back in the middle of the night to come and fetch us, and it was raining hard. A lorry lost control on a corner, went onto the wrong side of the road, and it flattened their car. They all died instantly, Craig, Josie, and little Judy."

"Judy...?"

"Their dog, but she felt like ours. She was the only pet we've ever been allowed to have, and we really loved her."

Carol sat back up. The twins looked into each other's eyes and tears rolled down the mirrored faces.

"That's a double bummer," Anna held out the box of tissues. "What are the odds of that happening, do you think? It must be millions... trillions to one. It's like winning the lottery, twice, only in reverse, if you know what I mean. It's mind-blowing."

Even her new best friend was quietly sobbing. That must be the hormones, she thought. She'd heard somewhere about how emotional pregnant women could get, and Verona was only a child herself. But still, she was the only one here with dry eyes and it felt oddly empowering. For the first time in her life, she felt a strong urge to take care of someone. And here were three who undoubtedly needed taking care of.

For an hour, no one spoke. The twins continued to sob quietly onto each other's shoulders and Anna amazed herself by recognising that they needed this time together to grieve. She watched Verona engrossed in her magazines and saw the girl's full lips moving occasionally to form a silent word. Then she lay back and closed her eyes. The four of them were all in one hell of a predicament, and no mistake, but she was going to take control. She was going to make the plans that would get them all out of this mess.

"I've been thinking," she couldn't keep her brilliant idea to herself any longer. Three pairs of eyes suddenly focused on her. "Listen… you two have no idea of what lies in store for you, and I know I haven't a cat-in-hell's chance of going home, let alone of finding decent foster carers, and poor Verona here is facing months of doctors and psychiatrists prodding and poking at her. What do you say to the idea of us all getting out of here – today – now even?" Three blank faces stared back at her and she felt a twinge of irritation.

"But… what about our mum's funeral?" Maisie mumbled.

"It won't matter to your mum whether you're there or not, will it?" She heard Carol gasp. "I'm sorry, that came out all wrong. I only meant that your mum would want you both to do whatever made you happy, wouldn't she? She'd want you to get on with life."

"It's too soon." Maisie added.

"Well I'm not hanging around here any longer than I have to. God knows what they're planning for me. Please say you'll all come with me."

"Where...?" This time it was the twins who spoke in unison.

"I have a plan, but I'm not telling until I know whether you're in or not."

The twins looked at each other for a full minute without speaking. She wondered if maybe they were telepathic. She'd heard of things like that in identical twins. They even began nodding in sync. "We're scared of where the council are going to put us." Maisie spoke for them both. "Count us in."

Without prompting, the three of them turned to Verona.

"I have nothing. All my life is scared. Count me in also."

"Brilliant," Anna clapped and beckoned them over to her bed. "Now, we should have enough clothes between us. Have you two got any money?"

"We've still got the house key," Carol answered. "We have savings accounts and we can get more clothing. The house is a rental but I don't think anyone will go there till after mum's funeral."

"Then we'll go there first. We'll have to be in and out fairly quickly in case they start looking for you. It'll be the first place the authorities will go. In fact, if we go at night we'll have more of a start. Tomorrow night, we'll make up our beds to look as if we're all asleep and then leave at the end of visiting time. You'll have to leave your fancy mobiles in case they can trace them. We can buy cheap, pay-as-you phones anytime."

"Couldn't we go in a morning, after we've had breakfast?" Carol was looking vague.

"And I am sick sometimes." Verona added. "I need sleep. They told me I must sleep."

Anna felt in danger of losing them. "Don't worry, I've got it all sorted in my head. Long before daybreak, we'll all be safe and warm and you, Verona, can sleep for as long as you need."

"Aren't you going to tell us where we're going?" Maisie at least, was still sounding keen.

"I'm coming to that. There's a small commune at Parsley Hedge, about eight or ten miles south of Buxton. It's a kind of eco-place, set in the middle of nowhere. About twenty years ago, four couples clubbed together to buy it, and they do have some rules, but none that will affect us too much. No more than one person from each family group is allowed to work outside the commune, and they are pretty much self-sufficient. I know a couple who've been there for three years. They took on some loans they couldn't afford to repay and got kicked out of their flat. The debt collectors have never found them and they love it there. They've even had a baby without going to the hospital, so I know it will be perfect for you, Verona. They've got their own midwife and a hospital ward and everything. Trust me, I've been there, I've seen how cool it is."

"Are you sure we'll all be welcome?" Carol still looked dubious.

"Of course I am. I'm not making this up. We'll have to work for our keep, in the vegetable gardens or something, and it's all a bit weird until you get used to it, so I'm told. But once we turn sixteen, and no one is looking for us any more, if we don't like it we can leave."

"I can't help," Verona looked at the others. "I have nothing and I can't work."

"You've got us. Don't worry, I have a plan." She put on her best French accent. "Now listen very carefully, I shall say zees only vonce."

The twins laughed and Verona's brow wrinkled.

"We'll casually walk out of here and into town. If we see people standing around, we'll talk in loud voices about going to London, then if they do start looking for us they'll be on a false trail. As soon as I can, I'll get us a car."

"Steal a car....?"

"Shut up and listen. I've done it loads of times. This is Chesterfield – there are unattended cars everywhere. The owners will get it back eventually, and if they don't, then they'll get the insurance. And if they're not insured it jolly well serves them right."

"We've never been in a stolen car before," Maisie was beginning to sound impressed. "What if the police chase us like they do on TV?"

"I promise I won't speed, not with Verona in the car. I'll stop and we'll all run in different directions. And if they do catch us, then we won't be any worse off than we are now. Look at this place, it's for infants – they've no idea what to do with any of us."

"But, Anna, don't you need medications or something?"

"Maisie thinks I'm crazy," she sang, laughing at her own rhyme, and relieved to see the others giggling with her. "No, I'm as sane as anyone here, just as long as I keep away from my whore of a mother. Don't worry about me."

The twins turned to Verona. "But she's so young to be having a baby. Wouldn't she be safer staying here and joining us after it's born?" Once again it was Carol doubting the plan.

"I told you, they'll take good care of her. We'll make the midwife promise to take her to hospital if she thinks it's necessary. But they often have babies there. They even educate the kids themselves because none of the younger ones go to school. They can if they want to, and some of the older ones do, but they don't have to. They've got all the latest internet stuff and the children who want to can study for the same exams as regular school kids."

"It sounds cool."

"We'll tell them we're all sixteen, and that we've all been abused. It's not that far from the truth, is it? I know they're suckers for a good sob story, and anyone who sees Verona will instantly want to take her in and look after her. We'll be treated well, just wait and see. Are you all in?" She raised an individual carton of apple juice, inviting a clink-free toast. "To the four musketeers," she said.

The twins joined in and Verona reached for her juice. "Musketeers... I think I know... a book?"

Anna wrapped her free arm around the girl's shoulders. "This is real life, sweetheart, and it's going to be far tougher on you than on any of us, but we'll take care of you, on my life, I promise. We're a foursome now, and that's the way it's going to remain, or my name isn't Anna Jenkins."

Chapter 7

PC Robert Bell drove his patrol car into the empty lay-by, taking care to avoid the rain-filled pot holes. He switched off his headlights and rubbed the back of his neck. Parked opposite the Cat and Fiddle, the second highest public house in England, where Staffordshire meets Cheshire and Derbyshire is only yards away behind the property, this had always been one of his favourite stops. Closed as a pub by the brewery in December of the previous year, 2015, the future of the building was uncertain. The A537, on which it sat like an atrophied cherry on an enormous, crazily-iced cake, had been dubbed as one of the most dangerous roads in Britain, and it certainly had more than its fair share of inclement weather, in particular, snow and fog. Average speed cameras had helped keep the number of accidents down, but occasionally youngsters still used the winding, open road as a racetrack.

The open moorland, falling away in almost every direction, made him feel on the top of the world. From this vantage point he could see across the patchwork moss, heather and grassy landscape to the lights of Macclesfield and then beyond to the distant lights and tower blocks of Stockport and Manchester.

Being just outside Derbyshire, the building didn't fall into his area of responsibility, but he'd enjoyed many meals here in the past, with his family, and liked to keep an eye on the place.

He opened his window to absorb some of the refreshingly cold night air. Six sheep strolled across the lay-by in front of him and continued on down the centre of the road. He wondered what might have disturbed them at this early hour. The shrill call of a snipe from somewhere close by startled him. There wasn't enough tree cover here for owls, apart from the occasional barn owl on a hunting foray, but he regularly saw a fox with a dead pheasant or a dead partridge gripped in its salivating jaws, heading back to its lair to feed its family.

Robert had grown up on the edge of the council estates of Buxton. Most of his family had been in the police force, his mother was a still a computer operator at the station and his father had been a detective. He'd considered other careers, but deep down he'd always wanted to emulate his father. For now he was a police constable at Leaburn police station, just fifteen miles south of his home town of Buxton, but he was studying to become a detective constable.

Growing up, he'd spent numerous cold nights camped out on these moors with his school friends, David and Thomas. He recalled how it had to be early in the year before the flies drove them off the moors, and always close enough to home to be back in time for breakfast.

He shivered, closed the window, and reached for his flask. He needed a shot of caffeine. It wouldn't do to fall asleep here, almost at the end of his shift. During the ten minutes he'd been stationary, the sky to the east had become noticeably lighter and the eerie chattering of a pair of black grouse signalled daybreak. He tucked his flask back under the passenger seat and wrapped his fingers around the warm, plastic mug.

Nothing major ever seemed to change on these moors.

It wasn't every officer's idea of police work, and he knew he'd been picked because of his detailed knowledge of the old moorland tracks, but it suited him perfectly. He was meant to be a deterrent, partly to the latest group of vandals, more commonly known as 'green-laners', who'd been churning up the moorland tracks and disturbing the wildlife with their four-by-fours, and partly to the poachers and sheep rustlers who'd plagued much of Derbyshire over recent months. But the only vans and four-by-fours he'd seen since midnight had belonged to people whose families he'd known since childhood. These were the families who had lived and worked on the moors and the surrounding farmland for generations. All the incomers, in the barn conversions and the renovated farmhouses, would be setting off for their places of work in the towns and cities over the next few hours.

His mind was drifting and when the radio crackled he spilt coffee onto his lap.

"A missing person's report has just come in," PC Katie Brown sounded tired; it had been a quiet night so far and those were the nights which always seemed the longest. "It's Derek Austen, the reporter for the Markon Advertiser. Are you still up on Axe Edge Moor?"

"Yes Katie, I'm parked up right now. How long has he been missing?"

"Only about eight hours, but his wife's very insistent that something is wrong. She says it's extremely out of character for him not to phone her if he's going to be later than they've arranged."

"Where was he last supposed to be, do we know?"

"As far as she knows he only had one interview arranged for last night. That was to be at The White Horse in Bakewell, something to do with micro-breweries and a real ale promotion the paper was planning. Mrs Austen phoned the White Horse just before midnight — she'd been expecting Derek home sometime between eight and nine last night. They told her he'd left their premises at around eight and mentioned to the barman that he was headed home. He remembered because Derek had refused a free drink. She also says that if he changes his plans then he always lets her know somehow."

"Yes, I know Derek. He's a family man, not the sort to play away, but I thought he lived somewhere just outside Bakewell."

"Apparently they're staying with her mother at the moment, close to Forest Chapel, as she's not been well. She expected him to have crossed the roads you've been patrolling."

"Has she said whether she's rung round their friends?"

"She has, and she's tried local hospitals. We've checked all traffic incidents for last night and found no sign of him. He's driving a Vauxhall Zafira… silver… if that's any help to your memory."

"I've seen nothing parked up where it shouldn't be, but I'll check the car park down by Derbyshire Bridge. I was on my way there next."

"Air Traffic Enforcement is on standby. They can cover the moors very quickly if the boss deems it necessary."

Why did this have to happen at the end of his shift? He'd known Derek since childhood. There was no way he'd be able to get any sleep today if Derek was still missing, not without downing several large measures of whisky, which he usually tried to avoid doing mid-week. He gulped the remainder of his lukewarm coffee, replaced the plastic mug and then turned on the ignition.

Turning off the single-track road into the narrow entrance, his headlights swept the lower third of the car park. Nothing appeared out of place. He drove slowly past the locked toilets block, on which was a noticeboard used by Park Rangers to inform tourists of special events, or to warn of the dangers of moorland fires. As he reached the upper third, from the far corner, his lights were reflected back. He pulled on the handbrake and picked up his radio. "I think I've found Derek's car, Katie. I'm parked in the Derbyshire Bridge car park. It doesn't look good. I'm checking it out now."

The Zafira was a good twenty metres away. His headlights shone directly onto it but the narrow beams had the effect of plunging everything beyond their reach into blackness. To alert anyone as to his identity he switched on the blues and two's, but by bouncing off the surrounding, leafless trees their beams created an illusion of movement and the siren seemed way too loud for the circumstances. He switched on his torch and slowly walked towards the car.

"Derek… Derek… it's the police."

As if anyone could be in any doubt!

"Are you all right?"

Silence.

He gripped the torch at eye level, doubling its use by making it a potential weapon of defensive.

Nothing moved.

With gloved fingertips, he touched the car's bonnet and saw five small droplets of water. The engine was ice-cold. He flashed the torch beam around the perimeter of the park, but could still only see inches beyond the gravelled area.

He stepped towards the passenger door and shone the beam onto the front seats. A phone lay on the passenger seat, with what looked like a set of car keys beside it. He resisted the impulse to try the door. Taking two steps sideways, he angled his torch beam onto the rear seats.

He turned one hundred and eighty degrees, instinctively stepping from the car and flashing the torch beam around the car park. Then he turned back for a second look. He prayed he'd been mistaken.

Wedged in the space between the rear seat and the two front seats was a blood covered hand. It was barely visible, but a small clean area towards the wrist shone white from the beam of his torch. Dark liquid on the remainder of the hand glistened. It was resting on something large and dark. "Steady, PC Bell," he muttered, only to break the sound of his own heartbeat hammering away in his ears. It wasn't yet daylight, he was alone, and his car was a good twenty yards away. "Deep breaths, son, deep breaths…" His heart continued to thump at his chest wall.

The protocol was never to disturb what may turn out to be evidence. He took one step towards the car, and then two steps sideways, attempting to retrace his exact footsteps, and then he turned towards his car and ran.

It was his first murder victim, but it couldn't have been just any victim – it had to be his friend lying there, waiting. Their last conversation had been conducted while standing up against the public bar of the Anchor Inn, exactly one week ago. No one knew how the place had come by its name because the nearest stretch of water had been a boggy swamp until a hundred years ago and the pub pre-dated that by at least another couple of hundred years. And in the heart of Derbyshire, the Anchor Inn couldn't have been any further from the sea in any direction. Maybe that was it, they'd both agreed on the possible explanation, a three hundred year old attempt at a joke. A watering hole anchored into the foot of the Pennines.

*

"I've retrieved a brown leather wallet containing a driving licence, several cards, and some bank notes," the young female police surgeon on her knees announced without turning to address anyone in particular. "The picture on the licence matches the victim, Derek Austen. There's a phone on the front seat if someone wants to bag it, and what looks like a laptop or a tablet is just visible under that same seat."

DCI Michael Forbes hadn't met this police surgeon before. Her name badge introduced her as Judith Horde. She looked young for a doctor but sounded efficient. She'd even beaten him to the crime scene. He leaned over the top of her just far enough to see the victim. Being tall sometimes had its advantages, but after a few seconds his back complained at the uncomfortable angle. There was so much blood that he could still only guess at the cause of death. He had to ask.

"Stab wounds, Inspector Forbes, multiple stab wounds, and many of them appear to be defensive so I'd guess that he put up quite a fight. The one to the neck was probably the fatal one. He would have died very quickly after that. And that's what caused all the blood spray that you can see across the rear seat – being alive when his throat was cut. That would do it for most people, wouldn't you say?" She looked up at him and smiled.

Now he could see what she meant, and he wished he hadn't leaned over quite so far. "And there's no blood anywhere else?" He asked her while moving away and straightening his back. "Do you think the attack was contained in the rear of his car?"

"As far as I can tell at the moment, yes, and your killer would almost certainly have been splattered with blood which would indicate that the vehicle wasn't moved after the murder, not by the perpetrator at least, not unless he or she had a change of clothing ready and could wash their hands. Not very likely though, is it?" She smiled at him again. "Not given the frenzied nature of the attack."

His Detective Sergeant, Adam Ross, had been listening. "I'll organise a preliminary search of the area, sir."

"A blood covered knife would be an excellent start," Forbes muttered, leaning back into the car slightly. "What is that smell? I mean apart from the blood, there's something of a chemical smell." As he spoke he hoped it wasn't the police surgeon's perfume, or her hairspray. He was very close to her again.

"That, Inspector, is the unmistakable odour of a rather cheap perfume, and in my humble opinion, probably worn by the bucket full. You can draw your own conclusions."

"Not the brand that Mrs Austen would have used then?"

"You're better placed to answer that one, Inspector, but from what I know of her, I wouldn't have thought so. I'll mention it to forensics and ask if they can isolate it. Though it may have dispersed somewhat by the time your scenes of crimes officers arrive."

*

PC Robert Bell was standing next to DS Adam Ross, his head bowed and looking stunned. Forbes knew from experience it wasn't an easy thing to deal with, being the First Officer Attending at the scene of a brutal attack, especially when the victim was known to you.

"Good work, Robert," he placed a hand on the uniformed shoulder. "I understand that you're familiar with all these moorland tracks and narrow back roads."

"Yes sir, this car park is a bit off the beaten track but it can get quite busy in the summer months, especially at weekends. There's likely to be all sorts of rubbish in the undergrowth."

"Quite... this road leads to the reservoirs, doesn't it?"

"Errwood and Fernilee Reservoirs, yes sir, and a couple of hill farms, but the road is one-way. We'd have to go back up to the main road, down the hill for about three miles and then turn right into Goyt valley to reach them. The road's very narrow in places and loops round in a semi-circle."

The main artery crossing the moors was already beginning to pulse with lights from the early morning traffic. Forbes shook his head. That was an image he could have done without. He turned to the uniformed officers who'd just arrived. "I want checkpoints setting up in both directions as quickly as possible, before the morning traffic builds up. Any reported sightings of this car, or of Austen himself, and you get statements. Now, PC Bell, hasn't your shift ended?"

"Almost two hours ago, sir."

"Then what are you waiting for? Get on home, get a stiff drink inside you, and get some sleep."

Forbes turned back to Adam, "Find someone to conduct interviews at the farmhouses along this lane to establish whether anyone saw anything unusual last night, then you and I will visit Mrs Austen. The family liaison officer is already on her way there."

He waited for Adam to fasten his seatbelt. "Ready?"

"Yes sir. Could the killing be linked to a story Austen was researching? I know he could be very persistent if he believed he'd got something worth pursuing. It's possible he ruffled somebody's feathers."

"It's the Buxton Advertiser, Adam, not a tabloid journal." One job at a time, he was thinking, and that job unfortunately, was shattering Mrs Austen's world.

They'd passed the officers setting up check-points before Adam broke the silence again.

"It looked like a pretty frenzied attack, sir. In my experience that often indicates passion. His work colleagues might know if he was less than the perfect family man that he had us all believing."

Forbes gave a mock sigh and Adam took the hint and kept the remainder of his thoughts to himself.

*

Forbes stood in the incident room for the afternoon briefing, aware that every officer in front of him had either met or known Derek. He tried to project some optimism – that was, after all, a part of his job. "The first few hours of a murder investigation are the most important. We've no murder weapon yet, although there's still a lot of moorland to cover, and the North West Regional Underwater Search and Marine Unit can begin searching the reservoirs if we think it necessary. A motive eludes us but we've ruled out robbery from the scene. Derek's bank accounts are temporarily frozen and are being checked. As for opportunity – well he was out alone, late at night, on an unlit moorland road. On the up-side, Mr Austen was a very well-known, popular, and recognisable figure in the community. It's far more likely for people to remember when and where they've seen a well-known figure. Mrs Austen says she was at home all evening with their two-year-old son. She has her own car but none of the neighbours we've spoken to so far can recall seeing or hearing anyone arriving or leaving. It's a quiet cul-de-sac but that doesn't entirely rule out the possibility. It isn't a cast-iron alibi, but so far she has no motive that we're aware of. Derek's parents live in Newcastle and they've been notified by local police. We understand Derek has a brother, somewhere in the Middle East, serving with the peace keeping forces. That should be confirmed for us later today. Then there are his work colleagues, and without exception they're claiming that Derek adored his family and that to the best of anyone's knowledge he never even looked at another woman after he met his wife, Fay."

"No one is that good," DC Jade Sharpe added from her desk at the side of the room. "If he never even looked, can we be sure that he didn't swing both ways?"

Forbes looked around the room. "Anything is open for discussion at the moment," he said.

"Just a thought," she offered for good measure, feeling her cheeks burn and wondering why she hadn't grown out of blushing by now.

"Derek's office equipment, his phones, laptop, and documents from his home will be sent to the forensics lab. We're also keen to hear any whispers of anything controversial, or damaging to anyone, that he may have been working on but not yet recorded. Oh, and we'll maintain the checkpoints on the A537 for the next few days."

DS Adam Ross stepped towards the board and pointed to the map. "One of the households on this lane remembered seeing lights at or near the car park sometime between eight-thirty and nine o'clock last night. They only noticed one set of headlights, so if we assume that the killer was already in the car with Austen, then either he knew his killer, or he was working on a story and didn't wish to be seen. Did he turn off the main road voluntarily? Either way, if the killer left on foot then we'd hope to find some sort of trail. SOCOs are still at the park but we need to widen the search. The nature of the moorland ground makes searching difficult so it's going to be slow and steady this afternoon. We expect every available officer to be out front and ready to go in thirty minutes to allow us a few of hours of daylight."

PC Jade Sharpe's comment had struck a chord and by the time they were approaching the crime scene again, his opinions of Derek were wavering. "Who can really know a man like Austen?" he asked Adam. "Is he really that lovable and squeaky clean, or is that just the public image he wants us all to see? The very nature of his job dictates that he must have 'the gift of the gab', as they say."

"His wife's a stunning woman," Adam hadn't known the Austen family as long as most of the other officers had. "Did he have a jealous streak, maybe?"

"Has the wife got a lover, you mean? She has a reasonable alibi, but it's something to consider."

"This may still turn out to be a crime of passion, sir."

It was a mild, bright, autumn afternoon. Because of the one-way system, they passed the reservoirs first. The Underwater Search Unit was still busy and he didn't envy them. The water looked very cold and very deep. They had a blue, rigid, inflatable boat about a quarter of the way across the reservoir, equipped with sonar equipment. That was being used to search for any other bodies while two divers searched within throwing distance of the shore for the murder weapon. Forbes remembered this reservoir being almost dry, way back in the seventies. He'd been a child but he remembered the hose pipe bans, the endless heat that never bothered him back then, and the rock-hard and parched ground. His father had brought him and his mother here to see it, but it all seemed so long ago and he couldn't recall how far the drop had been to give him any sense of how deep the water might be when the reservoir was full. No doubt there were some water level markers somewhere, but he couldn't see any from where they were standing.

They continued along the narrow, steep-sided valley that followed the River Goyt until the murder scene came into view, then parked on the grass verge and walked towards the car park entrance. A pair of mallard ducks waddled up from the running water. They obviously weren't accustomed to being driven away and were letting the officers know exactly what they thought of them.

"Has there been any progress?" Forbes asked James Haig, the crime scene manager.

"Yes sir, we think so. The river is little more than a stream at this point. It's within easy reach and it appears someone's knelt down here very recently. My officers have just finished taking samples from the area. It's possibly the place where the perpetrator cleaned the blood from his, or her, hands, because we believe we've found traces of it in the mud."

*

Anna marvelled at how happy Verona looked these days. Her cream-coloured and slightly misaligned teeth didn't detract from the glow of her face. She looked so overwhelmed with joy that Anna occasionally found herself just staring at the girl. She appeared so much younger than she had in the hospital ward. For the first time, her features matched her slowly expanding frame and she could easily pass for the fourteen-year-old that only Anna realised she probably was. The 'self-proclaimed' matron had tempted her with ginger biscuits each morning and the sickness had stopped. And since then she'd eaten every meal placed in front of her and won the hearts of everyone in the commune with her unending desire to learn the English word for absolutely everything that she saw.

The twins had gone the other way, and that concerned her. Their puffy cheeks and glassy-eyed expressions had remained unchanged throughout the weeks they'd been at the commune. The dark shadows around their eyes stood out against their pale skin and grey lips. Treble the grief obviously meant treble the tears, but just once, recently, she'd seen Maisie laughing at one of the cats in the yard as it chased a leaf. It had only lasted a second, but she hoped it signalled the beginning of their recovery. They were still in a state of grief and shock, and they obviously needed more time to heal. She silently promised to make it her mission to help them whenever and wherever she could. And if the last few weeks had proved anything to her, it was that anything really was possible. She'd brought them all to safety, hadn't she, and she was protecting them. She couldn't remember ever feeling as relaxed as she did in this commune, and as the tension had left her, so had the inexplicable fears and the uncontrollable, overwhelming rages. But there was something else; something she'd never, ever, experienced before, and that was the feeling of being in control.

It had only taken her a couple of nights to find the door that her commune friends had whispered about. The cellar was just as dark and cobwebbed as they'd described it, and she'd had to find a spare torch that she hoped no one would miss for a while. The hatch was never locked and it opened out onto the rear of the building in the shadow of the large orchard. From there she could easily slip unseen to the car that they'd arrived in.

She'd already driven it from here several nights without anyone noticing.

Chapter 8

Driving his silver Mercedes, with DS Ross as his passenger, DCI Michael Forbes was on his way to take another look at the scene of Derek's murder. Neither of them had spoken since leaving Leaburn and Michael's mind began running through the events of his morning.

His sister Louise, eighteen years his junior, and whose upbringing he'd been involved with since the sudden and untimely death of their mother when Louise had only been a few weeks old, had finally settled back into the family home with her two-month-old daughter, Gemma. Three adults and one fretful baby – there were bound to be the occasional disputes – but despite being early days, all was going well. Too well, Michael's father, Andrew Forbes occasionally mumbled when Louise was out of earshot.

According to Louise's school teachers, she'd been a bright pupil, destined to go far. That had never happened. For years, Michael had blamed himself for his sister's erratic, adolescent behaviour. He was obviously closer to her generation than their grieving father, and he felt he should have been able to communicate with her more easily, but she'd been a strong willed child, and on the day of her thirteenth birthday, what little chemistry they'd had between them had vanished without warning. She'd begun to spend days shut away in her room while he'd made little or no effort to engage with her. By the time her fifteenth birthday had come around, *a rebel without a cause* had taken up residence in the previously calm household.

"It could be so much worse," Michael Forbes had tried to reassure his father when she'd begun to stay away from home for days at a time. "She's with a peer group who promote a drug-free lifestyle, and that takes guts today. She'll come right eventually, and she knows we'll be here for her when she does."

In truth, during her painful teenage years, he hadn't a clue what was going on inside his sister's head. He only knew she'd lacked the comforting influence of a mother, but their father had made it quite clear that no one ever could, or would, take the place of his late wife. So Michael had concentrated on building his career and left the lion's share of the worrying to his father.

"One day you'll come crawling back," his father had prophesied on the day that Louise had packed a large holdall and announced that this time she was definitely, categorically, leaving for good.

Michael and his father had both been proved right.

It was a determined Louise who'd surprised both of the Forbes men at the breakfast table that morning.

"I know that I've got responsibilities now," she began.

Michael tried not to react. That statement alone would have been so out of character for the Louise of just twelve months ago.

She had their full attention, and she knew it.

"I've been researching some courses and I'm really hoping you'll both be pleased to learn that I've decided to start college in September. And before you say anything, they have a day nursery for Gemma. I've enrolled us both."

She paused.

Michael looked at his father, willing him not to utter one of the many sarcastic remarks that he knew must be on the old man's lips.

"What are you intending to study?" Michael pre-empted their father.

"Do you remember how I was always top of the class in science, because I found it easy? At least, I did until I lost my way. And before you say anything, I know now that it was my own fault. Well, I'm continuing with some of the 'O' levels I would have taken if I'd stayed on. I'm already enrolled for the three sciences, and maths and English. I'm hoping to get grades A to C. Also, if I can get a place, the college is running a new course on forensic science. I've put my name down for that as well, and I was kind of hoping... if I can get the grades I need... that Alison might help me to get a job in the mortuary, or in the laboratory. I was thinking of training to be a pathology technician. My eventual aim is to get a certificate in Anatomical Pathology Technology. It's something I think I could be good at. Well... what do you think?"

Michael glanced at his father, who looked as if he was struggling to swallow a mouthful of porridge. "How will you go on for money, have you looked into all that?"

"Of course I have," she snapped. "There are such things as student loans, you know."

That's more like it, he thought. The old Louise is still in there. "You won't find it easy," he said. If she's going to throw one of her old tantrums, let's get it over with. "You'll have night after night of home studying, instead of going out with your friends. And having a baby around will make it hard work."

"I know... I know... but I truly believe that I'm ready now. I feel that I want to do something useful with life, apart from bringing up my beautiful Gemma, of course." Her eyes softened a little and a smile twitched at the corners of her mouth. "Also... I've been looking at the possibility of a part-time job until college begins in September. In the evenings mainly... and I was hoping I could rely on you both for babysitting duties. I want to save up for driving lessons and a little car so I can be more independent, and I also want to pay my own way and make it up to you for some of the trouble I know I've put you both through."

"I thought there'd be a catch." Michael said what he knew his father was thinking.

"Oh please... a couple of the clubs in town are looking to recruit staff from next Easter onwards. I won't waste a penny of my wages, I promise. I'm determined to make something of myself before Gemma starts school. I want her to be proud of me. And I know it's going to take an awful lot, but I want you guys to be proud of me as well."

Michael's father finally spoke. "I'm sure you'll do well, as long as you're willing to work at it, but even the two of you working together won't solve every case involving a needless death. Some are never investigated properly. Some deaths are swept under the carpet and forgotten about."

"Dad, don't start. Louise is making the effort here. We can't change our family's past, but we can look to a more promising future, and I think we should give her our full support."

It was going to be a waiting game with his sister. Although if her demeanour over breakfast was an indication of what was to come, then he'd little doubt that she'd see it through to the bitter end.

The moor remained dotted with officers and the car park a hive of activity. Sharp gravel crunched beneath dozens of boots.

"Derek was killed in this deserted car park, late at night, so why was he here?" Forbes asked Adam without looking at him.

"Forced at knifepoint, seduced by sex, or an interview with someone who didn't want to be seen talking to the press, or maybe something he was working on led to a violent argument. But how many people walk around carrying a blade large enough to inflict that much damage on a person?"

"The knife could have been in Derek's car, we haven't ruled that out yet. People don't usually carry that type of knife around with them, not unless they're planning to use it."

"No… but sir, the fact that his trousers and the top two buttons of his shirt were undone, and that he was found in the back of his car…"

"His tie was underneath him, soaked in blood, don't forget that. His killer had the upper hand."

"And his injuries were a bit over the top for self-defence, don't you think, sir?"

"We need someone to look over all the unsolved rape and sexual assault cases over the last five years. We'll also need lists of everyone – male and female, accused or convicted of any type of knife crime. But first I'd like a word with the folks living along this lane. Let's see if what they tell us today corresponds with what we read in yesterday's statements."

*

Craig and Tony Havers stood side by side in their wooden front porch, minus their shoes, watching the tail lights of the police car bouncing out of sight down their long farm track and then turning out onto the lane. It was heading towards their nearest neighbour, half a mile away, and Tony couldn't supress a smile. "It's no use them going back to question old Bill Vardy again," he chuckled. "He's as barmy as a box of frogs. If it wasn't for the fact that he's too scared of the dark to leave his own front porch, most folks around here would be pointing a finger at him for that murder."

Craig locked his huge muscular fingers around the back of his brother's neck and squeezed. Ignoring the squeal, he forced Tony back into the kitchen and thrust him into the wooden chair. "But his sister's not so daft, is she? I told you that copper yesterday didn't believe that we hadn't seen anything. You're a bloody hopeless liar, Tony. If they come back here today to do a proper search, we're well and truly in the shit. We should have got rid of that stag and those damn sheep last night. We should have just dumped them like I said."

"Relax," Tony stood, rubbed his neck and reached around the back of the chair for his grey jacket, "we'll give them half an hour and then we'll move the carcasses out. We'll take them down the old quarry track to the gravel pit. I'll phone Lewis to let him know what's happened and tell him to be ready for an earlier than usual delivery. The coppers are chasing their tails investigating this murder, not looking for poachers."

Craig glanced at the long case clock that they'd inherited with the farm. "But the whole moor is crawling with coppers. What if they stop us?"

"Then we'll say they're our own dead sheep that we've just picked up and explain that we're off to the knacker's yard. They won't want to go poking around half a dozen stinking sheep carcasses, will they? We'll just have to make sure the deer carcass is well hidden."

"I suppose this murder could take the heat off us for a while, and besides, where could we dump them with all this going on?" He copied Tony and hunched into his jacket. "But supposing someone saw our lights last night? I told you to switch them off before we reached the park. You never sodding well listen to me."

"Bloody hell Craig, will you stop whining. We'd been parked on the top track, behind those trees, for a good fifteen minutes before that car showed up. No one saw us. And even if they did, we'll just say our old dog went missing and we were out looking for her. It's not as if we recognised anyone. It was too dark. Have you got all that in your thick old skull?"

"But... those God awful screams... they went on for ages," Craig lifted both hands to the sides of his head. "We should have gone to help."

"You prattle on like some demented old woman. It's done... over... you've got to forget about it. Now give me a hand getting those sheep into the truck. We need the cash from them if we're going to get that barn roof fixed before it snows."

The restored Land Rover had been Tony's pet project. He'd adapted and raised the exhaust to enable them to cross the stream in all but the worst of the winter rains. Once across, a two mile drive along one of the many overgrown tracks criss-crossing their land, took them off the moors and down to where the butcher would hopefully be waiting for them with a pocket full of twenty-pound notes.

*

"There were twenty-two stab wounds in total," Alison Ransom, the forensic pathologist, announced over the phone. "I thought you might have attended the post mortem yourself, Michael. Your new DC didn't look as if he enjoyed it too much."

"What can I say – we drew straws – I lost. Just give me the main findings, Alison."

"All the puncture wounds were in the upper body, none were below the navel and ten of those wounds were on his arms and only a couple of centimetres deep. I'd say he fought off his attacker for several minutes as the shallow wounds all showed considerable blood loss. Five of the stab wounds penetrated his vital organs and the one to his neck sliced straight through the carotid artery. That alone would have killed him in under a minute, but he couldn't have survived for more than a few minutes even without the neck injury. From the blood spatter across the rear seat of his car we know that he was alive when his neck was sliced open."

Forbes could never quite get used to the direct way that his long-term girlfriend, Alison Ransom, spoke to him over the phone. Her professional voice was consistently hard and edgy, recounting the most gruesome details as if she was reading from a text book. It was so different from the softly-spoken woman who accompanied him on his hiking expeditions around the Derbyshire Dales, and who loved to sit in his car and share freshly cooked fish and chips, even in the coldest of weathers.

"We found his tie very loosely wrapped around his left wrist – the left arm was wedged under the front seat a little way – possibly placed there after death as he'd used both arms in his attempts to defend himself. We also found an abrasion to his right wrist which may indicate that he was loosely tied up. It probably wasn't fastened tightly enough to hold him for long, but it could have hampered him just enough for his assailant to deliver some of the more immobilising blows."

"Loosely..." Forbes considered Adam's theory, "so we could assume that means voluntarily. Add to that the multiple, less forceful stab wounds and we could be looking for a female. Is there anything back yet on the perfume?"

"Not yet. We're also waiting for several DNA results which may throw some light on the sex of the attacker. So far we've only identified Derek's blood, but we have six blond hairs, all between three and four inches long, all clean but recently lightened very slightly with a commercial hair dye. Isn't his wife dark haired?"

"Yes, a dark brown with reddish tints if I remember correctly. Are we drifting into the realms of fantasy to consider her putting on a natural blond hairpiece before sneaking out, leaving her baby home alone, and murdering her husband in cold blood?"

"Very little about murder is normal."

"I'll ask the family liaison officer to have a discreet poke around for hair dye or a blond wig while she's at Mrs Austen's home."

"Are we still on for tonight, Michael?"

He was still picturing the newly widowed Mrs Austen – her glossy hair, her striking features, and her immaculately maintained home. "What... yes of course, but do you mind if we eat in? I know dad's got a casserole in the oven and he always makes far too much. I'll pick up a good bottle of wine on the way home, we'll finish off with a glass or three of that brandy that you like, and then you can stay over."

Even to his ears that last statement sounded crass and he could hear her laughing.

"You really do have the sweetest of chat-up lines, have I ever told you that? How could a girl possibly resist? Hopefully I'll be with you before seven."

"Before you go, I'll admit to you now, over the phone, that I do have an ulterior motive for asking you over to the house tonight. Louise has begun making plans for her future and I was hoping you'd talk some of them over with her." He knew that Alison believed Louise was more than capable of taking care of her own life, and that she was probably thinking he was being ridiculous.

"Louise... plans... those are two words which don't normally belong in the same sentence. I'm intrigued."

"She's talking about trying for a career as a pathology technician, possibly working in the mortuary. She seems deadly serious, if you'll ignore the terrible pun, and I was hoping you might be able to advise her. I know she looks up to you."

"I doubt very much whether Louise looks up to anyone beyond her own generation, but if you think she'll accept my advice and encouragement then I'm more than happy to provide it." She sounded pleased to be asked. "I'll download some brochures for her and try to answer any questions she might have. I'm pleased for you that she's beginning to think about her future."

DS Adam Ross was writing on the white-board when Forbes returned to the incident room. "We've just had two possible sightings come in from the roadside checkpoint, sir. The earliest was by a couple driving westwards along the main road at about ten-thirty on the night of the murder who noticed a lone figure walking up from Derbyshire Bridge, towards the main road. On the open moorland, and with a half moon, the figure had *'looked very out of place'* as the couple put it. They noticed that the person stopped walking as their car approached the junction to the lane. They couldn't say whether it was male or female, only that it looked on the small side. They slowed down and discussed stopping in case help was needed, but the lady in the car was quite nervous so they continued driving."

"Good choice; and the second sighting?" Forbes prompted.

"The second witness was a gentleman alone in his car, driving eastwards, returning from a hospital visit at somewhere around eleven p.m. This witness was feeling tired. He'd had a family member rushed into hospital with a heart condition on that day but he did remember seeing someone getting into the passenger side of a small silver car. A slender figure he said, though he couldn't give a more detailed description. He overtook the stationary vehicle and watched it through his rear view mirror. It set off behind him, slowly following, and he soon lost sight of it. He'd seen no other vehicles for a couple of miles so he wondered whether someone had been hitching a lift, and thought what a dangerous thing to do, for both parties."

"Was he concerned enough to…?"

"Yes sir, for those very reasons he tried to read the number plate but only managed a partial. It began with SX06. And he thought the car could have been a Ford Focus. It's our best lead so far."

"Trust you, Adam, to leave the most vital piece of evidence till last. So, are we looking for this silver car?"

"Yes sir, all traffic vehicles have just been alerted."

"Then I think we've time for another word with Derek's widow before we call it a day."

*

Applying gentle pressure to the widow Austen, now that she'd returned to her own detached property on the outskirts of Bakewell, wasn't proving easy. Forbes and Adam perched on the edge of a white leather sofa but Mrs Austen was refusing to be seated in her own living room. Despite the tears, she obviously wasn't in a mood to be intimidated.

"We have a large circle of friends, none of whom would ever dream of harming Derek. If he made enemies then it surely must have been through his work, and I really can't comment on that. And of course my husband was both faithful and straight. What an utterly, utterly absurd notion to think differently. I truly believe, on my infant son's life, that my Derek was faithful to me for the duration of our marriage." Her head tilted slightly, so that she was looking down at them, challenging them to dispute her words.

"The same questions apply to you, I'm afraid, Mrs Austen." There was something about this woman, newly bereaved or not, that irritated Forbes. "We will need to have a complete picture of your family lives, for reference and elimination procedures."

"Of course you will; I'd expected nothing less." Her smile was as insincere as it was possible to be without looking ridiculous, but possibly that was the effect of her grief. "I've seen enough detective shows over the years to know that. And you can write this down if you must – I have never, ever, been unfaithful to my husband; not gay, not straight, not even a wobbly line, and to the best of my knowledge, neither of us have ever upset anyone to the degree that they would wish us harm."

"That will be all for now, thank you Mrs Austen," Forbes stood to leave. "We are all very sorry for your loss and rest assured that we are doing everything possible to find your husband's killer."

"Of course you are."

He would have put money on her not allowing them to leave without having had the final word.

PC Tracy Wilson, the family liaison officer, was waiting in the hallway. He explained about the hairs found in Austen's car. "Search through what you can of the house and car, and take a discreet look through the rubbish. Look for any blonde hairs on brushes and combs, and have a good look in the bathroom. But be subtle, she seems highly strung. Do you mind staying here for the rest of the evening?"

"Not at all, sir, and I'll have that discreet poke around."

*

By nine o'clock that evening, Michael Forbes was starting to feel like a stranger in his own home. To be accurate, it was his father's home, but he'd never really left and never felt totally comfortable anywhere else. Even the weekends of his university years had mostly been spent back in the family home.

He'd never witnessed Louise engaged in a serious conversation with anyone for so long, and Alison was obviously enjoying her new role as mentor. The dining table had disappeared beneath files, books, and computer print-outs and neither of the women had even looked in his direction since the wine bottle had been emptied and the dinner plates cleared away.

His father had retreated to the local pub and Michael was considering following him. Just for the odd pint; they'd know where to find him if they ever noticed his absence.

Chapter 9
Twenty-five years earlier.
Part 1 – Mother and Baby.

Several events forged the career of DCI Michael Forbes, and kept him inspired during the odd occasions when he'd been disillusioned and considering a complete change of career. The first of these events happened shortly after he'd joined the police force and was still struggling to find his place in the team.

That day he'd seen his first suicide victim, and witnessed the only crime scene which had ever made him feel physically sick, an incident which in itself would have stuck in his mind, but he had no way of knowing then, how the following few hours were about to affect him.

*

PC Michael Forbes was responding to an early morning phone call from a dog walker. As it was the start of his shift, and in case it was a hoax, of which they'd had several over recent weeks, he drove the patrol car alone for the six miles from Leaburn to the stretch of woods alongside Long Rake Mine, west of the village of Youlgreave. After parking in a passing place he was directed by a distraught woman, who had kindly returned from the call box in the village, towards a man's body gently swinging from an outstretched branch of an old oak tree. An aluminium ladder lay at the foot of the tree and envelopes protruded from the dead man's pockets.

The ladder proved handy for relieving the tree of its burden and the letters revealed everything that the officers needed to know. The balding, middle-aged man was Ian Chester, and he had lived only a few hundred yards away.

PC Michael Forbes's sergeant walked past the line of cars, straight towards him. "You've done well this morning, Michael. That was a tough thing to witness and deal with, especially on your own. The man's letters state that he had a terminal illness, and that this was his chosen way out. If his doctor confirms the letters' contents then I'd say he had grounds for his action, though I doubt that Mrs Jones will ever walk her little mutt in these particular woods again."

He was starting to feel sick again and quickly folded his arms across his lower chest. Did the man die quickly, or did he struggle in agony for minutes before losing consciousness? He'd read somewhere that it wasn't easy to break your own neck in one swift movement. While waiting for back-up he'd struggled to keep his nausea under control, but it was threatening to take over again.

"Will you be all right to accompany PC Sandra Bennett," Sergeant Walker was still talking, "to inform his next of kin?"

"Yes sir."

"Good man. It sometimes helps to see these things through. We'll need a formal identification as soon as he's been tidied up, but one of the letters informs us that his wife still lives at Woodbine Cottage, only about a quarter of a mile back along the road. It's an area we covered when a young couple went missing during a storm, four years ago. That missing person's case is still open and I remember this man and his wife all too well. They were our prime suspects for a while so maybe it's better if officers that she doesn't recognise go to break this news to her."

PC Sandra Bennett was only a couple of years older than Forbes and was carrying slightly too much weight for a police officer. The previous year she'd given birth to a daughter, in the middle of the night, and alone. Her shocked parents had stepped up to help with the baby so that Sandra could continue with her chosen career. Forbes had tried to be friendly, but always steered well clear of the subject of the infant's father – there were still rumours flying around the station. But one thing he did know, all too well, was infants in general. He'd been helping his father to raise his baby sister since his mother's untimely death two years earlier, when he'd been just eighteen.

"He's gone and done it, hasn't he? I knew what he'd done as soon as I heard the police sirens." Mrs Chester's face was hard to read. "Weeks ago, he told me what he was planning. I tried to talk him out of it but he was determined. When I got up this morning, and he'd already gone out, I knew... I just knew."

"Mrs Chester, we're so very sorry," Sandra began softly. "May we come in for a moment?"

"No, you may not... and you're not sorry at all," she looked accusingly at them. "You people hounded my poor Ian. You dug up all our precious allotment and you ransacked our house and our sheds and then left without a single word of apology. Our neighbours shunned us for months, and it was all for nothing... nothing. It's because of your harassment that my Ian became ill."

He'd read about the case, but what he was hearing from Mrs Chester didn't tally. The wing mirror to the missing couple's car had been found on the driveway to Woodbine Cottage, and that had led the police to the Chester household. The couple admitted to taking the Brundell's into their house and feeding them, and so a search of their property had ensued. Spots of blood, the same type as Mark's, had been found in a first floor bedroom, along with hairs which matched the length and colouring of Katy's. But neither Mark and Katy Brundell nor their car had ever been found.

"Oh I can see what you're both thinking. You think you know all there is to know about Ian and myself, and what happened here on the day of the storm, but you don't. All we did was offer a young couple shelter and provide them with tea and biscuits and a bed for the night. For all we know, the man cut himself shaving the next morning, or had a nosebleed. We didn't harm them."

"The couple have never been found," Forbes felt the need to defend his colleagues, even though he hadn't been a part of the investigation.

"But you treated us like criminals." Mrs Chester leaned against the half-opened door and he watched her face passing through every shade of red and then back to grey.

"Is there anyone you'd like us to fetch – to stay with you for a while?" Sandra reached out and gently touched the woman's forearm.

Instantly it was pulled back, out of reach, and Mrs Chester stood straight while all the time maintaining her firm grip on the door. "No thank you my dear; that's sweet of you, but no."

Forbes heard a noise from deeper inside the house. He raised his eyebrows.

"My niece is currently living here. She's in the kitchen. Charlotte… Charlotte… would you come to the door please?" Mrs Chester's knuckles looked white against the black gloss paint of the door, which she was now using more as a physical barrier than an actual support.

Charlotte could have been in the hallway, waiting for the summons. A thin, devastatingly pale, fair haired young woman appeared in under a second, and without a word of acknowledgement to either Mrs Chester or the officers, managed to squeeze herself between her aunt and the heavy door. She adeptly slipped one arm around her aunt's waist and the other arm squarely against the back of the door. In one fluid movement, Mrs Chester was being guided backwards while the door was being firmly pushed into the PCs' faces.

*

On certain days, when he was driving through a similarly wooded area, the minutes which followed the closing of that door seemed as if they'd only just happened. He was never sure whether it had been his natural curiosity, his recently completed police training, or something else altogether that had made him hesitate before getting back into the patrol car with Sandra.

*

Something made him turn towards the rising sun, squint against the light and look up at the barred top-floor windows. The twist in his stomach was like nothing he'd experienced either before or since. For a few moments, every part of his body froze.

The emaciated face and tangled mop of straw-like hair could have been a child, with its face tilted down towards him. "Sandra, what do you think that is up there?" Tiny white hands, one on each side of the face, appeared to be pressing against the glass. If it hadn't been for one slight movement of one thin finger he might have dismissed it as a trick of the light on an old abandoned, but seriously spooky doll.

"A moth-eaten doll, come on, get in," Sandra leaned across the car seats to get his attention. "We've done our duty here, as best we can anyway if they won't let us in. We've got to report back."

"Can you see any children's things?" Forbes bent to Sandra's level. "There's nothing anywhere – no swings, no bits of coloured plastic, no toys in the grass, nothing to indicate that a child lives here."

"That's probably because no children live here," Sandra frowned.

"Look... you'll have to get back out... take another look up there."

"It's a doll, you klutz. It's nothing but a tatty old doll."

"No... no it isn't, keep looking." He lifted his arms above his head, waved both hands and smiled.

"Hell... you're right... it moved..." Sandra's voice cracked. "I definitely saw a hand move. It looked as if it was about to wave back, but then stopped. I'm sure of it. But the eyes are too large. It doesn't look real."

"No, keep looking, I think... I think it's the face that's too thin. Something definitely isn't right here. From what I can see, I'd say that child is starving to death. We've got to do something."

"I'll radio in with what we think we've seen and ask for advice while you go back and question the women. I agree it doesn't look right. I don't feel like leaving till we know what's going on."

Charlotte opened the door almost immediately. Was she waiting in the hallway again?

"Children… no officer, there are no children here. There's a collection of old dolls in the attic windows. That's probably what you've seen. There are mice and bats living up there, so it's no surprise you saw movement. There's only Aunt Elizabeth and myself here now, and if you don't mind, we'd both be grateful for some respect and some privacy." The door slammed shut again.

Forbes hurried back to the car. Sandra was in conversation with the duty officer and in answer to her questioning expression, he shook his head. He looked up at the barred window. There were dolls there, certainly, but the face had gone.

"Get in. We've been told to wait here till back-up arrives. What exactly did the woman say?"

"She was adamant that all we'd seen were old dolls and she blamed the movement on mice or bats. I think I'd doubt myself right now if you hadn't seen it too."

"We both have young children in our lives, Michael. I'd like to think that if anyone ever suspected that they looked anything remotely like that child up there that they'd be willing to stop and do something about it." Her eyes watered.

"This had better not be a fool's errand, PC Forbes," Sergeant Walker emerged from the first vehicle to arrive at the Cottage. "Social services have been contacted but they have no record of child endangerment on these premises. Depending on what we find, they have someone on standby."

"We both saw it, sir," Sandra answered, looking from Forbes to their sergeant.

*

The woods were actually a collection of trees along the roadside with the occasional acre of trees sprouting off into the pastureland. Ancient oaks and massive beech trees had grown there for generations, but as locations went for suicides, PC Forbes had thought, the area would never feature in the nation's top ten.

It was the aftermath of new recruit PC Michael Forbes's find in those woods, the swinging body of Ian Chester, which had grabbed the attention of the local media, rather than the suicide itself.

*

Mrs Chester stood next to her niece, Charlotte, glowering at the backs of PCs Sandra Bennett and Hazel Foster, the two officers who were disappearing up her uncarpeted stairs while PC Forbes and Sergeant Walker waited in the cramped hallway. The four of them listened in silence to fading footsteps echoing through the building, and when the rhythmic sounds stopped, Forbes watched the women exchange a glance.

In the tense minutes before they heard footsteps again, he knew they must have found something. If what they'd seen from the patrol car had been the antics of rodents, then the two PC's wouldn't be taking anywhere near as much time up there.

Slowly and deliberately, PCs Bennett and Foster descended the wooden staircase. Sandra was speaking in a gentle and reassuring, much softer voice than Forbes had heard from her before.

It should have reassured him, instead he shuddered.

The straw-like hair that they'd seen was poking out from the top of a grey blanket, and two very white, stick-thin arms were tightly wrapped around Sandra's neck. She looked awkward, hugging the blanket to her body almost as if it was empty. He felt an unexpected wave of emotion when Sandra's eyes focused on him and remained there for several seconds.

"Dr Jenson is already on her way and should be here in a few minutes," Sergeant Walker broke the spell. "And the social services are waiting for a call from me. Mrs Chester, Charlotte, shall we all go into another room?"

At the sound of an unknown voice, the tangled mop of hair moved from Sandra's neck. The child, it could have been either sex, appeared to be scanning the hallway. Forbes waited for the infant's scream, but none came. He watched Sandra whispering into the side of the unruly mop, but the child simply blinked and continued staring. Forbes smiled and raised one hand to shoulder height, self-consciously waving his fingers exactly as he'd done outside to convince Sandra, and himself, that it wasn't just a dusty doll that they were looking at. Outside, he'd been rewarded with a slight movement, but in here, with so many strange people watching, it produced only another blink.

What better place to bring up a child, he'd been thinking while they'd waited for the PCs to come back downstairs, than in this old rambling property, surrounded by nature. He'd met frustrated parents and bored youngsters in flats and council estates whose lives could have been transformed by living somewhere like this.

And yet here was a child, whose very existence had been denied by these two women, and who looked as if it had never been outside, much less climbed trees, searched for birds' nests, or chased butterflies through grassland in summer sunshine. The eyes were a deep blue, he could see that much. And he'd been right in thinking the main reason why they'd appeared so out of proportion with the face was that the pale cheeks were sunken and the skin almost translucent. He couldn't hazard a guess at its age.

Mrs Chester was blocking the doorway between the hall and the living room, and Sergeant Walker was forced to stop.

It was Sandra who moved next. Taking the initiative, she took two steps towards the women. Forbes wanted to snatch the child from her arms, but at the same time was fascinated by the women's reactions.

"Yes… yes…, all right," it was Charlotte who spoke, in a quiet and controlled manner, "she's my daughter. You can take her away with you. I'm not the maternal type. I don't need to see her again."

Mrs Chester, without a flicker of emotion, turned away from her niece and took one step inside the living room. "This has absolutely nothing to do with me."

As Sandra's jaw fell open, Charlotte walked past her and the silent child and reached for the front door. Without another word, Charlotte wrenched the door open and beckoned Sandra to leave.

"Wait in the car for the doctor," Walker instructed the two constables. "Call for assistance and make sure you keep that child warm. Ladies, this officer and I aren't going anywhere, so please move out of the way and let's all go through to the next room."

A dozen officers arrived and searched every disorganised, junk filled room, from the attic to the cellar. Dust motes swirled through the air and clung to their clothing.

Even the two drug detection dogs Sergeant Walker had requested had sneezed their way around the property. They'd arrived in a flurry of tail wagging and high pitched barking and then scrambled and struggled, checking out every item of woodworm riddled furniture and dusty cupboard in every room, before leaving, covered in cobwebs, disappointed.

When the dogs and the officers had completed the search, and the two women were at the station, PC Forbes and Sergeant Walker closed the front door of Woodbine Cottage with a sigh of relief.

"This could be the only case of child neglect I've seen which doesn't involve either drug abuse or alcohol." Sergeant Walker dusted off his clothes before he opened his car door. "They offered us no explanations. What we've witnessed here appears to be pure, selfish neglect, and there's never an excuse for that. Until today, three adults have been living in this mausoleum of a place, and one of them even claimed to be the mother. How has this been allowed to happen?"

Dr Jill Jenson slapped a slim file down onto the table. If it was an attempt to gain everyone's attention in the packed incident room, it was a needless gesture. "The young girl I've examined today possibly wouldn't have lived many more weeks without medical intervention. Knowing what it would mean to everyone here, I felt I had to come and deliver the outline of my report in person. After examining her as much as I could without adding to her trauma, I can say that it's the worst case of neglect that I've ever come across. It may take years for her to fully recover, both physically and mentally." She turned to Sergeant Walker. "I still don't know her name or her age – she isn't speaking and I don't want to put undue pressure on her."

"The woman claiming to be her mother, Charlotte Chester, told us she gave birth in April, at Woodbine, three years ago. She can't, or won't give us an exact date and she claims the birth was never registered with the authorities. We've contacted the registrar and they have no record of the birth, at or around that time for that property."

"PC Michael Forbes," she'd picked him out of the sea of faces. "I understand it was you who found her. You almost certainly saved her life. Well done."

"I looked up – that was all." He could never be articulate in the presence of Dr Jenson.

She'd been the first to respond to his emergency call, beating the ambulance by ten long minutes on the day his mother had collapsed, and hearing her voice always swept him back to that day. As an eighteen year old, he'd stood in the doorway watching Dr Jenson battling to keep his mother alive on their living room floor while his two-month old sister had wailed her little heart out in her crib upstairs. On the fifteen minute journey to the hospital, she'd lost the war.

He knew she was a very capable young doctor, and until that life-changing day he'd quite fancied the slightly older woman. Slim and attractive, with blonde hair firmly set in a Margaret Thatcher style, which at first glance had the effect of ageing her, he thought she probably had many admirers. He also thought the effect of her hairstyle was deliberate.

In the dark weeks following his mother's death, Dr Jenson had been a regular visitor to their house, encouraging Michael back into his studies, monitoring the health of his tiny, motherless sister and even bringing cooked food to encourage his father to eat. He'd stood by and watched her with her arm around his father, gently offering parenting advice. To his embarrassment now, he'd found some misplaced courage and offered up an inappropriate suggestion to his father. That was the closest he'd ever come to being punched to the floor. His grief had been so distorting. He'd instantly seen how wrong he'd been and apologised, and then for several embarrassing minutes father and son had hugged each other and sobbed as only the bereaved can. Then they'd pulled apart and for the first time in weeks, they'd laughed together.

Thank you, Dr Jenson.

She was still speaking. "Not only is she severely underdeveloped for a three year old – if we believe the mother on the birth date, but she has sores over approximately one third of her body. In her weakened state, several of them have become infected and even more painful. But something we rarely see today, thank goodness, is rickets. She has an extreme case, probably down to a very poor diet over an extended period. Because her bones are softer than they should be they too are painful for her and make it difficult for her to walk. We think her arms may have fractures, because of the rickets, but we don't want to alarm her today with the x-ray machines. Mentally, she's difficult to assess, but she is quite alert, although still very frightened. Even some brightly coloured plastic toys were enough to send her into a state of panic. I left her supervised and playing with some wooden building blocks, the kind you'd offer to a twelve month old child, and she seemed comfortable with them. The very least you can charge those women with is child neglect. There'll be no shortage of evidence. Have they offered up any explanations?"

Sergeant Walker looked impressed. "I appreciate your coming here, doctor. We were hoping for your initial report before we began formal interviews. Charlotte has been offering to give a blood sample to help confirm she's the biological mother, but she's still insisting that she wants nothing more to do with the child... the girl."

"What about the older woman, the one who's just lost her husband?"

"Mrs Chester still maintains ignorance about the child. She also still claims that Charlotte is her niece, but I'm not convinced."

"One, or possibly both women, could be suffering from a mental illness, feeding off each other's instability and thereby multiplying it. They'll need psychiatric assessments. Have they requested solicitors?"

"I very much doubt that, and no," Walker answered both questions. "But you're more qualified to assess their mental state than we are. We're interviewing the child's mother first. Would you care to sit in as an observer?"

"I'm on call, but I don't have to be anywhere for the next couple of hours, so thank you, I'd be fascinated."

Forbes had deliberately remained close to his sergeant and noticed an uncharacteristic twitch in the corner of his mouth. Here was another admirer of Dr Jill Jenson, he thought, and another with no chance. Walker, a balding, workaholic divorcee and take-away worshiper, and a confident and single, health food fanatic – he had *absolutely* no chance.

The Buxton Advertiser, Matlock Mercury, and Derbyshire Times, already had the gist of the story and were begging for more. Forbes hadn't sat in on any interviews as high profile as this case promised to be. He took his place at the table and was surprised at the intensity with which his sergeant scrutinised Charlotte's face, as if expecting to find answers written there. She was looking down at the table and under the glare of overhead lighting he saw that her wavy hair was the colour of ripened straw.

Only Dr Jenson had been aware, as she'd told him days later, of the fragile golden curls that had appeared in the hospital ward in response to a warm, damp flannel.

When Charlotte looked up, the same piercingly blue eyes they'd all seen in the child, stared back at them. Charlotte

Chester wasn't conventionally good looking, he thought, but her eyes and her cheekbones were striking, in a supermodel kind of way. Light in Woodbine Cottage had been poor, but in here every wrinkle and every blemish was visible. She fiddled with a strand of hair, and her dirty, worn-down fingernails told him she wasn't a woman who took care of her appearance. Maybe she was mentally ill and in need of some sympathy after all.

"You've been arrested and charged with neglecting a child," Sergeant Walker began, speaking more softly than Forbes had ever thought possible. He wondered if it might be for Dr Jenson's benefit. "It will help you if you co-operate from the beginning of this interview. So let's begin with your full name, shall we?"

She held Walker's gaze for a full five seconds before looking down into her lap and withdrawing her hands from the table. The overall effect of those high cheekbones that some models would die for, and the perfectly shaped if rather pale lips, was ruined by the length of her nose and the uncommon upward slant of those distinctive blue eyes.

"You see, I have this nagging thought which won't go away. I don't actually believe that Charlotte Chester is your real name at all." Walker paused for effect.

Forbes watched the pale lips being pressed together until they'd disappeared completely. Charlotte appeared to be battling inner demons, unable to decide whether to speak or to burst into tears.

If his sergeant had grounds for his suspicions, he'd no idea what they might have been. And glancing sideways at Dr Jenson, neither, he suspected, did she.

"Nor do I believe," Walker continued very slowly and very deliberately, "that you are actually related to either Mr or Mrs Chester. So... what we'd all really like to know is... what is your real name, and what are you doing, living at Woodbine Cottage, with your supposed child?"

The room remained silent.

"You're facing very serious charges, do you realise that?" Forbes thought he'd better add his voice, even though he didn't follow the line of questioning. "We're trying to sort out what's been happening in that house, and not speaking isn't helping you or us."

"You know who I am, don't you?" she whispered without looking up.

"Unless I'm very much mistaken... yes I do," Walker answered. "But for the benefit of the tape, will you please speak up and give us your full name."

"Where have you taken the baby?" she spoke without any emotion.

Dr Jenson leaned forward. "I'm a doctor and I've just come from the hospital after spending almost three hours with your little girl. She's in Calow Hospital, in Chesterfield, in a single room and she has someone with her at all times."

"That's as much as I need to know. I don't want her back. I keep telling people that."

Walker smiled. "She's just fine, and she's being well taken care of. Let's do this one step at a time, shall we?"

If this was what it took to get her talking, then for now, his sergeant was obviously willing to play along, as neither of the officers had seen the child since she'd been wrapped in several layers of blankets and whisked away from Woodbine, and even then they'd only seen above the tiny shoulders.

Dr Jenson persisted. "She's the most beautiful little girl – she has your blue eyes – she just needs feeding up a little. What's her name?"

"I... we never gave her a name, not a proper one... we just called her baby. I did care for her at the beginning. I fed her myself, from my own body for the first few months, but Elizabeth... Mr and Mrs Chester, they didn't like it. And they wouldn't let me out of the house. They locked me in that attic. You've no idea how that felt. I got so depressed that I stopped trying to feed her and the milk stopped coming. Every night I cried myself to sleep, and when baby wouldn't stop crying, I wanted us both to die." She hesitated and Dr Jenson reached out and touched her shoulder. "But I couldn't bring myself to hurt her, I just couldn't, and I was too much of a coward to kill myself. I know I'm pathetic. Elizabeth said so. She told me I was suffering from post-natal depression, and maybe she was right. She told me they had to lock me in that room for my own good, and that I was too messed up to understand. If you know who I am, then you must know what happened. Please… you must tell me… did you ever find my husband Mark's body?"

Forbes rolled his shoulders slightly. For the first time since joining the force he felt the hairs on the back of his neck actually move. A few months earlier, not long after joining the force, he'd read notes on an open case and seen the pictures. He'd known who the Chester couple were before knocking on the door of Woodbine Cottage, and he was familiar with the story of Mark and Katy Brundell, missing for four years, presumed dead. And yet here, without any doubt, was Katy asking about her husband's body.

"For the tape please…."

"My name is Katy Brundell," she spoke in a clear voice but without looking up from her lap. "They… Mrs Chester drugged me and when I woke up properly found myself lying next to Mark's body. He was stone cold."

Forbes realised that Sergeant Walker, for some reason, was looking at him. He asked the only question he could think of. "How did Mark die? Do you know?"

"I never knew. It didn't matter. He was dead… that was all that mattered. I think they kept me drugged, but I've no idea for how long. I never dared ask them about Mark – I was too afraid that whatever had happened to him would happen to me."

"Why did they keep you alive?" Sergeant Walker regained his voice and took back control of the interview.

"Why do you think?" She closed her eyes and whispered. "They were both sick – sick in the head. They raped me, hundreds of times over the years – both of them raped me – sometimes one and sometimes both. My swollen belly turned them on. How sick is that? After one of their assaults I began to bleed and they left me alone for a few days. Then baby was born. But just weeks after her birth, they began all over again."

Jill leaned forward again. "Was your husband the father?"

"Yes, it hadn't begun to show but I was four months pregnant on the day of the storm. Mark was so looking forward to being a dad."

"We searched Woodbine, and the woods around it, within days of you both being reported missing. Where did they take you?"

"I only remember travelling inside something small and dark, a car boot, or maybe a large box. I was drugged, but I do remember being next to Mark's body on the way there, and being alone on the way back weeks later, but I've no idea how long the journey took. They kept me in a dark room, underground I think. When it rained, water seeped in through the walls. They began to rape me in there. I told them I was expecting a baby but they didn't stop. I can't believe I'm finally telling someone. When can I see my parents?"

"Now we know who you are, Katy, we'll send someone to fetch them. Have you no idea how long you were you held in an underground room?"

"I know it was weeks because I felt baby growing inside me. They brought food and drinks, which at first I refused. But because of my baby, I had to give in and eat. I never knew whether it was day or night, and I was so scared. Then one day they dragged me out and took me back to Woodbine Cottage. They pulled me up all those stairs and locked me in the attic. I really believed I would die there."

She lifted her head and looked from Walker to Forbes to Dr Jenson, and then back to Walker. She wasn't showing any signs of fear now. If anything, her blue eyes were challenging. They were intelligent eyes, he realised, not clouded by a mental illness, but not filled with relief either. It was the briefest of looks, but it had the effect of cancelling out his growing feelings of sympathy. He'd seen that same look many times, usually on the faces of teenagers who'd mistakenly thought they were above the law, and it invariably meant that they were lying.

"Neither your car nor Mark's body were ever found. When was the last time that you saw him alive?" Sergeant Walker asked.

"Inside Woodbine, on the day of the storm, I was offered a drink and a biscuit in the kitchen while Mark went upstairs with Mr Chester. I thought the man must have wanted him to look at some building work. My drink was drugged. I remember not being able to move and then being carried upstairs, and then I remember seeing Mark lying on a huge bed. I think he was still breathing but I must have fallen unconscious. When I woke, he was cold. They came into the room and gave me another drink – I was too out of it to resist. Then they took us somewhere. You must believe me. I'm not the criminal here."

Dr Jenson made a throaty sound but didn't speak.

"Your tiny daughter was locked in an attic room, in the most appalling conditions and seriously emaciated state, and yet you were downstairs in the living area when my officers arrived." The subtle change in his sergeant's tone told Forbes he wasn't alone in doubting the story. "Why did you never try to go for help?"

"You must understand," she continued quite calmly, "that I was locked in the attic until several weeks after the birth. Then baby took my place as a prisoner – a hostage. I was allowed into the rest of the house, but only when they needed me to skivvy for them. They locked us in the attic room each night. They said that if I ever left the house they'd kill baby and remove her body and her few things so that no one would believe me. They said they'd tell people I was a drug addict and they'd only taken me in out of pity while I was trying to sort my life out."

"And you believed all that?" Forbes asked.

"Back then, they were still giving me drugs of some sort, but I had to eat. I couldn't think properly but I did the best I could for the child. They wouldn't let me feed her properly, but while she was alive, I had no choice but to stay. I always believed that one day we'd both get out of there. That's why I told you to take her. It was our first chance to escape together. But I don't want her back. She deserves a better mother than I could ever be, because I know I won't be able to look at her without reliving my long nightmare."

"My constable here was the first officer on the scene this morning, where Ian Chester died. How did the suicide make you feel?"

"How do you think? I was relieved, but I could hardly jump for joy while Elizabeth held the attic keys. One of them always had the keys. If I'd tried to ask you for help, she would have made some excuse to stop you from coming in. It only takes a minute to kill a small child, she always said, and if her body was ever discovered then they'd blame me. I never stood a chance against the two of them."

"Were you aware that Mr Chester was ill?"

"No one told me but I could see something was very wrong. I kept praying it was terminal. He mostly did Elizabeth's bidding, but he enjoyed it every bit as much as she did. They were both evil. She must know where Mark's body is."

If Dr Jenson felt affected by the interview, she didn't show it. When they left the room, her first words were a question. *Could she please sit in on Elizabeth's interrogation?*

Part 2   Elizabeth.

Dr Jill Jenson followed Sergeant Walker and PC Forbes into the second interview room. They sat opposite Elizabeth Chester and Dr Jenson pushed a box of tissues across the table.

PC Forbes waited for his sergeant to begin.

"Mrs Chester, surely you can appreciate how unbelievable your story sounds."

"But I swear to you, on my poor Ian's life, that I never knew there was a child up there."

"Elizabeth," Dr Jenson spoke softly, "your husband, Ian, hanged himself this morning."

"I know dear, I know, but I promise you, I was as amazed as anyone when your officers brought that little mite down our stairs." She clasped her hands together as if in prayer, "Please tell me the child's going to be all right."

Those had been her first words of concern.

"You haven't been charged with anything yet, Mrs Chester." There was that soft voice of Walker's again. "Let me reiterate that you have our sympathy over this morning's tragic events. The little girl will recover, eventually, but we need to hear your version of events from the very beginning, starting with the afternoon of the storm four years ago, and whether you'd ever met Mark or Katy Brundell before that day."

"No, of course we'd never met them, Ian... Ian told you that at the time. That storm was so violent. We didn't learn until a few days later that we'd been in the direct path of a freak tornado. The phone and power lines were down, branches were flying and trees were falling like rows of dominoes so when we saw that little red car bouncing up our driveway, Ian said to me, 'I bet there are trees down. Folks should have more sense than to drive this road in this weather.' And he was right of course, but that storm hit us so hard and so fast that day, that you had to feel sorry for the young couple. They were just looking for a safe place to stop until the storm passed over and the roads were cleared. But you know all of this."

"I'd like to hear your side of the story again, as would Dr Jenson who's examined the little girl. Please continue, Mrs Chester."

Her hands shook as she took a tissue from the box on the table. "I need to know – no one's told me – is that child really Katy's? I don't understand how that can be."

"That's what we're hoping to find out." Dr Jenson smiled.

"Well the couple sat in their car for about a minute. It wasn't safe for them to get out. Then the storm passed, all of a sudden, and they both got out and came to our front door.

They told us the road was blocked in both directions. Ian went down our lane to check, but said there were too many trees for him to be able to cut them a way out with his chain saw. So we gave them tea and biscuits, and when it grew dark we felt obliged to offer them a sandwich and a bed for the night. What else could we have done? The next morning the council workmen, private contractors, and in fact anyone with a chain saw or a tractor was out helping to clear the roads. You must remember what it was like?"

"I remember the storm very well," Sergeant Walker encouraged her. "My father's house was also in its path and he lost the roof of his garage. It landed in the neighbour's garden."

"We gave them tea and toast for breakfast and they seemed grateful and went out to their car. I remember it was a beautiful spring morning and the birds were flitting about and singing their little hearts out. They sounded so glad to be alive. There was no wind at all that morning, just birdsong and the echo of distant mechanical machinery. It was quite surreal. He was a decent man, you know, my Ian."

She was drifting. "Mrs Chester, are you all right?"

"Thank you son, yes, where was I? They had a car full of groceries and they offered some to us as a thank you, so we all had lunch together while they waited for the workmen to clear a way out."

"No one working on the roads that day could remember seeing their car leaving, Mrs Chester," Walker said.

"That's because they must have already cleared the trees from the direction the couple took. We had all these questions thrown at us years ago."

"Just continue, please."

"We thought they must have gone back to town for something. How should we be expected to know? We thought they were a decent couple... I can't believe I'll never see him again."

"Never see who, Mrs Chester?"

"My husband of course… my poor Ian… please may I see him?"

Walker nodded. "There'll be a post mortem sometime today, but you should be able to see him tomorrow. The coroner has been informed, and your doctor has identified him and confirmed the medical conditions that he names in his letters."

She drew in a sharp breath and closed her eyes for a second.

Doctor Jenson shifted forward on her chair. "You're not under arrest, Elizabeth. If you don't feel well enough to continue I can give you a sedative and you can take a break." She looked at Sergeant Walker. He nodded. "I'm sure a female police officer could be spared if you wanted to go home for a while."

Forbes suppressed a smile. He knew that wasn't why his sergeant had nodded, but neither officer spoke.

"The officers here need to understand what led up to today's events," the doctor added.

"Is Katy still here?"

"She's already been charged," Forbes answered softly. He felt she needed more encouragement. "We're holding her here, but we need your version of what happened after the couple drove away."

She didn't seem to hear.

"I've nothing to go home for now. You all know what happened next. You searched our home, you ransacked our sheds and you treated us like criminals. It was a frightening experience for us."

"We had a job to do," Walker defended his team. "They'd been missing for a day before the alarm was raised and their families were desperate for any news. You must understand that."

"People for miles around us shunned us in the street — some of them still do. A public apology would have been appreciated when you failed to find anything. That's all we wanted. Was that too much to ask?"

"Then as the senior officer here, on behalf of the force, I sincerely apologise. If you've done nothing wrong, Mrs Chester, then you've nothing to fear by continuing."

"It's come too little, too late. You harassed and bullied us every day for a week. Then you just left and we prayed it was over. But it wasn't, and this is the part that you don't know. Ian and I were still busy clearing up your mess, a week after you'd left us, when there was a desperate banging on our front door. It was Katy... you have to understand... she was in a dreadful state and so thin and dirty that we barely recognised her. We wanted to call the police straight away but she begged us not to. And after the way we'd been treated, the last thing we wanted was to see any more of your lot. So we fed her and ran her a bath and then she told us what had happened."

"You really should have contacted us, if only for her family's sake. Until today, they believed she was dead. Her father had a breakdown."

"I told her we'd seen her parents on the television news, desperately asking for any kind of information, but she begged us, over and over, not to call anyone at all. You've no idea what she was like."

"So tell us now."

"She was terribly bruised and battered. She described how her husband had turned violent the moment they'd left our property, locking her in the car, driving like a maniac out onto the moors and then dragging her out of the car in the middle of nowhere and beating her. She said he'd accused her, over and over, of making eyes at my husband."

"And did you think that she had?" Forbes had only seen the man swinging from a tree, but he couldn't imagine, even four years earlier and without the stretched neck, that the man would attract any young woman, let alone an attractive, pregnant newlywed.

"The idea was ludicrous. And if she had, then I'm sure Ian would have told me. She described how Mark had dragged her back inside the car and driven to an old barn, in the middle of the moors, she'd no idea where."

"She told us how he'd tied her up, and how he'd eaten what they'd bought at the supermarket while she'd starved. Did I tell you they'd been on their way home when the storm began?"

Walker smiled and nodded.

"And they both drank rainwater when the beers ran out, she told us. They existed like animals for a fortnight, that's what she said, like animals. For the first week he threatened to kill her and then kill himself. Then he began telling her he was going to leave her to die. It sounded to us as if he'd gone crazy. Looking back, I can't say that I'm too surprised; he made me feel quite uncomfortable. There was something about his eyes, something not quite right, if you know what I mean?"

"A few minutes ago, Mrs Chester, you were saying that you thought they were a decent couple."

"We did... they were... it was just his eyes; they were kind of piercing."

"So when Katy returned to Woodbine," Sergeant Walker wasn't sounding convinced, "are you saying that you both totally believed what she told you?"

"We had no reason not to, especially given the state of her. She described how she'd dug a rock out of the earth floor with her bare hands while Mark had been sleeping, and how one night she'd hit him over the head with it. She'd freed herself from the ropes but couldn't find the car keys, so in a panic she escaped on foot. She'd been walking a while when she heard the car engine and saw headlights sweeping the fields. She lay down, hidden by a stone wall, until she heard him drive away and then she tried to find us. She said she thought this was about the last place he'd think of looking for her. He couldn't have held her too far from here, but it was still a miracle how she found us. Can you imagine how distressed she was?"

"But we still don't understand," Forbes added, "why didn't you at least contact her family?"

"She pleaded with us not to. I must say I never noticed an accent, but when she'd had a rest she explained that Mark came from a rough, gangster-type, Glaswegian family. If he was alive, she told us, then he'd hunt her down and kill her, and if he was dead, or in prison, then one of his family would do the job for him, and she was frightened for the safety of the rest of her family. She begged us to let her stay for a few days while she decided what to do. She was very convincing."

"She must have been, given that that was four years ago." Walker added.

"The days became weeks and then she became ill for a while. I wanted her to see a doctor but she was adamant that she wouldn't. She kept being sick, not just mornings but right through the day. Well you can't kick a sick person out of your house, can you? And it wasn't as if we hadn't got room. We lived on the ground floor and let her have the attic. It's a self-contained space up there but we never had any need for it. The middle floor is only used for the storage of old clothes, carpets, furniture, and stuff that we've inherited or we just don't want to throw out. But we were very glad of that first floor space after she'd been living in the attic for a few months. Ian made the mistake of letting her have an old radio, just for a bit of company he'd said, but she never, ever, turned it off. Day and night it was on, even when she was downstairs with us. I told her we didn't like it, but she argued that it brought life into the old place."

"She doesn't appear to be sick now, so why let her stop so long?"

"After a while, I really can't remember how long, her health seemed to improve and she offered to work for her keep. She cleaned the house, cooked all the meals and brought the old vegetable plot back to life. We've hardly bought any vegetables in the last couple of years. She never mentioned her family and I suppose it got where we couldn't do without her, especially when Ian became ill. She helped me to nurse him. She became like the daughter we never had. If anyone came to the door, she'd tell them that she was our niece and just helping out with the housework. It was her idea to use a false name – she used our surname and we felt flattered."

Sergeant Walker shook his head. "That still doesn't explain about the little girl."

"I've been thinking about that and a lot of things have fallen into place. At first Ian thought she was sponging off us, but she never asked for anything. I offered her some of my old clothes, despite them being several sizes too big for her, and she accepted them and altered them, but then we noticed she was gaining weight. We put it down to the good food she was always cooking for us, but then she did seem to lose weight quite quickly. We were afraid she was becoming ill again, but in the end we decided she must have been slimming and we simply hadn't noticed. Don't you see what that means?" She looked at Dr Jenson. "She must have given birth all alone in the attic, and the music covered the sound of the baby's crying. I can only think she must have thought we'd have asked her to leave, or contacted her family, if we'd known about her pregnancy."

Her lower lip trembled and her grey eyes watered.

"You say that you never knew," Walker said, "but are you absolutely certain that your husband didn't know?"

"What are you suggesting? My poor Ian never suspected; he'd have said something to me – I know he would. And if you're thinking that the child could be his, then you're wrong."

"How do you feel about Katy, now?" Walker asked.

"I can't get past the idea that such a shy, quiet, and kind young woman could keep a baby locked away like that, and for so long. Perhaps she'd been more traumatised by her husband than either of us realised. Do you think that's possible? It hurts to think that she couldn't talk to us. The poor girl must have felt so desperate and so alone."

The tears were in free-fall. Dr Jenson looked at Walker. He nodded again and she stood and gently placed an arm around Elizabeth's shoulders.

"I'll take you home now and make sure you're not left alone," she said.

Forbes flinched. He'd heard her speak those very same words once before, while she'd been cradling his infant sister, Louise, in her arms.

A soft, slow rain was falling as the two women walked towards the doctor's car.

"Two women from the same household," PC Forbes addressed his sergeant who was looking down on the women through the window of the first floor incident room, "but with two wildly differing accounts of what led up to today's rescue. Do you believe either of them, sir?"

"Like I believe in the fairies at the bottom of my garden, Michael, but we won't let them know that. Neither of them will be going far until we have some answers. And well done today, you did a sterling job."

PC Sandra Bennett's shift was officially over but she sat in her own car in the station car park, looking over her notes. Every few seconds she looked up and peered through her rain spattered windscreen. She waited until he was walking directly in front of her car, with his head bowed against the rain, then gave one short blast of her car horn and laughed at him. "Get in for a minute, Michael. You did well today, partner. They may not all show it, but everyone at the station was proud of you. If you hadn't taken a closer look, then a child who never officially existed would have died alone in that filthy room. Do you fancy following me to the pub for a quick pint on the way home? I won't be able to stay for long though. Mum's looking after Rose."

"That sounds good to me. I can't stop long either, Dad's had Louise all day and she's a bit of a handful now. Sometimes I'm worried that he's barely holding it together. She's my sister and I love her, but there are times when she's a mixed blessing."

"I know what you mean, but it's all right to feel out of control occasionally after what you've both lost. It will get better."

The Bull's Head was quiet, with one young couple standing at the bar, engaged in a serious conversation, and four teenagers in the games room, playing an equally serious game of darts. Trade had been gradually falling off over the past ten years, Forbes had been told. Without their two darts teams and an ageing domino team, it would hardly have been worth opening the pub doors during the winter months. It was still early for most of the regulars, and the quiet venue was perfect for a drink and a chat after work. Sandra paid for a pint and a half of Marston's real ale and they took their drinks to the fireside and sat down.

"So the only charges at the moment are those involving the child," Forbes explained. "We've two wildly differing accounts as to what happened to Mark Brundell and we're no closer to finding his body – that's if he is actually dead. If Elizabeth is to be believed, then Katy could have been the last person to see Mark alive, possibly before he killed himself."

"But no remains or suicide letters ever turned up," Sandra argued. "Even if he threw himself into the river and got washed away, you'd expect something to have been found by now."

"If Mr and Mrs Chester killed him, then his body could be at the bottom of an old lead mine shaft, or weighted down in a lake or a reservoir somewhere. Also, though I find this part hard to believe, Katy claims she's still afraid of a revenge attack from his gangland Glaswegian family."

"So who's telling the truth?" Sandra picked up her half pint glass, took a good long drink and then looked towards the bar. It was unstaffed.

"Sergeant Walker doesn't believe either of them. That part of the investigation involves covering old ground. Elizabeth is sticking with her original story and Katy can't prove any of her claims. Even if we do find Mark's body it may not prove which one of them, if any, killed him."

"We only visited Woodbine once and you spotted the child. I'd suggest you enquire about Mr and Mrs Chester's eyesight.

Even if they couldn't hear her, surely they could have seen her. I know the child was weak, but that can't have been the first time that she'd stood at that window." She took a second long drink and placed her empty glass on the table.

"That's a good point," Forbes wiped condensation from the side of his pint glass, saw that the barman had returned and slid two pound coins across the table. "Have this one on me."

"Ever the gentleman... cheers," Sandra smiled, went to get her glass refilled and then returned with his change.

"Both of the women's stories are quite detailed," he began. "Do you think it's possible they could have worked on them together? Let's say his body had been found at some point. With each of them blaming the other, and without any evidence or witnesses, they might have expected that we could never charge either one of them with Mark's death."

"I suppose it's possible, Michael, but where's your motive?"

"Maybe it was an accident, or an argument that got out of hand. There was never any evidence to suggest they'd known each other before the day of the storm. Any of the three of them could have killed him – maybe they were all involved."

"But why treat a child like that? What if all three of them were monsters? I wish I could get that poor child's face out of my head." She picked up her glass and examined the contents. "I don't think we're going to solve anything tonight. Can we please talk about something else? I'm a bit of a real ale freak and this beer's particularly smooth tonight, are you sure you wouldn't like another?"

*

PC Vivien Harrison closed, and then locked and bolted the front door of Woodbine Cottage. She leaned her back against it, listening to the doctor's car pulling away. The place had a musty smell and the air felt damp and cold. Vivien was used to her light, bright flat on the High Street – cheap and cheerful just like her personality, her friends had laughed, when she'd first described it to them.

"She's in bed," Dr Jenson had explained before she'd driven away. "I've given her a sedative and assured her she'll be able to see her husband's body tomorrow. Any medical concerns, however small, don't hesitate to call me on this number and I'll be straight here."

"I was surprised she was willing to go to bed so quickly," Vivien whispered, "I thought she'd want to go and look in the attic. If I'd been in her situation it would have been the first thing I'd have wanted to do. When you were with her, did she even ask about it?"

"She never mentioned it. It's as if she's resigned to the situation she's found herself in today."

"Or maybe she was well aware of what was up there."

"I may be speaking out of turn here, Vivien, but if I was you, I wouldn't want to sleep in this house. If they ask you to stay overnight, make sure you have a lock on your bedroom door, or failing that, have something solid and heavy wedged up against it."

Chapter 10
Present Day

Anna Jenkins leaned back on the sofa and watched the twins. They were almost unrecognisable from the sad specimens of a fortnight ago, and that transformation was largely down to her. Life at the commune was OK, but she had bigger and better plans for the four of them, and this was just the beginning. With a little encouragement from her, the identical pair had found employment in the largest, in fact the only decent nightclub in Leaburn. Add to that the flat which came with the job and Anna was even starting to feel a twinge of jealousy, even though it was a cramped, two-roomed space over a smelly fish and chip shop. She couldn't leave Verona. She wriggled on the scratchy, charity shop blanket and grinned at them. "Wow… you two look hot."

Carol blushed. "They told us these outfits are made from pure silk. Do you think they are?" She stepped towards Anna, inviting her to touch the gossamer soft folds.

Anna ran the blood-red fabric between her fingers. It felt like silk, but how would she know. "They're not brand new though, are they? Even if they are pure silk, which I doubt, I bet someone else has danced in these outfits. Who knows, they may even have had sex in them… Yuk! I wouldn't want to wear them without washing and disinfecting them first," she teased, but Carol didn't notice her smile.

"Of course we've washed them, stupid," indignation flashed across her face. "Anyway, they're ours now and we adore them."

Anna ignored her and instead turned her attention to Maisie. That didn't make her feel any more comfortable. The girl was stroking her cheek with a black fur wrap while fluttering her eyelids and swaying her body to the soulful sounds coming from the CD player that their dance teacher had loaned to them to practice their dance moves.

Gross… but Carol obviously didn't think so. She was smiling at her twin as she took a slow, sultry step towards her. The air felt charged with electricity and Anna's skin prickled as she watched the girls delicately touch fingertips and begin to sway together to the slow rhythm. No wonder they'd found employment in a seedy club. Their presence filled this small space, and she imagined they'd look drop-dead amazing on a proper stage with subdued lighting. They were totally mesmerising.

Carol finally pulled away but continued swaying her slim hips in time with the music. "You looked so natural on stage today, sis, so sexy and so relaxed while in rehearsal. I'm fine with it while we're here in the flat, but in front of strangers I feel self-conscious and stupid."

Anna instantly felt better.

"Rubbish, we need to practice to this old-fashioned style of music, that's all." Maisie stroked her sister's cheek with the edge of the wrap. "Didn't the instructor say that we're both naturals? The boss wants to see identical twins on his dance floor, that's what he's paying the extra for, and that's why we've been given this flat. How many people of our age get a chance like this?" She laughed, rather awkwardly. "We're every man's fantasy, the instructor said. And I say – if you've got it, flaunt it. Trust me, sis, it will all be all right."

Carol's hip gyrations slowed, out of sync with the music for the first time. "All the customers are bound to be drinking. There'll be alcohol everywhere once we start doing it for real. I'm afraid, Maisie, I'm afraid we might turn into a pair of alcoholics. I read somewhere that addictive personalities can be inherited. We can't end up like mum. I couldn't bear it."

Her intensity appeared to take Maisie by surprise and Anna watched as she placed her hands onto Carol's shoulders and gazed into her eyes. "That is never, ever going to happen to either of us, do you hear? Mum was alone in the world because we were too young to help her. We'll always have each other's backs. That's the promise we made when mum died. Remember... you and me against the world?"

Anna forced a gentle cough.

"And now we've got Anna and Verona on board – the four musketeers. This is scary for me too, but it's also exciting, and I intend to make the most of every moment. If mum is looking down on us, then we'll make her proud."

"Too right, you will," Anna couldn't keep quiet any longer. "You have a flat, a job, and your health. Your mum was poorly for a long time, by the sound of it, but we are all young and fit, and we have to make the most of this time. I'll even make another promise to you both, that if Verona and I can get jobs, then the four of us will save up to buy a flat of our own. Then we'll be dependent upon no one, and nothing will ever come between us."

She rolled off the bed, onto her feet, and embraced the twins.

"Come on, practise with us," Maisie tugged on her hands. "There's bound to be another job vacancy. We'll teach you the moves."

Carol moved to the wardrobe and opened the door to expose the full length mirror. They followed her and swayed to the music together. Anna prayed they'd be proved right, and that Verona would soon be a part of this.

"Sway a little more. Don't be shy," Carol laughed. "I know... I know... that's rich coming from me, but try and make a figure eight with your hips. That's it, now imagine you have an audience and push it out like Maisie does."

Maisie was the more natural, relaxed dancer. She'd slotted easily into the role of exotic dancer, even her voice sounded softer and sexier. "Brian says this is what the customers pay to see. Don't be shy, Anna. Sexy but sultry, and always towards the audience, that's it... that's the way." Carol giggled but Maisie wasn't about to be distracted from her project. "You have to tease them. You aren't doing your job if you don't send them home to their wives and girlfriends all hot and horny," she purred, swaying and writhing her way across the floor towards the window. Anna and Carol took advantage of the distraction and sat on the bed watching her.

The late afternoon sun directed a spotlight into the bedroom and Maisie gyrated her way towards it. "If any pervs are out there looking, this should be getting them all hot and sweaty."

"You're taking it too far, come away from the window." Carol said.

"We've got to get used to being ogled by dirty old men. Stop scowling like that you two. It'll be fun." But she moved back to the bed and sat down.

"We're out of reach while we're dancing on stage," Carol was still frowning, "but it's squeezing between tables and chairs, armed with trays of expensive drinks that I'm not looking forward to. When the room's full I'm not sure I'll be able to manage."

"I've thought about that too," Maisie answered. "But the other girls do it, so I'm sure we will. Just try not to let them touch you."

Anna thought of Verona and all that she'd suffered. She sat up straight. "Seriously though you two, if anyone ever tries to hurt you, or make either of you do anything you don't feel comfortable with, you must promise me now that you'll tell me straight away."

"What...?"

"What can you do about it?"

"Oh, I'll think of something! I'm going to make it my mission to look after everyone in our little group. We're a family of four, and no one will ever mess with any of us – at least not more than once. Now, do you promise me?"

"I promise."

"I promise."

Chapter 11

PC Robert Bell lowered his patrol car window a couple of inches and drew in a deliberate, deep lungful of the early spring, icy, moorland night air. His skin tingled, but in a good way. He felt alive, and slightly emotional. It was almost four months since he'd found Derek Austen's body and he still liked to take a quick look around the moors above the Goyt Valley occasionally. He drove steadily, off the frost covered moors and down the winding road through the tiny village of Earl Sterndale, past the pub which didn't look like a pub and which was named very aptly for the village – The Quiet Woman. From there he re-joined the A515 and headed back towards Leaburn.

Mid-week, things were normally quiet once the one club, the two public houses and the British Legion had emptied. He blinked at the street lights and his eyes stung. The air in the small town was slightly warmer than that on the moors, but it was making him shiver. It felt dirtier and damper, and tainted by the fingers of wood smoke from the log burners that seemed to be latest craze in domestic heating. He closed his window.

It seemed a world away from the city of Manchester where he'd trained, but the hills and dales of the Peak District were where he felt he belonged. He'd once heard someone quoting: *'nothing good ever happens around here after two in the morning'*, and from his own experience, not much bad ever happened either. So far this week, in the small market town, he'd carefully driven around four rambling badgers, been forced to brake hard for a couple of fighting, ginger tom cats, flashed his lights at a gang of three foxes attempting to break into dustbins and stopped to remove a plank of wood from the centre of the road.

He turned very steadily into Anderson Road and blinked his dry eyes. There was definitely something on the edge of the pavement ahead, just on the next bend. He leaned towards the windscreen, and blinked again.

As his car followed the curve of the road, his headlights skimmed the scene. His right boot squeezed down on the accelerator, and then on the brake. Only then did he reach for his radio. The shape had taken on human form. It was curled into a foetal position and lying in the centre of a dark stain.

*

"On first examination, this is strikingly similar to the attack on Derek Austen," Judith Horde, the same young police surgeon who'd been called to that incident, began telling Forbes. "The driving licence in his wallet identifies him as Carl Deakin, and this invoice I've just taken from his jacket pocket suggests that he's a local, married man. The address on it is for one of the cottages on the edge of Leaburn, only about half a mile away. He's suffered multiple stab wounds to his upper body before having his carotid artery cut. Also, his tie is wrapped around his right wrist. That suggests it's been used for something other than its intended purpose. I can't speak with any authority on the subject, but I wouldn't have thought bondage would be too popular with your average prostitute."

"There's a trail of blood leading back to the alleyway," Adam Ross nodded towards the officers who were taping off the scene. "Either he tried to fight off his attacker, or was dragged towards the road."

"He has some internal bleeding as well as what you see on the pavement. I'd suggest he crawled from the alley – take a look at his hands and knees, but then look at the blood spray on the pavement. The fatal blow to the neck happened right here at the side of the road."

Forbes was still studying the tie. "Which means our killer must have been in the vicinity for several minutes at least."

"Correct, and once again we can rule out robbery as the motive. His wallet contains exactly two hundred pounds, and he has a quality watch and two mobile phones."

"Carl Deakin, does that ring any bells with anyone this time?" Adam asked.

"I can't say that I recognise this victim. And what was he doing here? All the cars on this road are on private driveways. Where's his vehicle, and what did he do for a living? Did he have any association with the Buxton Advertiser, or with Derek Austen?"

"He could have been walking home, sir. It's not that far."

"Then let's go and find out."

One hundred yards from the junction of two country lanes, a short driveway led them to a parking space and a wooden, double garage which looked like an afterthought stuck onto the side of the converted chapel. Lights in the small, leaded, downstairs windows showed that someone was probably up and about, while the equally small, first floor windows were all in darkness. There were very few citizens out of their beds at this hour, and Forbes wouldn't have been one of them except for the body on Anderson Road.

The arched front door swung open before any of their boots touched the gravel. A woman stood, fully dressed and with the light radiating from the hallway behind her, looking at their vehicle as if she'd been expecting someone else.

"I knew something must be wrong," she said quite calmly once they'd identified themselves. "What's happened? Please tell me where my husband is."

The oak panelled hallway led into a high ceilinged, open-plan living and dining area. Despite being occupied, the property had somehow managed to retain the atmosphere of a musty chapel, the tiny windows managing to make the spacious living area feel claustrophobic.

They told her what little they knew and then allowed her a minute to digest the news.

"I couldn't sleep. That's why I'm fully dressed, in case you were wondering. I've been phoning him for the last hour and I was about to start ringing the hospitals. Oh the stupid, stupid man. He's never late without calling me. I knew something bad had happened... I just knew it."

"Pardon me, Mrs Deakin, but you don't seem too surprised. Was your husband concerned for his safety?"

"Not that I'm aware of. I just meant that I couldn't think of another explanation for him not calling me. I need a coffee. Can I get you two officers a drink? I've an opened packet of chocolate biscuits in the cupboard that I really don't want to finish by myself. I'll fetch them."

Adam stood. "I'll do that for you, Mrs Deakin."

A large, unframed picture of the Carl Deakin, reclining on a sheepskin rug with his arms around his wife, was the only wall furniture. It blended well with the rest of the modern furniture, but not with the style of the property. It was as if they'd recently moved from a modern apartment filled with modern fittings and brought all their furniture with them.

"We realise this is a distressing time for you," Forbes began, though he'd seen more anguish resulting from the death of a family moggy. "A family liaison officer will be with you shortly. She'll stay with you today and keep you informed with what's happening, but we need to ask a few questions now, if you don't mind?"

"No... I don't mind," she sighed and sank back into the leather armchair.

"Do you have any idea what your husband might have been doing in Anderson Road? We haven't found a car and there were no keys with him."

"His car... but he went out in it last night... that must be it then, mustn't it? Someone mugged him and stole his car. It's a black Peugeot 208, and he's only had it a few months. I'll fetch you the paperwork, I'm hopeless at remembering models and registration numbers. I won't be a minute. Carl keeps everything neatly filed away and I know exactly where to look."

She was looking less composed when she returned, with the documents in one hand and a handkerchief clutched in the other. She held out the papers and then flopped back into the chair. "What the bloody hell was he doing there?" She broke the silence just as Forbes had hoped. "I know he occasionally goes to the wine bars in the Manchester city centre after work, but he prefers the local pubs. But… there aren't any on that road, are there? I can't think of any reason for him to be there. I don't understand."

"How often does your husband go out drinking, Lisa?"

"He's not a heavy drinker – please don't think that. He has a glass or two of wine and then goes onto soft drinks. He has a stressful job and he goes out to relax. I always have his tea ready for him, and then he goes out… four, sometimes five nights a week. But he's normally back well before midnight. I don't mind. I get the television to myself and I prefer the quiet life. I go out with him maybe twice a month, but I'm a home bird at heart."

Her revealing blouse, seriously tight jeans and what looked like freshly applied make-up, made him doubt that statement. Maybe here was one of those women who breathed a sigh of relief when widowed.

"We'll be checking all the CCTV cameras in the city centre, as well as in Leaburn. If he was there then we'll find him." He waited for Adam to call in the vehicle details. "You have a unique home, Lisa. What did your husband do for a living?"

"He's the manager at Makin's, the kitchen and bathroom suppliers on the Harpur Hill Industrial Estate. The business is doing well. Sometimes they're so busy he has to work until eight or nine o'clock at night. There are new houses going up everywhere at the moment, but he always says he enjoys… he always enjoyed his work."

"Do you work?"

"I've two children upstairs, both under five. No, I don't work." She smiled, adjusted her blouse and brushed her manicured hands down her thighs.

"We're just collecting background information. It's routine in a case like this."

"And you're thinking nice house and two cars, how can they afford it? Well I expect you'll hear it from someone, so I'll tell you before one of the neighbours does. At a time when we'd been struggling financially, my husband inherited a considerable sum of money and it raised a few eyebrows. Four years ago, when I was about to have our first child, we were in a rented cottage up in the hills which we could barely afford to heat. The building trade was just picking up but Carl was still on a three day week. He was depressed. To keep himself occupied he began helping out our nearest neighbour. She was well into her eighties and Carl began fetching her groceries and doing odd repairs on her house. There was plenty that needed doing. It was an old run-down property just like the one we were in, but it was in a stunning location with a field and five acres of woodland. He cut down dead trees for her, filled her sheds with logs, and chopped endless piles of sticks. In return she let him take as much firewood as we needed."

Adam stepped back into the room.

"Please sit down," she said. "Do you need to write any of this down?"

"If it becomes relevant then we'll need a statement."

"Her name was Ivy Botham. She was a sweet old lady and always telling us how she hadn't seen any of her family for over twenty years. We certainly never saw anyone visiting. Anyway, one afternoon she announced to Carl that she had made a new will leaving everything, the house, the land, and all her savings, to him. We didn't take her seriously, of course. We dreamed, who wouldn't in our situation, but we decided it must be her way of ensuring Carl continued helping her out. One afternoon Carl found her dead at her kitchen table and it turned out that she'd had a massive stroke. When the will was read we were flabbergasted. She really had changed it in our favour and her family was seriously pissed off."

"Do you know where her family lives now?"

"Somewhere in Cambridge, our solicitor has the address. For a long while they were threatening to sue us, claiming Carl had coerced or brainwashed the old dear, but he'd done nothing of the kind. We'd been only too pleased to get free firewood and she was such a nice old lady that fetching her groceries along with our own, felt more of a privilege than a chore."

"The legal action was dropped... when?" Forbes asked.

"After a year they just seemed to give up. We sold her estate and bought this house outright, with enough money left for a car each. Then the building trade picked up and Carl was promoted to manager. It was a turning point for us, but Carl had genuinely been fond of the old dear."

"We'll look into it; were there many relatives threatening you?"

"Ivy never married, but there were two cousins and four surviving nephews and nieces who each thought they should have had a share of the pot. It's a shame really that they all neglected her for so long — it must have really hurt the old dear for her to have left nothing at all to any of them. But the estate was settled almost three years ago. Why would any of them come after Carl now?"

"It may turn out to be nothing to do with them. I have to ask this Mrs Deakin, but did you go out at all last night?"

"No, you're surprised at the way I'm dressed at this hour of the morning, I suppose. Carl likes me to look smart when he comes home. I almost always wait up for him."

"I see," Adam joined in. "Would you know if he ever had any dealings with the Buxton Advertiser?"

"The company Carl worked for do advertise in the local rag, and he knew the reporter who was stabbed to death a few months ago. He was talking about it only yesterday. But then everyone in the town is still talking about it, aren't they? I mean, things like that are usually confined to the cities, not little market towns like this." She paused. "But... you said that Carl had been stabbed... you don't think Carl's murder is connected to Derek's, do you?"

Forbes gently placed his mug onto the polished coffee table. "It's far too early to say. If we could have a recent picture, it will help to establish his movements last night."

"A picture... of course," she hesitated, "when will I be able to see him?"

"There will have to be a formal identification, so possibly this afternoon, unless you'd prefer a family member to do that."

"No, I'll do it," her voice quivered.

*

Jane Goodwin, special constable, mother of six year old Lucy and sole focus of DS Adam Ross's romantic leanings, was now an orphan. The mourners who'd attended her mother's funeral, a few of whom Jane hadn't seen for at least as long as Lucy had been on the earth, had all returned to their own homes, or to hastily booked hotel rooms, and Jane finally had the living room to herself. She was an only child, the same as both her parents had been, and suddenly she felt very alone. She gazed through the window at the birds enjoying the left-over, curled-up sandwiches she'd just put out for them.

A crash from the kitchen startled her, and then she smiled at the mumbled swear word, hoping the noise hadn't woken Lucy. Adam had offered to wash the pile of plates and the lipstick smudged glasses while she waved off the last of the mourners. She turned from the window, walked into the kitchen and crept up behind him, wrapped her arms around his firm torso and leaned into his shoulders. "I'll dry them later, if there are any left to dry," she teased. She could feel by the slope of his shoulders that he was tired. "Leave the rest. We'll finish off later. Go and get your head down for an hour or two and I might join you." She handed him a towel. No arguments, she was relieved. After Lucy's heart rending tears in church, and then refusal to leave the graveside, Jane's powers of persuasion were exhausted.

It was fifteen days since she'd found her mother lying cold on the kitchen floor. Only one thing could have made that day any worse, and that was if Lucy had been the one to find her. Her daughter, who normally ran on ahead, had paused. A friendly cat had been playing with leaves on her grandmother's lawn and distracted Lucy just long enough for Jane to enter the house first.

Jane had ordered a special wreath, shaped like a cat, and with Lucy's name on it.

She sat at the kitchen table and looked around. It had been one of the worst days of her life, but she was smiling through the tears. Her mother had always liked Adam, and his young son, Ryan.

Chapter 12

Two whiteboards, for the moment linked only by the manner and the ferocity of the killings they displayed, vied for attention in the incident room of the Leaburn Police Station.

"How is Jane?" Forbes was studying one of them as he greeted Adam. "Did the funeral go to plan yesterday?"

"I think she was on auto-pilot for most of the day. She's still adjusting, but she's getting there, thanks."

"We're going to need some of the special constables to deal with two murder enquiries. Do you think she'll be available for the occasional shift?"

"I'll ask if she'd like to come in. Have there been any sightings of Deakin's car yet?"

"We've found it on last night's city centre cameras. Deakin is clearly the driver and his manner suggests he's on the lookout for someone. We haven't found footage of him parked up, but tapes are still coming in. The last sighting we have of him was logged at ten past eleven on the Buxton Road, and he was heading back into the city centre."

"His wife says he prefers wine bars to pubs."

"He isn't looking for either. Never trust a man who belittles a good traditional pint of real ale, Adam. We're circulating his picture but it is early days. If he went inside any of the bars, I'll be very surprised."

"And whether he did or he didn't, things are pointing towards the prostitute theory?" Adam wrinkled his nose.

A quick bunk-up down some stinking alley wasn't his Detective Sergeant's style. "Don't look so bloody superior," Forbes muttered, after checking that no one was in earshot. "For some poor blokes it's all they can get, and for some women it means the difference between feeding and not feeding their children."

Adam looked at the two boards. "If Carl Deakin had left his car somewhere in Leaburn, it should have been reported by now. If the killer drove away in it, there's a slim chance that we'll see them on camera."

"We need more on Deakin's private life. His wife was no more emotional at the formal identification yesterday than she was at their house when we first broke the news to her. She was dressed more casually and the make-up was minimal, so perhaps she was telling the truth when she claimed she always dressed to please her husband, but something wasn't right with that marriage."

"So… an unfaithful, controlling husband and a wife who now has a motive for murder – I think it's unlikely, but it is a possibility." Adam said.

"PC Rawlings interviewed the staff at Makin's kitchen and bathroom supplier's yesterday afternoon. Deakin was well liked but some staff said they thought he liked the ladies a little too much for a married man. Unfortunately, they couldn't give us a name of anyone he might have been having an affair with. Also, Carl had two outstanding parking tickets, both within the last fortnight and both on the outskirts of Manchester. His firm pays most fines without questioning them, but they'd rejected these two."

"Which means they weren't work related?"

"Exactly – and at different times and different locations and so we're looking into them."

"What about a link between Mrs Deakin and Mrs Austen, sir? We could be looking at two wives, both aspiring to be widows. If they didn't do it, maybe they knew a man who would."

"You've been watching too much television, Adam."

*

Anna Jenkins had learned at an early age how to retreat from reality, happily wiping entire hours from her memory. The only person she'd ever been tempted to place her trust in had been a young social worker with a stutter, and that had only been because she'd felt sorry for the woman and actually thought they'd become friends. But as with the others, she'd regarded Anna as just another case. What was it that people sometimes said, *'the past is a foreign country'*? Too right it is. For the first time ever, she had true friends, friends who needed her at least as much as she needed them. Together they had a promising future, as long as she could keep them safe.

It was a dark night, the sky peppered with distant galaxies but no moon. Only blackness and the occasional rumble of an aircraft filtered through flimsy curtains at the huge house of assorted souls who made up the commune. Apart from Verona's rhythmic breathing, the house was silent. Anna thumped her pillow and wriggled down the narrow bed.

She felt herself drifting.

It seemed like minutes, though it could have been longer, when she woke feeling uneasy. She thought of the twins and the feeling intensified. It didn't make any sense. They were happy and starting out on a new life together. She was even slightly envious of them. She hoped her positive thoughts would dispel the anxiety. They didn't. It was ridiculous.

Then she realised. Verona had a small army of people fussing around her while the twins were alone out there. They were the ones who needed her the most. They should be her priority.

She pushed back the bedcovers and swung her bare feet onto crumbling lino. The floorboards below creaked under her weight. She placed her feet down slowly, testing each one.

It was time for her to leave.

Verona opened her eyes and smiled when Anna sat on her bed.

She'd put off this moment for too long. Placing her hand on Verona's pillow, she spoke very quietly. "Verona, I haven't forgotten my promise, and before too long we'll all live together again as a family. But I have to go now. I swear, I'll make a place for you out there, but this is the safest place for you until you've had your baby. You must stay."

"I don't understand... why now?" Verona's English had rapidly improved in the months at the commune. "Please don't leave until after the baby is born. You are my best friend."

Anna looked around the room. The dark furniture smelled musty and the few scattered rugs were threadbare, but none of that mattered. "The folks here love you and will take better care of you than I ever could in your condition. I'll visit regularly until you're ready to leave, with or without your baby." Seeing traces of that scared child from the hospital bed, she squeezed further onto the bed and put her arm over the girl. "When you wake in the morning, I'll be gone, but please don't worry. I'm organising false documents for you and I'll find work we can do together. Have faith in me, Verona. I don't make promises too often, but when I do I always keep them."

"And I promise also," Verona whispered back, "that when baby is born I will be ready for a new life with my friends. As soon as I am strong again I will follow. You are a best friend and I know I will not want a baby with me."

"You don't know that for certain, not yet." Anna felt very grown-up and unexpectedly maternal. "Women sometimes feel differently after having a baby. It's the hormones; they take over your body and turn you into a slave. They can fall in love with the ugliest of babies – I read that somewhere. Just wait to see how you feel and don't let anyone bully you into a decision. If you want to keep it, then we'll look after it together – all four of us."

"Please, Anna, promise me two things."

"Just name them, girl."

"Promise you will keep your mobile phone charged up."

Anna laughed, "And....?"

"Promise me that you'll take care out there."

Carrying the heavy blackthorn staff she'd taken from one of the sheds and left beside the cellar door, she trudged through the strengthening wind, her few belongings in a frayed tartan bag slung over her shoulder.

Until her eyes adjusted, she regretted leaving the car keys under Verona's pillow. The twins had left the car for her so she thought it only fair to pass on the favour, especially since Verona had so quickly picked up the basics of driving around the commune yards, and had obviously loved every second of her very basic lessons.

It was a long walk, five miles at least from the commune to the town of Leaburn where the twins were in for a surprise. Multiple layers of clothing hampered her and the trees and lawns sucked in what light there was from the stars. Heart beating faster, she finally reached the metal gates marking the commune's boundary and was able to increase her speed.

By dawn she'd reached the comfort of the first streetlights. The icy wind had become a cool breeze and she switched from a brisk march to a gentle stroll. She'd had some weird thoughts while covering the lonely miles. Was it love that she felt for Verona? Warm feelings towards another person, one you didn't depend on for your daily existence, were a new and slightly scary experience.

No... she felt sorry for the pregnant girl that was all, with her big puppy-dog eyes and her shy smile. Everyone at the commune had fallen in love with her, hadn't they?

Was it possible that her past life had made her gay? Hell no... never! She swung the blackthorn staff into the air and bounced it off the top of her head.

She was screwed up, that was all, and her evil mother was to blame for that, her mother and every one of her mother's stinking men friends.

As the first car of the morning approached, she hesitated and squeezed the top of the wooden staff.

The car didn't even slow down.

Chapter 13

Michael Forbes was wrestling with the idea of questioning the area's prostitutes, most of whom were known to the police and one of whom could potentially be a killer. It was an uncommon role reversal.

"Mrs Lisa Deakin is already known to us," Adam walked into his office waving a sheet of paper. "She was arrested and cautioned for possession of cannabis on five separate occasions, between six and eight years ago. She was charged just once with dealing but charges were dropped, and here's the interesting part, we have her on record as being cautioned for soliciting on three separate occasions, in Manchester. She was well known to the vice squad there when she was in her late teens and early twenties."

"How old is she now?"

"I believe she's thirty. The prostitution angle could be coincidence."

"No such thing in my experience, so I wonder whether she still has any contact with that world. Could that be why she was dressed so provocatively at three in the morning? Has she taken her business indoors, so to speak, and is that what her husband was involved in?"

"None of the neighbours have commented unfavourably on the Deakin's lifestyle. Someone would have noticed cars coming and going at all hours wouldn't they?"

"Not necessarily... with the hours the pubs and clubs can open now, people take less notice than they used to. Most neighbourhoods don't give the night traffic a second thought."

"Are you thinking we may have stumbled on a brothel in rural Leaburn?" Adam sounded surprised.

"Why not... our killer could be an irate wife or husband – it's a thought, but not one I want to hear repeated outside this room, not yet anyway."

"Austen was a journalist, sir, so his working hours were bound to be unpredictable."

"Have we any background yet on Austen's wife?"

"Nothing useful, and nothing that might link her to Deakin's widow, but then we've only just begun looking for a connection."

"Check their leisure times. They live approximately fifteen miles apart and both have a young family. They may have met. Did either couple play golf or go to a gym, or did they share a table for their pub lunch on the occasional Sunday? At the moment their husbands are only linked by a four inch, double edged knife, and a possible bondage game. We're still not releasing details of the ties. We don't need copy-cats, and it's hard enough to get the local sex workers to talk to us."

Forbes was about to begin his morning briefing in the incident room of Leaburn police station. Someone had eaten a bacon sandwich. He swallowed. "From the vehicles we stopped in the days following Derek Austen's murder, we gained only two leads, and we're still looking for that silver car. Also, Carl Deakin's black Peugeot 208 is still missing. Both killings suggested a sexual element, but that fact still isn't public knowledge, and if anyone from this station uses the words 'serial killer', then they'll be demoted to traffic duty for the foreseeable. Is that clear?"

"I'm surprised the press haven't connected the murders already," a female voice came from the back of the room.

"I've asked Manchester Vice Squad for their input. They tell me there have been no identical killings in or around their city in the last five years so we're concentrating on our own local area. Having said all that, I expect you all to be extra vigilant. And gentlemen, please keep in mind that our killer may be a young, attractive female, though I wouldn't expect anyone here to become side-tracked by fluttering eyelashes and a cute smile."

"As if...," a male voice came from somewhere in the centre of the group.

*

"That police sign is still up on the main road, Craig... you know... the one asking for information about that first murder." Tony Havers kicked off his wellington boots, adding only marginally to the mound of dried mud and dead leaves in their wooden porch.

The stained mug Craig had only just rinsed out bounced off the dull metal draining board, smashing into pieces on the stone slabs of the kitchen floor. "But that silver car that they're looking for, I keep seeing one just like it on our back lane."

Tony took three long strides into the room, kicked the pottery remains against the wall and grabbed his brother's shoulders. "I've told you before; we're not going to get involved. You've got to keep that big trap of yours shut."

Craig shook him off and persisted. "But I saw it twice last week, and cars don't use that rough back lane if they don't have to. And I'm pretty sure it was a girl in the driving seat."

"We agreed the registration didn't match the appeal on the telly, didn't we? Now stop wittering on about the damn thing."

"That means nothing." Craig continued. "Number plates are easy to change... and there's been another murder only twenty miles away. At Bakewell market yesterday, everyone was talking about them, saying they must be linked. There's a killer out there who could be driving right past our bottom fields. Doesn't that scare you?"

"It's you talking nonsense that scares me. Why would anyone come here and harm us?" Tony hesitated. "But if you're really worried, then from now on we won't go outside alone, and we'll keep all doors and windows locked whether we're in or out. That will take some getting used to."

"So you are worried?"

"Nope... it's what I have to do to shut you up. And if it will make you feel better, we'll start taking the shotgun and the rifle with us whenever we go outside."

"And Tess can sleep in the kitchen?" Craig added hopefully.

"And the flea-bitten mutt can sleep in the kitchen."

*

Louise Forbes felt ashamed to admit to herself, that at the age of twenty-six, she'd never even been interviewed for a job. She'd changed clothes at least a dozen times before setting off, but looking at the regular waitresses now, she felt overdressed. Their lunchtime shift was over and she walked across the changing room to introduce herself. "Hi, I'm Louise... I'm starting work here next week; have you girls worked here for long?" She was wondering how the blonde girl remained inside her in blue Lycra top if she had to reach over the tables, or even bend down, for that matter. "I'm starting college in September. It's going to be expensive and I need to earn some money for driving lessons and a little car."

"Good for you," the fair-haired girl raised one eyebrow to emphasise her sarcastic tone. "I'm Anna. Wouldn't it be nice if we all had that luxury? I'm starting today but the twins have been here for a few weeks." She sniffed and looked Louise up and down. "They expect us to work in pairs."

"So they told me." To break this ice, she was going to have to find some common ground. This could be the girl she was going to be paired with and on the surface she didn't seem too friendly. "You're younger than me," she'd no idea of the girl's age, but no one beyond the age of twenty should be dressed like that. "You've plenty of time for the serious stuff. I was a real stroppy little mare when I was around your age."

"Are you trying to be funny?" The girl was positively glowering now.

This was going from bad to worse. "No, not at all, but you're young, so have some fun. I only meant that anytime you decide to, you can try to do something different with your life. There are student loans you can apply for – I could show you how if you were interested. I'm just being friendly. Don't tell me you want to be a waitress all your life."

"No, I have plans." The words were said grudgingly, but with less of a scowl on her made-up face.

Finally, she had a small breakthrough. "Speaking for myself, I wasted too many years," she didn't really consider having her beautiful daughter to be a waste of time but she wasn't about to admit that. "I dropped out of school early, and I fought with my dad, and there were loads of times when I stayed away from home for days at a time. I never did drugs – they're only for the idiots, but at one point I could drink the best part of a stolen bottle of vodka in a day. And I hung around in a gang for a while, the sort you wouldn't want to take back to your family – not at any price. And then to top it all, I got myself pregnant, had a daughter, and I've not got a clue about who her father might be."

"You've got a little girl? Was it really horrible, giving birth?" Her face opened up and her eyes widened.

"Oh yes, and it's not something I intend repeating any time soon. But I've been lucky, my family stood by me and now I'm living back at home. But I can tell you this much – my daughter has made me look at life differently. I needed to do life my way, but it turned out to be the hard way and I wouldn't recommend it. I know what an idiot I've been."

"I don't have a family any more. I don't believe my mum ever knew who my father was, either. As parents go, she was a complete nightmare and her sort should never be allowed to have kids. For years everyone said I was ill, but I know she was trying to slowly poison me. In the end she tried to get I locked away, but I walked out of the hospital ward before they could do that and took refuge in a commune."

"Wow… did the police ever charge her with poisoning you?"

"No, they wouldn't listen to me and I could never prove it. But I know that she was. I was in and out of clinics for years, and every time I spent any time at home, I got sick. I believe she's dead now though, and I hope her death was really painful."

"Are you still living in a commune?"

"No, I only stayed a few months. I'd never seen such a bunch of losers and weirdoes." The girl laughed for the first time since Louise had entered the room. "Looking at me, you'd think I'd fit right in, wouldn't you?"

Louise laughed with her. "So where do you live now, how do you manage?"

"I've just moved into a flat with the two girls you see there." She pointed to the twins. "It's a bit cramped and I have to sleep on the sofa, but we're managing, and we don't have many expenses. They were given a one-bedroomed flat because of their jobs here, and the rent is taken straight out of their wages. But don't mention that to anyone because I don't think the boss knows I've moved in with them. We're saving up to buy our own flat one day, something cheap in town, with another room so I can have my own bedroom. We look out for each other."

"Buying a flat… that's way more ambitious than I could ever have been at your age. Well done you."

"Well from what you've just told me about yourself, that wouldn't be difficult, would it?"

The ice was shattered. They both laughed and Louise tugged the front of her new blouse down.

"I'm Anna Jenkins, by the way."

"Louise Forbes, I'm very pleased to meet you. Who are the girls you're shacking up with?"

"Maisie and Carol Evans – they're identical twins. They're dancers, a few months older than me, and not been dancing for long, but they're very good. You'll like them. They applied for work here as waitresses but the boss thought the punters would come flocking in to see them because they're so pretty and so alike. He's a sleaze, but he's right, the customers love watching them."

"I think I saw some posters on the way in, they are pretty."

"They use loads of make-up, but yeah, they are. Their mother was almost as bad as mine. I say almost... she didn't try to kill them... but she neglected them from the day they were born. She was an alcoholic prostitute who eventually died from liver failure... I think. They were lucky for a while though, they had nice foster carers to turn to. Until the weekend that their mother died, that is. On their way to pick up the twins, a lorry squished their car and they were both killed. They lost everyone in a single day, and I was with them on that day. Can you believe that? That's why we get on so well, we've all suffered."

"And I thought I'd had it tough; I do at least have a Dad and an older brother. They raised me after Mum died. I was only a few weeks old, so I have no memories of her. I felt loved, but I always felt I was missing out. I admire you all for the way you've coped with everything." Her new friend looked suitably impressed, but she'd meant every word. It had taken her a long time to get to this point, but these teenagers were one giant leap ahead of her in the independence stakes. They even had plans to buy a flat.

For the first time since Gemma's birth, she felt resentful of her daughter.

Chapter 14

Saturday morning was still and overcast, but with a definite scent of spring in the air. Tony and Craig stepped outside their rather shabby farmhouse and observed the low clouds hovering over the moors. Everything around the farmhouse, every blade of grass, tussock of heather, and spike of gorse had overnight been cloaked in gossamer thin, jewelled cobwebs. Nothing around them had been disturbed for hours.

They breathed a combined sigh of relief.

Before breakfast, they routinely checked the sheep. It had been a rule of their late grandfather's, handed down from the generations before him, on the family farm.

"Always remember boys, you look after your livestock and it will look after you." Grandfather had patted the young boy's heads in exactly the same manner as he'd patted his beloved sheepdogs.

Carrying a gun each and scanning the skyline as they walked, they headed towards the tractor shed.

Craig battled with the steering wheel of the old red Massey Ferguson tractor as they bounced across rutted fields towards the sheep. Tony sat on the wheel arch behind him, clinging on with his left hand. Tess was the only one afforded any kind of comfort – she sat on a stained cushion, originally part of an old sofa, leaning against the opposite wheel arch and watching for rabbits. She had to be lifted into the tractor these days, and it wouldn't be too long, Craig thought sadly, before they'd have to be lifting her out as well. But she was still eager to work and it didn't seem right to retire and replace her just yet.

Tony's right hand rested on the guns. They were wrapped in a hessian sack and wedged upright in the corner of the tractor beside him while he had the rifle bullets in his left coat pocket and the shotgun cartridges in his right. He felt the rims of the cartridges pressing into his leg through the fabric of his worn jeans.

"That don't look right, bruv," Tony raised his cold backside from the unforgiving metal. "Doesn't that look like smoke coming from our gravel pit?"

Craig slowed the tractor to a crawl and wiped condensation from the side window with his gloved hand. "Bloody hell, I think you're right. That's thick black smoke all right. That's not good. It looks like it ain't been burning for too long either. Unwrap those guns and I'll get us a bit closer."

"Take it steady, I've a bad feeling in my guts."

"That's what happens when you eat crisps and pickled onions last thing at night in bed."

"Stop joking, I'm calling the fire brigade. And then I'm loading these babies."

The small hill running parallel to the road hid the cause of the smoke. Craig eased the tractor into bottom gear and turned the steering wheel to climb higher and hopefully get a clearer view.

Their gravel pit consisted of a pocket of hard shale and sandy gravel, gradually excavated over decades to provide hard-core and a concrete mix for field entrances, farmyards and buildings. It had slowly expanded to about half an acre, a conveniently sized and levelled area for some of the locals to park in when they wanted somewhere quiet to walk their dogs. The brothers had no problem with that, as long as the dogs didn't disturb the sheep. Many of the area's younger motorists had nocturnal uses for the makeshift park, but that too was OK.

But located on the narrow back road, it was rare for strangers to the area to stumble across it.

"The smoke's getting thicker; it looks like a proper blaze now. Have you got a signal?"

"Hold up... just getting through... fire service please... and maybe the police and ambulance as well."

*

DS Adam Ross had slept surprisingly well. It was the first time that both he and his son, Ryan, had slept over at Jane Goodwin's house. He'd expected to be woken during the night, his son being in an unfamiliar room, but light was already filtering through the floral curtains and the house was blissfully quiet. Jane was lying on her stomach. He gently slid his arm across her shoulders and she began to move towards him.

"Mmmm....," she purred. "This is nice, and the children are both still asleep. We must do this more often. What time is it?"

"It's getting light, but beyond that I neither know nor care," he whispered into her neck.

He felt her beginning to turn towards him, and for a second he tried to blot out the noise. Reluctantly, he pulled away from her and reached for his mobile.

"I'm sorry to disturb you, sir," PC Philip Coates was obviously on night duty, "I know you're not on call, but I can't reach DCI Forbes. A burning car has been reported on the Havers property. It's located in the gravel pit about two miles across the fields from where Derek Austen's body was found. All emergency services are on their way, but in view of the location we thought CID would want to be informed straight away."

"Thank you, I know the place. Would you remind all officers attending that it's a potential crime scene, and that nothing is to be touched once the fire services have made it safe. I'm on my way but keep trying to contact DCI Forbes." He could feel Jane wriggling up the bed and pulling herself into a sitting position.

"I heard most of that," she whispered onto his bare shoulders. "I'll take care of Ryan while you check it out. It may be nothing to do with your murder cases, but you won't know till you get there. Now just go."

"I'll call you when I know something. God only knows where Forbes spent last night." He kissed the top of her head, finally found his shoes, on the landing of all places, gathered up the previous day's clothing from the bedroom floor and crept down the stairs, praying that Ryan wouldn't be too upset when he woke.

What remained of the car was barely recognisable as a black Peugeot 208, but part of the charred registration plate was just legible. They'd found the vehicle Carl Deakin was seen to have been driving on the night of his murder, and now the scene required both scenes of crimes officers and a senior detective. But for the moment, the Chief Fire Officer was in charge of the scene. Adam was organising his thoughts, planning his questions for the two brothers he'd met the day after Derek Austen's murder, when a car pulled up behind his.

Forbes, who'd driven well above the speed limit most of the way, climbed out of his car and ran the fingers of one hand through his short hair.

"I didn't hear the phone," he muttered, hoping, but not really expecting that Adam would believe him. "Is there anything at all left inside that car?"

"No obvious bodies, if that's what you mean, sir. SOCOs are on their way but I doubt there will be any residual evidence. It should be cool enough by the time they get here."

"Who called it in?"

"Tony Havers called the emergency services. He was with his brother, Craig. I asked them to return to their tractor. They were checking their sheep, as they do each morning, when they saw smoke coming from their land. All the ground on this side of the gated road is part of their farm. We've interviewed them twice since Austen's murder but each time they maintained they hadn't seen anything."

"I remember; no one else lives at the farmhouse, do they?"

"They said they lived alone, sir. They were brought up by grandparents and neither of them has ever married."

"Two healthy males, there must have been women somewhere along the line, or are they happy to pay for what they need?"

"They could be gay, sir."

"Well let's find out, shall we?" Forbes studied the twelve-foot wide, timber field gate, fastened shut with a length of frayed, orange baler twine. It looked sturdy enough, and easier to climb over than to unfasten. He wouldn't have thought twice about climbing it if he'd been in his hiking gear.

Once over that obstacle, it was only a short walk to the tractor. He could see Adam hesitating. "Wait here; there's no point in both of us getting dirty footwear."

The mud around the tractor was deeper than it had looked from the lane and some of it was seeping inside his polished brown brogues. He tried to ignore it. "Gentlemen, I'm sure we can find somewhere more comfortable than this to have a little chat."

"We'll have to get the old dog back to the farmhouse," Craig muttered. "Our Tess doesn't like to be left alone in the tractor, do you girl? And we've left a pan of porridge on the back of the Aga; we've had no breakfast yet. Have we time to eat it?"

"It's just an informal chat, Mr Havers. We can have it in the comfort of your kitchen, unless you've been up to anything illegal that you'd like to tell us about."

"No, it's just… you sounded so serious."

"This is a serious business. If you're at home for the rest of the morning, someone will call round to take your written statements." Forbes grabbed a steel handle and hauled himself up onto the tractor's metal step and out of the mud. "Are those guns licenced?"

Tess let out a low rumble.

"Take no notice of her, she wouldn't harm a fly. A big coward, she is. Tony and I are hill farmers so we were practically born holding firearms licences. The foxes will take our lambs, given half a chance, because there's hardly any rabbits left for them. The trigger-happy idiots keep coming from out of the big towns at night, shooting at all the poor little buggers, and there's nothing we dare do about it. The foxes are going hungry so we have to control their numbers to stop them taking our livestock. In our granddad's day there were hundreds of rabbits and hares on these moors. We practically lived on rabbit stew and the foxes rarely took any lambs or chickens."

"Did either of you see anyone around here either last night or this morning?"

"No." Both men shook their heads.

"Or at any other time... anyone here who shouldn't have been?"

More head shaking.

"You can go and get your breakfasts now."

"We've got a locked gun cupboard, if you want to see that. We're all legal." Craig added.

"I'm sure that you are."

Forbes stepped down and squelched his way back to the road. He'd have to change his socks and shoes now before he could concentrate fully on anything. As he picked his way back towards the gate he heard the brothers arguing, but couldn't quite tell what the argument was about.

"Craig, you idiot, why did you go gibbering on like that, you never give the police any information that they don't directly ask for, you know that. We don't want them poking around the farm, do we? That Inspector guy was being too nice. I don't trust him, and you shouldn't either. Good girl Tess."

"But there's nothing for them to find now. We agreed we're not going poaching again till this has all blown over. The police just make me really nervous."

"Yes, and they know that, dummy. They use that fact to try and trick you. Why else would they be coming back for a statement when all we did was call the emergency services? They think we're withholding information, and that's a serious offence. If we tell them now about the car park, or the silver car, we could land ourselves in a whole heap of trouble."

"All right... all right... I get it; we've seen nothing except one burning car."

*

"It will get easier, Verona, I promise," the smiling woman crooned at her. "You've had a difficult birth. You just need time to get used to the idea of being a mother."

However many times they pushed the squirming bundle in her direction, she knew she could never love it. That was never going to change. She'd finally pushed it out of her swollen body and as far as she was concerned, that was that.

The blue eyes everyone gushed about made her feel physically sick, and the first time they'd tried to put the screwed-up face onto her breast she'd thrown up all over his clean white blanket. It wasn't his fault, but then none of this had been her fault either.

The whimpering finally stopped and she felt herself drifting back to sleep. Someone must have fed him.

"Just take a peek at his chubby little cheeks, isn't he adorable?" She woke to the sound of the woman who'd taken him away and the sight of a tiny pink face just an inch from her own.

She'd prayed that the agony of the last day and a half would bring her long nightmare to an end. It was the only thing that had kept her going. Why couldn't they just leave her in peace now? No, she didn't want to hold him or give him a bath. No, she didn't want to give him a name. She wanted to forget that he'd ever existed.

In her occasional, happier dreams over recent weeks, she'd pictured a beautiful little girl, a bit like herself, with soft dark hair and a loving smile, and if those dreams had been prophesies, then perhaps she would have felt differently.

"You've got a little boy!"

That one sentence still rang in her ears. It had sealed her future.

Lying back and staring at the whitewashed ceiling she felt an overwhelming sense of relief. There was no difficult decision to be made. "I am still a child," she muttered into the void. "I can't do this. If I stay, they'll expect me to look after him and love him as a mother should, and I know that will never be possible." She pictured her mother's face and continued whispering. "I need to go, but dare I leave him here with these people? They know me. They may come looking for me. I know they all want to do what's right for him, but I daren't risk them finding me and bringing me back to him. I can't be a prisoner again. I just can't. You'd understand, mother, I know you would. I must take him away from here. We have to leave together."

*

The unmistakable fragrance of tinned spaghetti in tomato sauce and burnt toast greeted Adam Ross when he opened Jane's front door. The children were merrily twirling their forks, gathering more strands than either of them could possibly fit into their hungry mouths at one time and Jane was standing at the kitchen sink, scrubbing out the stained pan. The children each spluttered an unintelligible greeting and Jane turned from the sink. She looked tired. She was still very much wrapped up in her grief and maybe it was too soon for them both to be staying over.

He kissed each of the children on the top of the head and then walked over to her. His arms automatically slid around her inviting waist.

"Dinner won't be long. Was it definitely one of the cars you were looking for?"

"It's been confirmed as Carl Deakin's Peugeot. SOCOs are still working on what's left of it. It's a fair old walk from there back to civilisation so we think another vehicle must have been involved, which means another driver."

"And you're thinking of the missing silver Ford Focus, the one seen possibly picking up Derek Austen's killer?"

"Yes and the arsonists wouldn't want to be seen once the car was ablaze, so they'd need a quick getaway. That gravel pit is an ideal spot for firing a vehicle, hidden from almost every angle, set into the hillside and with a wood opposite. It's unlikely there'll be any witnesses unless there were early morning ramblers in the vicinity."

"No one's come forward from the television appeal, have they? If the silver Ford is being driven on the road, then they must have changed registration plates."

"That's what we're assuming. Vehicle cloning is more common now we have the Automatic Number Plate Recognition cameras and can do instant checks on the roads. They're possibly driving it about right under our noses."

An empty plastic beaker and a fork clattered to the floor, followed by a feeble, "I'm sorry... it just slipped."

"It's all right, buddy," Adam hugged his son. "I should have been paying you more attention, shouldn't I?"

Jane smiled at the three and then wiped butter and tomato sauce from the tiled floor. Then she watched the children disappearing into the garden together.

Adam finished the omelette Jane put in front of him and wondered whether to ask for a bacon sandwich, nicely crisped and smothered in brown sauce. Perhaps he'd better wait. "I haven't seen any stabbings quite as brutal as the two we're investigating now. Neither were random muggings, but we're still without a motive, and we've found no links between the victims that might point to one."

"A motive....?"

He looked up; maybe this was all too much for her at the moment.

"Are you staying over tonight?" she seemed distant. "I've got chicken nuggets and pork chops in the freezer."

Adam hesitated and looked through the kitchen window.

The children obviously enjoyed each other's company; most of the time anyway. It seemed a shame to uproot Ryan, and he very much wanted to spend the night. "As tempting as chicken nuggets sound, maybe we should leave and let you have some peace."

"I haven't cried today, honestly, and peace is overrated. Besides, if there's a knife wielding maniac in the vicinity, I'd much rather it was you that he tackled and not me."

"Now how could I refuse an offer like that? Did I see some bacon in the fridge?"

Chapter 15

Louise Forbes stood in the floodlit lobby of the Kirby Club, in the centre of Leaburn, watching the late night taxis and hoping Brian wouldn't keep her waiting too much longer. She cocked her head to try hearing what the muffled male voices coming from just inside the club were saying. What was it about men? Once they got talking they were almost impossible to stop. She wished she'd listened to her father and brought a coat. It was well past midnight but despite the cold she felt good. Her first shift was over. She'd enjoyed it more than she'd expected, once she'd learned to keep on the move and not be drawn into conversations with customers.

Brian Haws was a retired boxer, she'd been told, and his features certainly bore out that story. From doorman to club security, and ensuring that any girls who needed a lift home got one, he was the longest serving member of the staff. She shivered and turned to go back inside when his bulky frame filled the doorway.

She followed him to his electric-blue, two-year old BMW 3 Series, X-Drive M Sports car.

Seriously impressive, she thought as she fastened the seatbelt.

"The boss put you on with Anna Jenkins, I noticed," he said as the car purred out of the staff car park. "Had you met her before?"

"No, but she seems nice enough. Why do you ask?"

"You're only working here for the summer, so I'm told. Just… err… just take some fatherly advice, will you, and don't get too friendly with that girl."

"I'm starting college in September and I have a little girl at home, so I don't have much time for friends. I've seen the twins she shares a flat with. They seemed nice enough, and they're friendly with her. What's her problem?"

"I've only known her a few weeks, but from what I've seen she's got a rather short fuse. She likes to control people. The twins seem happy with that, but I've seen her lose it a couple of times already, and what I witnessed her doing would make even your hair curl." He looked at her long, straight hair, neatly secured over one shoulder.

"I've done a few crazy things myself in the past. How do you know that I'm a truly balanced person?" This was turning into an odd conversation.

"Trust me, love, there's something not quite right with the wiring in that girl's head. The boss hasn't seen that side of her yet, but he will do if I've got anything to do with it. Don't get drawn into her world, that's all I'm saying. I've seen how friendly she can be when she turns on the charm, but I wouldn't trust her."

She turned her head to look out of the passenger-side window. Taking advice had never been one of her strong points. "This is fine, thanks. You can drop me off here, it's only a short walk and I could do with some fresh air."

"Not likely, I've been given strict instructions to deliver you to your door and to watch you go inside."

He didn't say from whom, but she had a good idea. "OK."

"It's more than my job's worth to leave you at the roadside. There's a knife wielding maniac on the loose in this area, haven't you heard?"

"Yes, I've heard. That's my house, the one with the red gates." She wondered whether he knew that the Chief Investigating Officer on the case was her big brother.

"Will you take Anna and the twins home?"

"That's my next run, but it's only a five minute journey now the boss has them in one of his flats."

"Anna thinks the boss doesn't know she's stopping there."

"Oh, he knows."

*

"Brian, where have you been, we've been freezing our butts off out here waiting for you?" Anna opened the car's rear door and shoved the twins, one at a time, into the back.

"I'm here now. I had to take the new waitress home first."

"I bet you went the long way round because you fancied her," one of the twins giggled while Anna climbed into the front seat. "What do you think, Anna? She's got a few years on us, but she's still proper fit."

"And she's got a little kiddie, Brian," Anna leaned towards him as far as her seatbelt would allow. "So you might be in with a chance."

"Shut up, all of you, I'm a happily married man. I won't put up with any more of your nonsense." He'd been watching the twins in his rear view mirror, and now he glanced sideways at Anna and saw that her expression had changed since she'd got into his car. They were three stunning-looking girls, and no mistake, but the one beside him made his skin crawl. It wasn't just her short temper, or her dominating manner. It was something he couldn't quite define.

"I'm sorry, Brian, we were only teasing," the *butter wouldn't melt* voice came from the back seat.

"We respect you, and all that," Anna placed a hand on his knee and he quickly brushed it away, "and we know how much the boss respects and listens to you. We don't want to sound ungrateful, but we've been thinking... most nights that flat that we're in really pongs. Is there any chance of us having a different one? We've heard he's got loads of properties and we could use something a fraction larger. We'll work more shifts to pay any extra rent, won't we girls?"

"You were lucky to get that one. You have to prove yourselves as good tenants and good workers before you can hope to get anything better. You've only been with the firm five minutes." He wouldn't pass on their request. There was no way these girls were getting their feet any further under the table.

"The thing is, Brian... we have this friend," Anna persisted, "a really sweet girl, and we know she's been very badly abused. She's had a far worse time than any of us and her English isn't that great, but it's improving. Any day now, she'll have nowhere to go. We want her to move in with us and we were hoping she could work in the club. She'll do any kind of work, pot washing, cleaning; she'll take any job that's on offer."

"Where is she now?"

"She's with friends, but she can't stay."

"How old is she?"

"Sixteen, but she looks younger, she's really pretty." Anna wasn't sure whether even Verona herself was certain of her real age, but it was close enough.

"Is she an illegal?"

"She says she was born in Moldova, and that's part of Europe now, at least she thinks she was, but she's no papers and no family. She was trafficked and sold, but escaped. She really is the sweetest girl, you'll like her. She's not forward like us three, I promise."

"Leave it with me, I'll see if I can organise some papers for her, but my contacts will need paying up front. And we never had this conversation, right? Her feet and yours won't touch the ground if the boss finds out she's not legit. Not a word to anyone!"

"We won't," three voices spoke in unison.

"Brian, you're an angel. We knew you'd help." Anna touched his arm and he instinctively pulled away.

*

Carol lay with her eyes closed, listening to the scrabbling noises inside the bedroom walls. At least, she hoped they were still inside. She was finding the night time disturbances harder to live with than the smells from the take-away chip shop downstairs. She'd got used to those, but the scratching and gnawing sounds seemed louder each night. She pulled the duvet tight around her legs.

There were still times when she wanted to call out to her mother, and wondered whether Maisie ever felt the same. "Are you awake?"

"I am now, what do you want?"

"When everyone we loved went and died, do you remember how they offered us counselling?"

"Huh....?"

"Don't you sometimes wish we'd hung around long enough for that?"

"We'd have been plonked into some place full of soft toys and then expected to talk about our feelings to some pasty faced, vegetarian social worker getting paid a fortune just to listen to us. Anna's told us all about them and we don't need them. We've had to grow up fast, I'll give you that, but we're doing all right, aren't we? How many sixteen-year-olds have a flat and a job and freedom? Of course I miss mum, and Mr and Mrs Stevens, and little Judy, and I expect we always will, but we've got Anna. She's street-wise and sassy, and I trust her judgement – most of the time, anyway. We have to get on with life and make the best of what we have. Now go back to sleep."

Anna was also wide awake. Her brain felt as if it wanted to explode out of her skull. She was sixteen and already had a job, and that was something her mother had never had in the whole of her pathetic life. She was even learning from the twins how to cook proper food in their tiny kitchen. Who would have thought that two wall cupboards, a tiny sink and draining board, a two-ring gas stove and a folding table which doubled as a worktop could excite her? But it was clean, and it was theirs, and she was happily turning into 'a domestic goddess'. It was amazing! She was determined never to eat another jam sandwich, or another dish of 'own brand' mushy peas with dry bread, ever again. For years she'd tried to persuade her mother to watch the cookery programs with her, and to actually cook something, but it had made no difference. Tinned fruit and proper vegetables had been a novelty, only available when her mum had a new man. Once, she'd found a five pound note on the pavement. Instead of chocolates or make-up, which most girls of her age would have bought, she'd gone to the supermarket and proudly brought home a whole chicken and a cauliflower and some broccoli and frozen peas, and placed them in the fridge as a surprise for her mother.   But five days later, the fridge stunk and so she'd thrown everything she'd bought into the dustbin.

Last night the club had been busy, she'd earned enough in tips to buy three chicken portions and have change left over. She swung her legs off the sofa.

The twenty-four hour supermarket was eerily quiet, the shelf stackers all looking as if they'd rather be anywhere but there. She paid for three chicken portions and a packet of frozen peas, picked up a free magazine and then sat on the plastic bench just inside the door. There was a children's recipe section featuring pancakes and scrambled eggs. Pancake Day was a week away, but she'd need to practice first with the recipe. Most of the ingredients for scrambled eggs were already in the cupboard back at the flat. She looked at the change left in her hand. There was enough for some eggs and with a bit of luck she could afford to buy the free range ones.

A perfect morning beckoned.

She would rattle the plates and pans when food was almost ready, and the twins could wake up to the sounds and smells of her new culinary skills.

Carol prodded her phone. What the hell was Anna doing at this time of the morning – it was barely light? The air beyond her bedclothes was cold and she could hear Maisie stirring beside her. It was far too early to get dressed. She pulled a jumper over her pyjamas and padded into the small room which housed the cooker and television, and the sofa which doubled as Anna's bed and which was still hidden under a duvet. She pulled two cushions from under the bedding, dumped them side by side on the floor and switched on the breakfast news.

Anna was already dressed and engrossed in her cooking – if she wanted help, she'd ask.

Carol turned her focus back to the small screen and her eyes widened. "Hey, you two... come and look at this! Look at the news! A new-born baby's been dumped outside a newsagent's shop on the edge of town this morning. And there's CCTV footage of a girl in the street. Quick, come and look! It looks like Verona! Anna, you must see this... be quick!"

Maisie dropped onto the cushion beside her. "All right, Carol, calm down. The pictures are a bit fuzzy, I don't know, but you could be right."

The scene cut to a conference room, the background boarding displaying a clear picture of a new-born baby boy with a wrinkled face and a grainy picture of a slim, dark haired girl. There was a web address and a phone number for the Leaburn Police Station along with the anonymous Crimestoppers number. A serious looking, uniformed PC was speaking and holding up a white blanket and a holdall.

Anna handed plates of food to the twins, stood with her hand over her mouth, and then flopped onto the sofa. "My God... I recognise that bag. I knew she must be nearly due. She looked huge last week. I should have gone back but it's such a long walk after getting off the bus, and it rained every time I thought about going. But she never even hinted that she was thinking of dumping it."

"You can't blame yourself, Anna. None of us thought she'd do anything like that."

"I wanted to surprise you both with breakfast, but Verona's surprised us all. We must find her. Eat up and then we'll go."

Carol swallowed her last mouthful. "The breakfast's still a surprise, Anna, thank you. You know you're not personally responsible for Verona. You've already done more for her than we have."

"And she's got that cheap mobile so she could have called if she'd needed us," Maisie added.

"She could be out of credit, or she could have lost it. Eat up Maisie. We've got to find her before the police do. If she's dumped the sprog then she must have left the commune for good. She's only been here once but I reckon she'll be heading for this area right now, trying to find us."

"But won't the commune call the police? They'll see the news."

"I doubt it," Anna had the last piece of her food on her fork. "They won't want the hassle. We've got to find her ourselves. Like the policewoman said, she might be in need of medical attention. Today we have to put her first."

Maisie wiped her plate clean with the last corner of bread and butter. "She's must be driving the car. What if she's lost?"

"I'll "borrow" us another car. This is an emergency. I don't know how much fuel was left in it for her – I wasn't expecting her to drive this far."

*

Louise Forbes lay in bed watching the same news report. She looked across at her own daughter, fast asleep and breathing steadily. That child could sleep through anything as long as her tummy wasn't totally empty. Someone was up and about in the kitchen and the smell of toast was tempting. It was time to get up.

"Michael, have seen the news? Someone's abandoned a new-born boy. How could anyone do that? Is there any chance you'll be involved in the enquiry?"

"We've got our hands full with two murder cases, so it'll be handled downstairs. In cases like that it's the general public we appeal to first. Don't be too judgemental, it's not something that anyone does without a good reason."

She took her toast through to the living room. It wasn't so many years since she'd stopped feeling abandoned and angry at her own mother for not being around. The mother that she'd never known hadn't been given a choice, and she realised now that at least some of that anger had been fuelled by her father. He'd always believed that someone should be held accountable, that someone was to blame, in fact he still did. He'd never accepted the assurances that his wife's death had been a natural, and totally unpredictable, tragic event. But it had hurt so much, for so long, watching her friends at the school gates with their doting mothers. It still hurt. Perhaps that went a little way towards explaining why she was a girl of such extremes, and why once she'd decided on a certain course of action, nothing could stop her. Her mother had suddenly stopped. But she wasn't going to. And if there was an afterlife and she was looking down on her grown-up daughter, then she was going to make her mother proud. Once she'd decided to continue with her pregnancy, she'd sworn to be the best mother that she possibly could. For now at least, that meant accepting the help and support of her father and brother, but as she listened again to the news report she considered how lucky she was. That girl on the news could so easily have been herself. Easter was only a month away, and with her first wages the only thing she intended to buy was the prettiest egg she could find in the shops, for her Gemma. "I'll take a breakfast tray up to Dad to thank him for babysitting last night," she shouted through.

*

Verona felt weak. She hadn't slept. She'd waited until the building was quiet before loading her few possessions into the car and forcing herself into the nursery to pick up the sleeping bundle. It was just something that she had to dispose of. She couldn't think of it in any other way.

The walk between the parked car, and the shop that had lights on in the room above, and then back again, had sapped the last of her energy. All she had to do now was turn the key and drive, but her legs trembled. She had to be clear of the busy roads while most of the people who knew how to drive properly were still in their beds. Hoping she could remember the area where Anna and the twins were living, she took a deep breath and turned on the ignition.

Chapter 16

The Easter holidays were finally over and as he drove slowly through the familiar, poorly lit back roads of Leaburn, his dipped headlights picked out one female after another, after another. They all looked so alike, and so boringly predictable, all of them waiting to catch sight of the next set of brake lights, and all trying to look provocative, rather than desperate. Stale odours of tobacco, alcohol, and cannabis mingled with the cheap perfume and he wrinkled his nose as the mixture seeped in through the ventilation system of his car. Most nights he wondered why he still came here, until that moment came when he saw long, bare legs folding into another man's car. It was the only thrill some of those poor sods ever got and he pitied them. They were the ones who were compelled to come here, not him. He had a pregnant wife waiting at home, and a three year old daughter who'd been stuffing herself with chocolate Easter eggs all afternoon. But this was a separate part of his life. It was just a little harmless fun. After all, he worked hard enough, and what his wife didn't know couldn't hurt her.

He spotted a discreet place to park, on one of the side roads and in front of another car but with an unobstructed view of the road junction.

Headlights off, he leaned back into his seat.

Mid-week, and almost two hours until the witching hour, the Castle Public House was filling up. He needed to be patient. He watched some pub-goers passing the girls, and he heard their obscene remarks. "Careful boys," he muttered, "any one of those could be your sister, or your daughter, or even your old slapper of a missus."

He smiled to himself. He was more particular. He was willing to wait for a new face, for someone whose sad, drug-riddled life he hadn't already subsidised. Memories of the ones he'd already had played through his mind like the loops of an old film reel. It was a mild enough evening and still early – he intended enjoying the process of making his selection.

A noise, very close by, startled him. A female face suddenly appeared in his wing mirror. It jolted him from his reminiscences and he turned his head to look into the eyes of a young girl – a sweet, innocent looking young girl with her delicate fist raised and about to knock on his car window. She had such a sweet smile, he was sure he'd have remembered having this one before. But she almost looked too young. He scanned the street for anyone who looked out of place. If she really was sixteen, then it wasn't by much. He felt a familiar stirring as he opened the car window.

Neither of them spoke as shops, buildings and walls were replaced by trees and hedgerows. Heading towards his favourite spot, a disused gravel pit where there was plenty of room to pull off the road and from where they'd be practically invisible to passing motorists, he prayed no one else would be using it.

It was often used during the day by dog walkers, but for at least half an hour tonight, the only simpering dog would be the one almost wearing that skimpy dress.

He was in luck.

His breathing rate increased.

Very carefully, he drew into the park, turned the car so that he was facing to leave, and then switched off the engine. A slight, rocking movement of the girl's legs sent a tingle through his thighs. Seatbelt released, he eased himself towards her and the movement stopped. He stroked the inside of her leg and her young muscles felt firm, but tense.

He considered himself a good judge of women. "This is the first time you've sold yourself, isn't it?" he whispered into her neck. The few words increased the pressure in his trousers.

"Yes it is. I'm nervous. Can I ask your name?"

"Peter… just Peter…"

"Well, just Peter, I think I'm ready now, are you?"

Was he ever – his vision had adjusted to the light level now and his eyes rested on pale shoulders as she slid off the straps of her dress, one at a time, and allowed the soft fabric to crumple around her waist. He saw she was wearing some sort of slip. Gently tracing the top edges of her bra and slip with one hand he leaned closer. "It's all right, I'll be gentle," he whispered. "I won't do anything that you're not comfortable with. Allow me to teach you a few things, my little one." This was going to be so good. "You're such a sweet little girl."

She turned her head and looked into his eyes. "Are you married, just Peter? Do you have children at home, tucked up in their beds?"

He pulled back. So she wants to play games, does she? Well why not, if nothing else it would make the experience last a little longer. Perhaps she wasn't as innocent as she looked. "I love my family, if that's what you're asking, but that has nothing to do with what's happening here and now." His hand moved downwards, gripped the hem of the dress and pulled it up.

The harder he pressed into her flesh, the tighter the muscles in her pale thighs became. She wasn't yielding to his fingers as an experienced prostitute should. Playing games was one thing, but now he was starting to feel more than a little frustrated. He took a deep breath. There was no way he was paying a timid little tramp for a bit of a grope. "Come on now love, give a little. I can't hold this in all night." He took hold of her right hand and moved it onto his groin. She held it there but didn't move. And she was still looking at him.

"You're not wearing a tie," she whispered.

"What the hell are you on about? This isn't a bloody fashion show. I only wear ties for weddings and funerals, and this definitely isn't either of those." A gentle movement from her right hand made him close his eyes. At last he was getting somewhere.

"Could we move onto your back seat where there's more room?"

"Anything you like, my little one, just as long as you deliver the goods." He stroked her face but she didn't offer to move. And she remained perfectly still while he opened his door, got out, and walked around the front of his car. He had to smile – a street girl with airs and graces, actually waiting for him to open the passenger door for her – he'd never even done that for his own wife, if he didn't count the time she was in labour and couldn't get out by herself. "Out you get, your ladyship," he held the door open and watched flimsy fabric slowly sinking down her body and revealing her skin coloured slip. Now he was really tight.

"Would you get in the back first?" she purred. "Some of my best moves are when I'm above, and I know you won't be disappointed."

He felt one index finger lightly tracing the outline of his chest and nipples through his cotton shirt and tried to steady his breathing as he felt her hand moving south. This was the moment he'd been waiting for. His eyes automatically closed when he felt the cool fingers of her right hand slide inside his waistband. "Now you're talking my language," he whispered, fumbling with the button.

Before he unzipped, he decided to turn and open the car door – it wasn't cool, even with a prostitute, to have your trousers falling around your ankles.

His hand gripped the door handle, but he couldn't move. His shirt felt too tight. He couldn't draw breath, almost as if he'd been winded, as if he'd been punched in the back.

A heart attack, he thought, I'm having a bloody heart attack! What a rotten, sodding time to be having one of those! He wanted to turn, to ask for help, but felt his legs begin to buckle.

Another blow, only this time his chest bounced off the car and his legs crumpled.

It wasn't his heart.

It was the girl, and there was nothing he could do to stop her.

For Christ sakes, why was she doing this? He tried to speak but his breath came out as a gurgle.

Another blow, everything happening in slow motion, he felt the blade slide in between his ribs, tasted blood, and then fell back.

Dark branches zoomed in and out of focus. He couldn't understand why he couldn't draw even a single breath. He only knew his chest felt on fire.

The last thing he was able to focus on was one long, white, naked leg.

"I warned you my best moves came when I was above," was the last thing he heard. He barely felt the blade drawn across his throat.

The road was quiet and the knife was easy to clean on Peter's trousers. There was no immediate rush for her to leave. She opened her purse and took out the small plastic bottle of soapy water and some wet wipes. She'd come well prepared.

The fall-away dress had been an accident, but a convenient one. She removed her slip, in case it was blooded, and stuffed it into the plastic bag with the used wipes. Then she stepped back into the dress and brushed off the dust.

The car bonnet was warm. She leaned against it and drew in slow, deep breaths of moist, night air. A sudden, soft breeze tingled against her exposed skin and her head tilted towards a rustle of leaves coming from somewhere in the trees on the opposite side of the road.

There would be no movement from the blood soaked mound beside the car. The foxes and badgers would soon be tempted by the smell of fresh blood, and the off-chance of a free meal, and good luck to them.

The whole operation had only taken a few minutes. No cars had passed by, and even if they had, the occupants wouldn't have been likely to want to disturb a courting couple. She smiled. That was funny. This man's courting days were well and truly over. She leaned into the vehicle for the keys, but they weren't in the ignition.

They had to be on him, probably in his pocket – keys hadn't been the first thing on his mind, after all. "Not so full of yourself now, are you just Peter?"

What was she doing, talking to a corpse? She lifted the keys and moved swiftly back to the car.

It was time to go.

*

"Sir," PC Katie White was holding a phone at arm's length as Forbes walked towards the front desk of the Leaburn Police Station. "The body of a man has just been reported by a dog walker, in a small park close to Hartington Meadows Nature Reserve. The caller says there's an awful lot of blood."

"I know where that is. God bless the nation's dog walkers, what would we do without them. Is DS Ross in yet?"

Katie opened her mouth but then pointed towards the swing doors. "He's here now, sir."

"Is the caller still at the scene?" He took the phone from her.

"Yes, sir."

*

Forbes drove his Mercedes along the main A515, turned left towards Hartington and then left again down a sloping, narrow road. Only one police car had beaten them to the scene, and by less than a minute judging by the body language of a woman dragging a dejected looking spaniel towards it.

He saw a convenient field entrance. "That bad feeling I had after the second stabbing just got a whole lot worse."

Adam nodded. "If this turns out to be another fatal knife attack, the press are going to be all over it."

"He's in there," the woman shouted and pointed into an area appearing to be a dumping ground for a farmer's rubbish.

"Adam, go and check whether he's actually dead."

"I'm really sorry, but Bessie was sniffing all around him for several minutes before I realised," she gasped as Forbes guided her back to her car. "I called her away and put her lead straight back on. I hope she hasn't disturbed anything. I thought it was a dead deer at first. It gave me a real shock when I realised it was a man, but I called you immediately and I've been on the phone talking to your officers ever since. No one's come past while I've been here. It's very spooky waiting with a dead body just a few yards away and my poor Bessie whining because she's still expecting her morning walk."

"It's all right Mrs Booker, you did the right thing. Just try to relax. Take deep breaths. You've had a nasty shock."

"He's covered in blood. I only took a quick peek, but it looked to me as if his throat had been cut. His eyes were open and staring, and his skin looked grey. I didn't need to feel for a pulse to see that he was dead."

"So you didn't touch him?"

"No, I couldn't get back to the road fast enough. For all I knew, the person who'd done that terrible thing could have been hiding in those trees, watching me."

"Where have you walked from this morning?"

"I live in the centre of Hartington, a little over a mile from here."

"Wait here with this officer please, Mrs Booker, while I take a quick look." He could hear reinforcements approaching and wanted to see the body before they arrived.

The gravelled entrance led to flat area surrounded by heaps of rubbish, which in turn was surrounded by a steep rocky bank.

"There might be more evidence here than around the last two victims." Adam was trying to sound optimistic.

"No car," Forbes stated the obvious, "but recent tyre tracks very close to the victim. Let's hope our killer got careless this time."

"His trousers are in a similar state of undress to the other victims."

"Hmm... no obvious signs of bondage this time, but he wouldn't have been wearing a tie with that jacket and tee shirt, would he? So the victims aren't selected because of what they wear, and the killer doesn't appear to bring anything other than a knife."

They'd left the woman in the police car, but with the car door wide open and the dejected spaniel on the ground beside it. When they walked back, the dog looked at them hopefully, but then looked away.

Forbes bent down and fondled the dog's ears. "Are you certain that you didn't see anyone either on foot or in a vehicle, on your way up here?"

"No, it was barely light when we set off, but I'm sure I would have noticed. It's a quiet road. Bessie loves it up here, don't you girl?"

"I've only had a brief look," Judith Horde, the young police surgeon who'd attended the first two victims told them, "but the main differences between this stabbing and the previous two are that there are no obvious defensive wounds, and he's been stabbed multiple times from behind. The lungs have been punctured several times and it's doubtful that he would have lived for more than a minute or two after that, but just as with the others, the fatal blow was to the throat. We've found no ID this time, so that's over to you I'm afraid."

"Would it take a powerful individual to inflict those types of injuries?" Adam asked.

"Not if the blade was sharp enough, and if the victim was unaware and presenting his back to his assailant, which is certainly how it appears to have happened. One sharp, slightly upward thrust and the victim would have been incapacitated almost immediately, and totally unable to defend his back from subsequent blows."

"Can you estimate the time of death for us?"

"I'd say probably no earlier than nine o'clock last night and no later than one o'clock this morning. Also, when we were looking for any form of identification, we found a wedding ring in the inside pocket of his jacket. Whoever did this is likely to have considerable blood spatter on their clothing. Interestingly, we found smears of blood on the legs of his trousers, in a pattern which would suggest the murder weapon had been wiped on them. We didn't see that on the other victims. That's all I have for you until Alison does the post mortem, but he'll take priority when we get him back to the mortuary."

Forbes stared into the rock face, picturing his sister as he'd seen her not so many years earlier. Some of the images he'd tried for a long time to blot out, came flooding back. In the two years she'd spent away from home, he and his father had been called to the Accident and Emergency Department of the local hospital on three separate occasions, each time finding her battered and bruised but refusing to speak out against her attacker. Her clothing and lack of denials had told them all they'd needed to know, but they'd been powerless to help her. Louise had always been strong willed and each time refused to listen, much less accept help or advice. It had been a dark time, especially for his father. He guessed she'd probably been to places like this, maybe she'd even been here, and with married men just like this latest victim. "Let's head back," he said.

"The public don't want their serial killers to be young women," Adam broke the silence on the return journey. "It's taking equality a shade too far."

"Assuming we're right, we're looking for the very antithesis of what the public expect a serial killer to be. But let's wait and see what the post mortem turns up before we start using those two words. And let's hope the press do the same."

"Could it be a revenge killing by someone who's had a family member or a close friend killed while working as a street girl?"

"I've already got a list of all known prostitutes working the area. Perhaps we should backdate the list and cross reference it with the known relatives of rape victims, and then do the same for violent deaths. Any link to these latest victims, and any matching surnames, and I want to know about it." He quietly prayed that he wouldn't see a Miss Louise Forbes on any of those lists. "Any incidents in our area over the last twelve months to begin with, and any related hospital incidents which we were called to attend, whether they resulted in charges being brought or not. We need names."

They were in sight of the station when the call came in.

"A missing person report has just come in, sir. Mrs Tania Stansfield has reported her husband, Peter, as missing since seven o'clock last night. She woke to find he hadn't come home, called hospitals and family members, and then called us. They live in Ashbourne."

"Send us the co-ordinates and organise a liaison officer. We're already on our way."

*

Jane Goodwin woke from a fitful sleep, at the end of a disturbing dream that she knew wouldn't go away for at least the next few minutes. She looked at the bedside clock. It was 9 a.m. She'd slept in. Adam's side of her bed was cold and the house was silent. He must have gone to work early without waking her and that meant there were two sleeping children in the next room.

She tiptoed to the bathroom with the remnants of the dream trailing behind her, helped along by a creaking floorboard.

They'd discussed the knife attacks and the lack of progress made on the cases until they'd fallen asleep last night, and perhaps that hadn't been the wisest thing to do. There'd been knives in her dream.

Since her mother's death, she'd been having concerns about remaining a special constable. A young female constable she'd trained with had recently been stabbed while on crowd control in Manchester. Fortunately she hadn't been badly hurt, but Jane had been rocked by the news. The thoughts of her precious daughter, Lucy, being raised by anyone other than her was too disturbing to contemplate. Lucy's father was seriously wealthy but an emotional vacuum, and her beautiful daughter needed love and care, not expensive gifts and live-in nannies.

The children's bedroom door was slightly ajar, just enough for her to peep through. They were both still sleeping so she crept downstairs and switched on the kettle. Then she switched on the television in the living room, adjusted the volume, and began preparing breakfast.

The words 'knife attack' jumped back into her thoughts. But this time they'd come from the direction of the television.

"Breaking news from the Leaburn area of Derbyshire this morning…" the reporter was saying, "…a third male victim, in this beautiful tourist area in recent months…"

She moved across the kitchen to the living room doorway.

"And now over to our local reporter, live at the scene."

The immaculately groomed face of a young female reporter almost filled the screen.

In the background, she could just see Adam with DCI Forbes, talking to a woman in white overalls. The kettle switched itself off. She wasn't listening to the words, instead she watched the two men trying to leaving the crime scene, being jostled by the gaggle of reporters. Adam hated that side of his work.

"…knife crime victim in this quiet rural area, in the very heart of the Peak District National Park, has all the hallmarks of a serial killer at work. Residents and tourists alike are being urged to report anything at all suspicious, and to remain vigilant until this person is apprehended." The reporter sounded full of concern. Jane could imagine the face of DCI Forbes if he ever saw that news report.

Chapter 17

Forbes manoeuvred his Mercedes through the renovated gritstone archway, into a large paved courtyard, and parked beside a white delivery van. It was getting so you couldn't go anywhere without finding them taking up valuable parking spaces, he thought. What had once been the main cattle market for this rural area, and the central hub of the small, but busy market town of Ashbourne was now a dozen, occupied flats. As flats went, he'd seen a lot worse, but in his experience they were rarely faultless. The architect couldn't have been expected to foresee the mushrooming of the numbers of dustbins, let alone predict the variations in sizes and colours. They spilled out of their purpose-built designated areas and blocked the walkways as effectively as a legion of armed warriors, leaving barely enough room for residents to walk, and as far as he could see, nowhere had been designed for small children to play in safety.

The Stansfield family lived on the first floor. Forbes paused to listen to raised voices, followed by the piercing screams of an infant. He walked past the doorway of the war-torn flat. They weren't here to settle a domestic.

The smell of bleach, washing powders, and stale tobacco contrasted sharply with the damp, crushed-grass perfumed air of an hour ago. He allowed himself a few seconds of rare self-indulgence while they climbed the concrete stairs, and considered how lucky he'd been in his life, despite it not always being easy.

As Mrs Stansfield opened the door, Forbes saw Adam wrinkle his nose and tried not to do the same. The woman was obviously oblivious to the air quality. He looked at the child's tear-stained face and thought that maybe he'd be crying too if he had to live in this atmosphere.

At a guess, the boy was about eighteen months old, and once settled on his mother's knee he quickly calmed down, maybe deciding that the two strange men were suitable entertainment for the moment.

The loud exchange from the flat below seemed to have run out of steam.

"We realise this is difficult, Mrs Stansfield, but it would help us if you could answer a few questions. Is there anyone nearby who could take your child for a while?"

For a moment she looked stunned, as if this was her lot in life and things were only about to get worse. He wondered how old she was. With clean hair and make-up, and a good night's sleep, she could probably pass for mid-twenties, but slumped in that chair, with the news that she was now a single parent, she looked to be on the wrong side of thirty-five. For the second time in as many hours, he thought of Louise.

"I'll phone my cousin. She lives across the yard so she can be here in a minute, and she knows I've called you. She works nights but she hasn't gone to bed yet."

The wide-eyed child was still taking everything in.

"Do you have a recent photograph of your husband, Mrs Stansfield?"

She held out her phone. "These are the most recent. Can you take some off there?"

Forbes looked at a smiling picture of a man holding his infant son. The man he'd just left.

She sat still for a few moments, hugging her child. Then her eyes widened with a sudden flash of doubt. "You could be mistaken, couldn't you? Peter doesn't take a very good photograph, he never has. It could be someone else. He had no reason to go out of town." She looked into both men's eyes and then looked at her son and her face fell.

"We need to ask whether your husband went out in his own car last night, and whether he was alone when he left here, or whether he mentioned that he was intending meeting anyone."

"He drove away alone and he didn't mention anyone. He goes out once a week on his own, but only when he's not on call. He's a part-time fire fighter. We're trying to save up for somewhere better for the children to grow up. It's difficult to get a babysitter. He's a loving husband and father – I can see what you're thinking... but he wouldn't do something like that... he loves us too much."

"You said children, have you got more than one?"

"We will have five months from now... he'll never get to see..."

"We're really sorry, Mrs Stansfield. A liaison officer will be here very shortly to keep you informed with what's happening, but we will need the details of his car."

"I don't understand... you said you'd found him."

"Yes, and again I'm sorry, but we don't have very much information at this point. He was found in a fairly remote spot, where people frequently park, but there was no vehicle. It appears he was attacked in the open air, and someone, his attacker or an opportune car thief, then drove off in his car."

"That must be it then. A car thief must have made him drive out of town to rob him. He must have tried to defend himself. But it's an old car, and he never carries much money. Why would anyone kill for such an old car?"

Ross was in the hallway, briefing the cousin who'd arrived with another infant in her arms, when strains of classical music began drifting from the flat below. What began as background music was becoming louder by the second. From the same general direction, a man responded with verbal abuse and a row erupted again. Mrs Stansfield stamped both feet three times on the laminate floor, the poor child bobbing up and down each time in her lap. Quite understandably, he began screaming again.

They left the young widow to her dismal life, but in the care of neighbours. Adam spoke first. "I reckon that if Mrs Stansfield was to stab her husband, it would be inside that flat."

"I won't argue with that. If he regularly goes out once a week, then we've got to go through all that old CCTV footage again, as well as last night's. Find out where he goes and whether he meets up with anyone. Just because she denied the possibility of an affair, it doesn't rule it out. She's probably sleeping by the time he gets home. Organise door to door with friends and family, but make finding his car a priority."

"Is it too early for an appeal to the public?"

Limestone walls and overgrown hedges beside the main road rushed past them. "Let's wait for the post mortem. If it is a street girl gone bad, then we don't want to frighten her indoors. We'll increase patrols around the public houses in Leaburn and see what the next twenty-four hours of forensic work throws up."

He sensed Adam wasn't in full agreement, and knew why, but gossip would rapidly spread around the pubs and clubs and most male punters would soon be aware of the danger, without any need of a police warning.

*

The incident room felt as airless as usual. Forbes looked at the newest pictures on the board and announced a lunchtime briefing. He wanted to be sure every possible angle of the enquiry was being covered. He realised that he'd missed lunch and suddenly felt hungry. Although his work often revolved around some gruesome crime scenes, not to mention extremely unpleasant smells, nothing ever affected his appetite as it did with some of his colleagues. Maybe that was a trait that he shared with his sister. He went into his office in search of the cheese biscuits and chocolate bar that he hoped were still there from yesterday, just in time to take an internal call from a police constable downstairs.

"Sir, I think we may have found this morning's missing car already. Fire officers were called out to a blaze half an hour ago on wasteland beside Harper Hill Industrial Estate. It's well burnt out, apparently, but I've asked them to secure the area until we arrive, considering that Dakin's car was torched."

He shoved his meagre lunch into one jacket pocket, and his car keys into the other.

*

The misery in the air was almost as tangible as the lingering smoke. They might not have pulled a body from this burning wreck, but the fire crew had heard the breakfast news and recognised the car of a colleague. Forbes walked towards the Chief Fire Officer, a giant of a man who'd played rugby for his native Scotland before joining the Derbyshire Fire and Rescue Service.

"It was well ablaze by the time we arrived, Michael. We can't get anywhere near the VIN number, not yet, it's too damn hot, but it sure looks as if someone tried to destroy Peter's car, along with any evidence."

"Do you know who called in the blaze?"

"Staff at the Pelican factory over there saw the fire and called it in."

Harper Hill Industrial Estate consisted of a recycling centre, a council yard, several kitchen and bathroom distribution units, two building and timber merchants, and the usual assortment of smaller, independently run units at the far end. But to reach any of those meant passing the largest unit on the estate, and a major employer of local workforce, Pelican Industries. They produced tapes, discs, and various other spare parts for the computer industry and were the only unit with employees on site overnight.

The Scotsman stood his ground; he was a man of few words, more comfortable giving orders than information. Presumably this was as helpful as he was likely to be, so Forbes turned his attention to Adam. "Get all the surveillance tapes from this area, and find out whether any one from any of the other units saw anything. I'll find the person who called in the blaze."

"Mr Johnson called the emergency services," the youth on the fork lift yelled down at him. "He thought someone might want to talk to him so he's waiting in the canteen. The rest of the early shift has already gone home. It's straight down the corridor, second door on the left. Keep walking between the yellow lines or the health and safety officer will be after your blood."

Forbes pushed open the double doors and squinted. Presumably lighting was reserved for when people were actually eating, and the two small roof lights weren't having much of an effect on the large space. There were muffled sounds of plates and pans coming from somewhere close by and it smelled as a canteen should. His stomach rumbled again. He scanned the seating area and saw something on one of the tables which could have been a mobile phone.

"Mr Johnson, I'm DCI Forbes, may I have word with you?"

The head of a middle-aged man appeared from the far side of the table.

"Just give me a moment, officer, I was fast on." He swung his legs to the floor, pulled himself into a seated position and then yawned and stretched. "My wife works nights at the hospital, so I didn't want anyone calling round to the house and waking her. I thought I'd try and get forty winks here while I waited. The name's Joe, by the way."

"Joe, would you mind telling me exactly what you saw today?"

"Did you say a DCI, there wasn't a body in that car, was there?"

"No, but it may be linked to a serious crime. What time did your shift start?"

"We have three, eight-hour shifts here at the moment, and this week I'm on from six in the morning till two in the afternoon. I aim to get my work area cleared at least half an hour before I finish. Then I can go outside for a quick fag before cleaning my work station and setting up for the next shift, which normally takes me a further twenty minutes. When I went outside at one-thirty, I noticed a small, dark car going really slowly, and I thought it was old Mr Simmons. He has a car very similar. He's the part-time caretaker and he sees to any small repairs, cuts the grass, and generally keeps the place tidy. It was the slow speed that made me notice it. I wondered what the old bugger was up to, driving off like that towards open ground. I came back in, did what I had to, and then Tom and I went outside together for another fag at five minutes to two. That was when we saw the fire."

"Did you see anyone near the car?"

"No, I ran back to phone the emergency services, and Tom ran to the car to see if anyone was trapped. He said it was too hot to get up close, but he couldn't see anyone inside."

"When did you know for certain that it wasn't Mr Simmons?"

"I was still on the phone when the old bugger pulled into the yard. He came in here waving his arms about and yelling, demanding to know who was responsible for dumping and burning rubbish without his written permission. I reckon he needs his eyesight testing. I wouldn't take too much notice of his claims that he saw someone running from the industrial estate."

"Has Mr Simmons gone home?"

"His wife worries if he's not home on time, but he's left his address and phone number in case to needed to speak to him. He's a daft little man who likes to feel more important than he really is."

"Did he say whether he recognised the person?"

"All he said to me was that he saw someone running, and that they got into a small silver car that seemed to be waiting at the junction. After he'd watched the car moving away, he noticed smoke coming from the waste ground. But like I said – his eyesight isn't what it should be. I don't think he should be driving, or still working, come to that."

*

"Please relax, Miss Forrester," DC Harry Green had entered interview room number one, but not before he'd been reminded that Miss Forrester was a reporter and therefore to be handled with caution. "I understand that you'd been a colleague of Derek Austen's for several years?"

The spikey-haired young woman from the Buxton Advertiser was perched on the edge of her chair. She had the expression of a startled rabbit. "Yes, I've been with The Advertiser for three years, I went there straight from college and I've worked alongside Derek for most of that time. I haven't much to tell, not really, but I know you've been hearing all kinds of gossip since you last spoke to the staff on the Advertiser, and I felt I ought to come and defend Derek."

"We appreciate any information you can give us."

"He was a good man; a real family man who had told me on numerous occasions that he had no ambitions to work for any of the national newspapers. He was *'Derbyshire born and bred'*, as he liked to say. He loved the Peak District, and he loved his wife and his children. It's embarrassing for me to admit now, but when I first started work I developed a little bit of a crush on him, and he knew that, but he took me aside and we talked, and he put me straight. That's why I find all these rumours about him using prostitutes so hard to believe. He just wasn't that kind of a man. He quite literally lived for his work and his family."

"You'd be surprised how many times I've heard that cliché, Miss Forrester. Have you had any thoughts about who he *might* have picked up that night? Whoever he'd arranged to meet may not necessarily have been his killer."

"No, I wish I had some ideas, but I do know that he'd been trying for quite a long while to find someone. He wouldn't say who, only that it was a human interest story he might have been able to sell to the larger tabloids. A few days before he died he told me that he'd got a new lead. I got the impression money was involved, but I'm not sure whether Derek was the one doing the buying, or the selling."

"I don't suppose you've come across anything else in his documents, anything we might have overlooked, or have any idea where he might have got this new information from?"

She shook her head. "No, and believe me I've searched. He had a reputation as an investigative journalist. People would occasionally contact the paper and ask specifically for Derek, offering a story for cash or asking for his help in digging something out that they thought may be of interest to him. He was becoming something of a minor celebrity in the area and it was good for our local rag, but he never enjoyed being in the limelight. He would have hated all this attention on his private life and all the gossip."

*

"I've found footage of Stansfield in his car last night, sir," PC Gary Rawlings was one of three officers sitting at their desk and staring at grainy CCTV footage.

Forbes and Adam walked over.

"In this one he's watching the pub's clientele arriving." Adam said. "Is he looking for someone in particular or is he waiting for those pedestrians to move away?"

It didn't look good either way. Forbes pictured the pregnant woman they'd left in that flat a few hours earlier, and grunted. A different camera picked up the car as it slowly drew away and indicated for a sharp right turn.

"There are a lot of flats and empty shops down that road," PC Rawlings told them. "It snakes round and ends up back in the town centre. We expected to pick him up again at the junction, but we didn't. Now watch this second camera. Thirty minutes after he's turned right, there he is, coming back up."

"And, surprise, surprise, he has a passenger." Adam slapped PC Rawlings on the back. "Well spotted Gary."

"The close-ups on these screens don't show anything very useful I'm afraid, sir. It's as if the passenger's aware of the cameras and doesn't want to be seen."

A small hand and part of a hood were where the face should have been.

"There are no rings, no markings or nail decorations, sir. But they do look more like the fingernails of a woman, or a girl, than the fingernails of a man. They appear nicely manicured, although that doesn't necessarily mean a lot today."

Forbes turned to Adam. "So someone quite small, in relation to Stansfield, but then it doesn't take any great bulk to stab someone from behind. That could be our killer right there."

The mood in the incident room was changing.

It wasn't distinctive, but it was their first possible sighting.

*

One hour later, Forbes addressed the incident room again. "We now have two timelines. At nine-thirty last night, cameras recorded what could be the last person to see Peter Stansfield alive. And at one-thirty this afternoon, his car was driven onto wasteland where it was set alight." He paused and looked around the room. "Beginning with the females, I want everyone associated with the first two murders revisited and questioned for an alibi for those two times. Then we'll double check them."

"And keep in mind," Adam reminded them, "just how lethal a pretty face can be. We don't want to hear of any officers entering properties alone. Remember, not everyone is a walking advertisement for their trade, all of the time. Also, we'll need officers to conduct a search and a door to door enquiry along the road our latest victim spent time on. Someone may have seen something useful. The person seen in the car last night, and again at the bonfire today wore an indistinguishable hooded garment, and yes I know, there must be hundreds of them in this town alone, but one of them is almost certainly hiding a killer."

Chapter 18

Waiting for the others to get their coats, Anna leaned back on the sofa and allowed her mind to drift into the not-too-distant past. She felt thankful that grief wasn't an emotion she'd ever suffered from. She'd seen it in the twin's faces, week after week, and it definitely wasn't for her. So what if the woman she'd always called *mother* had gone and killed herself – how sodding stupid was that? But it had had no effect on her. The woman had made it abundantly clear that there was nothing left between them. The council had seen to her funeral and her manky ashes were stored in a pot somewhere, if she could be bothered to find out, which she couldn't. That part of her life had been over for months.

It had simply been rotten luck, all those months ago, when that reporter had been at the hospital sniffing around for a story on Verona. He'd had the nerve to ask the duty nurse about the other girls in the ward, and that nurse been stupid enough to give him their names. That sort of thing should be a sacking offence, at the very least.

And it had been even more unbelievably rotten luck a few months later, when he'd been the only reporter ever to be invited into the commune. Of course he'd recognised Verona – and her, wasn't that the way her life always went? Covered in dusty overalls and helping to muck out a ramshackle henhouse, miles from anywhere, and this reporter guy she'd never even seen, had recognised them. What were the odds?

She'd had to admire his persistence, pretending to be her long lost relative, and continuing to visit. Most people who came into contact with the commune took one look at the huge dogs, and the bearded men on the ends of the dog's leashes, and never came back. But this reporter kept on filling his pockets with dog biscuits and bravely knocking on the massive front door.

And once she'd had time to digest every aspect of his news, she'd felt a begrudging gratitude towards him.

But he'd served his purpose, and he wouldn't be interfering in anyone's life again.

It was what to do with his news that she was still undecided about.

"Anna, are you asleep? Verona can't find her hat." Maisie's voice cut into her thoughts.

"I can't be responsible for all of you," Anna stood and straightened her shoulders. The small living space was more of a tip than usual, but the mess could wait. Keeping control of the group was her priority and it wasn't as easy as she'd imagined it was going to be. If they were to stay together indefinitely, and that was her long term plan, then she would have to create a tighter unit. "I've been thinking – we have to dispose of that car. We can't afford to get caught driving it. The club won't employ anyone with a record."

"But we've been moving it every day. It's never been parked in the same place, on the same street, more than once." Maisie and Carol held hands, making their joint appeal. "And you used it the other day, Anna."

"Stop doing that." She pointed to their hands. "When you were six it may have been cute, but now you're sixteen, it's just plain creepy."

The twins stepped apart, but Carol wasn't giving up. "We don't drive far, and the number plates are false. And anyway, we keep them dirty so the machines can't read them. Please, please, let's keep it just a little while longer. My driving's getting much better, honest."

"You're a soppy pair." She couldn't help but smile. "I can get another car any time we need one, and right now we don't. We walk into town, or catch a bus if it's raining. Besides, we can't risk bringing trouble to the flat now we have Verona to take care of. I know she sometimes seems a little weird, but that's because of what's happened to her. I'm making it my mission to help her get better, and I expect you two to support me."

Verona's head appeared around the bathroom door. She saw the girls looking at her and took one tentative step towards them. "I didn't know I was a little weird. Can you really help me? I'm trying very hard to belong here, with you three."

Anna beckoned her over. "You're weird in a funny, beautiful kind of way, and we all love you for it. No regrets – remember – that's what we all said when we walked out of that hospital – the four musketeers, together for ever. You already belong here, you soppy mare."

The twins were still pouting.

Anna held out her hand. "You have to trust me on this, but I am getting rid of that car today."

They all pulled on woollen hats and charity shop coats, and the twins led the way.

They walked along three streets into a more residential area and Anna stopped them when she saw the car. "We can't risk all been seen together, not too close to it. Wait here till you see me drive away, then walk back into town. I'll meet you in the square in an hour. If I don't get there, go home and wait."

*

Jane Goodwin had defused the latest confrontation between the two youngsters, but the stairs now resembled an obstacle course. She'd put the subtle changes in Lucy's behaviour down to her grief. She found herself struggling with her own emotions occasionally, so she could understand her six-year-old experiencing problems, she just wasn't sure how best to deal with it. She blinked away an unexpected tear and ushered the children into the kitchen. Adam was arriving home and the casserole was ready. Tidying up would have to wait.

"There's going to be a mountain of checking and cross checking of statements over the next few days. Would you like to come in for a few hours if I can persuade mum to take care of Ryan and Lucy?"

Jane hadn't expected to be called in to the station just yet. She'd barely left the house since her mother's death. Maybe it was Adam's way of easing her back into the world, but her confidence had been knocked more than she'd realised and the thought didn't appeal. "I've been wondering about a change of direction – career-wise," she said, "maybe into wildlife crime. What do you think?"

"But I thought you loved all wild creatures," he pulled a face at the children and laughed at her.

"Oh, you know what I mean. Ryan, your daddy is so silly at times."

The children were both giggling – tantrums forgotten.

As she opened the cupboard for her mother's dishes she couldn't help picturing the grey-haired lady, woolly hat pulled down over her ears and torch and plastic container in her hands, feeding the local badgers over the wall at the bottom of the garden with the day's leftovers. She'd done it for as long as Jane could remember, to the annoyance of some of the neighbours whose gardens were occasionally raided. Mr Collins, three doors down, had had to dig up all his strawberry plants and transfer them to buckets and pots, and then build a rack to keep them out of reach of the creatures.

Then there had been the years when the badger numbers had mysteriously dropped and her mother had fretted over them.

"It was only a thought for the future. Of course I'll come in if your mum's willing to do the school run. But speaking of the future," she hesitated, "I really think we should sit down and work out some structure to both our children's routines."

Adam grunted. "Whatever you think will work."

He was looking tired. Yesterday was the first time she'd noticed shadows under his eyes, and today they were even more pronounced. It was going to be down to her to make the decisions. "Sit down and I'll dish up the casserole," she said.

Adam scooped up the wriggling infants and sat them both down at the kitchen table. "Now then you two, who's for an extra-large plate full?"

Ryan was giving them his *please don't make me* look, while Lucy was shaking her head with the fiercely determined expression that she'd been perfecting lately. Adam hadn't any surplus fat to lose, so she divided what was left between the adults' plates.

It was another couple of hours before the children were settled into their beds and Jane and Adam had the sofa to themselves.

"We're interviewing all known prostitutes in our area, male and female."

"I bet that's going down well," Jane smiled. "I never told you why I got into police work, did I? It was as a direct result of a poster on the community centre wall promising a safer neighbourhood. You see, I knew a couple of women just like the ones that you're interviewing. They'd been school friends of mine, and they were afraid for their safety on a daily basis. If the girls I knew ever suspected that one of their own had become a killer, I know they'd come forward. After all, it can't be doing their business much good."

"That's true. But if it's not a regular, where does that leave us?"

"Looking for someone posing as a prostitute, maybe? You did say sex never actually took place."

"But where's the motive?"

She tried to sound indignant. "When one of the girls I mentioned finally spoke out about a well-respected friend of her father who'd been abusing her for years, no one in her family believed her. In the end, she left home. I believed her story, because I saw how angry and upset she was. And I've no idea what happened to her after we lost touch a few months later. How about revenge killings by a badly treated woman? Could that be a motive?"

*

It was Saturday morning. Forbes had woken early and, as was his custom, had spent a couple of hours in his office while the building was relatively quiet. He leaned back in his chair. The sun had risen into a clear sky and he decided that ninety minutes of sitting at his desk was enough. He wondered whether Alison would be up and about yet and decided to risk phoning her.

"Fancy a brisk walk on the moors later today... if you're not working? We could have an hour or two of fresh, clean air and then follow up with fish and chips."

"You read my mind, Michael. I put my wax jacket and walking boots into the car yesterday, but didn't get a chance to use them. See you at the usual place?"

"I've got to call home first, so I'll see you there at about eleven."

Some last minute paperwork that he really didn't want to leave for Monday morning delayed him, but he was accelerating away from the station by ten o'clock.

Louise was opening the front door as he walked up the garden path.

"Off to work," she informed him as she breezed past. "I've got a double shift today because someone's called in sick. I won't be home till late, so don't wait up."

"Hold it right there, lady," he knew she wasn't about to stop. "What about Gemma?"

"Dad's offered to feed and bath her, and get her to bed. He's got my number if there's a problem. Relax... he loves it, besides, it's all arranged now. Give her a goodnight kiss from me. Bye," she yelled from the pavement.

He closed the front door on her and headed towards the sound of his father's singing. "All right Dad? Do you think you can manage if I go back out for a few hours? You do know Louise is already taking advantage, don't you?"

"I love spending time alone with Gemma. Stop fussing. Your sister's going to work and earning money. After the last few years, I count myself lucky to be able to say those words."

"Point taken, Dad, but give me a call if you need me. I'm going for an hour's walk at Minninglow – hoping it will blow some cobwebs off."

"Alone?"

"Hopefully not – do you want fish and chips bringing back?"

"Text me when you're on your way. I'll have three plates warming."

*

On the main road leading to Winster he turned left at the hamlet of Pikehall. Driving past Gotham Grange Farm always made him smile, remembering the television series featuring Batman and Robin and thinking how he'd once dreamed of being a law-enforcing superhero. A DCI in Derbyshire was as close as he wanted to get to that dream now. He turned off the road onto the gravelled car park and then onto rotting leaves squelching beneath his tyres. The filtered spring sunshine hadn't been sufficiently powerful yet to have any real effect on the gold and brown mulch. Four unoccupied cars were parked, their owners probably either walking dogs or riding pushbikes on the High Peak Trail. Assorted birds were enjoying the containers of birdseed and suspended nets of fat balls and peanuts that the good people of Derbyshire regularly left there for them.

Alison's car was at the furthest point of the park. She was sitting perfectly still, head back and eyes closed. He felt a brief moment of panic, but as he approached her car he smiled. Her gloved fingers were tapping out a rhythm onto her denim jeans.

He knocked on her window. "Ready to go...?"

She blinked and removed her earphones.

He watched her slow sexy smile developing, the one that had first made him notice her.

"What kept you?" She pulled a very unsexy bobble hat down over her ears before locking her car, and when she turned to face him he couldn't resist pushing the hat back from her face and giving her a long kiss.

"I hope they have some strong air fresheners in those vehicles," she was looking back at two muddy spaniels being loaded into the rear of an estate car and a tail-wagging, equally muddy collie being coaxed onto the back seat of another.

Grey moisture splashed the backs of their boots and trousers as they strode out, both aiming to raise their heart rate as they braved the crosswind to reach the far side of the viaduct.

Alison stopped first, leaning her back against a massive, stone gatepost and gasping for breath. They watched two more dogs leading their owners back towards the car park.

"That was exhilarating," she puffed. "The car park will soon be empty. Do you think they know something we don't?"

"If they do, whatever it is can wait. Now we've got the blood pumping we can take it a bit steadier."

"I hoped you'd say that. We'll take in the view and then steadily complete the circuit. Let me get rid of this stitch first." She rubbed her right side.

The final leg of the hike was on tarmac, and he could see something was bothering her. "Are you going to tell me what's on your mind?"

"I didn't want to bring it up while we were out here, we get so little time alone together during the day and I didn't want to spoil it, but seeing as you've asked... I loaned Louise a pile of text books last week on forensic science and pathology, and while I know some of them were a bit advanced, even a touch gruesome, I thought she might have been back in touch with some questions. I've heard nothing at all from her, not even an e-mail. Do you know whether she's been reading them?"

"Reading them... she's been absorbed in them too much. Dad had to stop her from studying them at the breakfast table. You wouldn't have told me until last night that anyone would be able to study some of those full colour pictures while eating a plate of liver and onions."

"And what's wrong with that? I'll bring some of my case work for her to look at if she's showing a genuine interest. She stands a chance of a good career if she can get good grades and show that she's become a responsible adult. You can be proud of her, for once." She put her hand over her mouth.

"Sorry, that came out wrong. I know how much you've both always loved her."

"Only time will tell, but at the moment she's working all the hours she can and saving every penny. She seems happy enough, and when she works late she gets a lift home." His thoughts were returning to the incident room and he felt Alison watching him.

"Hey, we agreed no talking or even thinking about knife crime while we're out here. What time does the chip shop open?"

One of the things he liked most about Alison was her ability to almost read his mind. This time though, she didn't expect an answer – she was following the direction of his gaze. They were still walking along a tree-lined lane but facing the car park and he could see smoke. There was no mistaking the dark mass spiralling up into the clear sky. A vehicle was ablaze.

His hands shook as he fumbled with the double zip on his coat pocket.

*

Blackened leaves swirled around the park, and wherever they stood the throat-burning smoke seemed to find them.

"There were two separate calls, sir, both from the same gentleman," PC Robert Bell told Forbes, "six minutes apart and concerning a silver car being erratically driven by a young woman in a residential area. The traffic department alerted the incident room. We were about to contact you, sir, when you called in the fire."

Streaks of grey snaked up between scorched branches, taking with them potentially valuable scraps of evidence.

"Well I'm just thankful that our cars were at the far end of the park," Alison had checked hers over and come to listen to PC Bell.

He wanted to put his arm around her again, but it wouldn't have been professional. "When exactly were the calls logged?"

"The second call was twenty-two minutes before you called in, sir. It's about a ten minute drive from where it was seen, to this park. Allowing a few minutes to make sure no one was around, and then lighting the fire and making sure it took hold, until the time that you first saw the smoke, I'd say the time frame fits and it's probably the same vehicle."

"Did the caller recognise the driver?" That would have made it too easy.

"I only know that he said a young woman was at the wheel and that he couldn't see any passengers."

"You said that he made two calls?"

"Yes sir, he first called it in because it had been parked in front of his house overnight where his wife normally parks, and none of his neighbours knew who it belonged to. He'd asked around and one of the residents told him they'd seen it a few days earlier, parked in front their daughter's house overnight. There'd been a burglary not too far away and people were understandably suspicious. When someone mentioned that they'd seen our appeal for a missing silver car, he offered to make the call. He returned outside just in time to see a young girl climbing into the driving seat. He thought she must have had keys, but she wasn't a good driver because she pulled out in front of an oncoming vehicle. That car had to swerve to avoid a collision and that's when he made the second call. PC Rawlings is at the caller's house now, sir."

"SOCOs can finish off here." He turned to Alison, "I'd better go and have a word with the caller. Dad's waiting for his tea but I've already texted him. Will you call for the food and put mine in the oven. I'll be as quick as I can, but I must talk to this eye-witness."

He didn't like sending her off like that, she looked pale, but she'd be well looked after by his father. With any luck, she'd have helped to get Gemma bathed and settled for the night and be in front of the television keeping his father company, by the time he got home.

*

He opened the living room door onto just that scene, with the added bonus of the unmistakable odour of fish and chips. "You look comfy. Can I get either of you a hot drink?" He felt he needed to compensate for the afternoon.

"I'd love a hot chocolate... unless you've got to go back to work," she said without turning to look at him.

"All right, I asked for that. Now that you've got it out of your system, would you like half milk or all milk?"

"Half milk please. Those chips were good and I'm afraid I ate too many."

He smiled. Their relationship had spanned almost twenty years, and somewhere, in the mists of time, they'd declared that they were both dedicated career people and so most nights Alison slept in her own flat in town. She had tried to help out when Louise had been *the toddler from hell*, but she'd told him then that she would happily spend all day on her feet with a room full of corpses, in preference to spending an hour with one disruptive toddler. Her natural affection for Gemma, however, was obvious, and the last time he'd seen her with Louise they could have been mistaken for lifelong friends. It looked as if Alison might, for the first time, be enjoying being a part of his dysfunctional family.

Chapter 19

PC Rawlings stuck his head through Forbes's open office doorway. "A couple have just walked into reception, sir. They say they may have some information regarding Saturday's vehicle fire. Katie is showing them into interview rooms one and two."

"Tell them we won't keep them waiting," It was a job for a less senior officer, but Forbes wanted to take at least one of the interviews himself. It would be good to get Monday off to flying start.

In interview room one, he saw a young, clean shaven hospital doctor, not someone likely to be attention seeking.

"This may be nothing, but my wife and I noticed a young woman, a teenager possibly, riding a pushbike from the direction of the park where the car was set alight. She was going far too fast for safety, and that's why we remembered her. When we passed the park we saw a small amount of smoke, though we never considered a car might be burning, or naturally we would have stopped. We thought someone had lit a camp fire, an irresponsible thing to do in a public place, especially around all those beautiful trees. We wondered if it might have been travellers, though we couldn't tell from the road whether there were other vehicles there. Then last night we saw the local news report and wondered whether the girl we'd seen might have been responsible."

"We'll need a description of the girl, of what she was wearing, and also of the bike if you can remember."

Jane Goodwin had been allocated a desk in the corner of the busy incident room and didn't lift her head when Forbes and Adam returned to the room.

"Unfortunately, the press are already leading with the title, 'the high heeled assassin'," Adam was saying, "and the public houses are complaining that trade is at an all-time low and unlikely to improve until we have someone in custody."

Forbes couldn't help thinking that the livelihoods of the women on the streets would probably have taken a nosedive as well. "Maybe we should take another look at the more rural properties. Let's begin by revisiting where this all began... let's take another ride out to Bakewell where Austen was last seen alive."

There was a low haze. Grey and purple light tones merged into the open grassland, totally obliterating the horizon. Motorbikes of varying sizes and models roared along the twisting, open road, blissfully unaware of the occupations of the driver and passenger of the car rapidly disappearing in their rear view mirrors.

Despite being early, the roads into Bakewell were snarled up with slow moving cattle trailers, tractors towing trailers loaded with bleating sheep, and even a convoy of buses ferrying Japanese tourists around the ever popular British Isles.

"It looks like market day, sir."

"You don't say. We'll have to make a courtesy call at the local station. It's right in the centre of the market and only a short walk from there to The White Horse where Austen was last seen alive."

"I already put everything I remember about that night into my statement," the landlord ushered them into an empty room behind the bar. "We have regular entertainment here and it pays to advertise. I knew Derek Austen through the Buxton Advertiser."

"But he was a reporter, not a salesman." Forbes said.

"It's only a provincial newspaper, despite what the editor says. When Austen first started work there, his main task was to sell more advertising space. That must be ten years ago, or more. And over the years he's become another of my occasional customers, even when he's not officially working.

Though I suppose you can never really be sure with a reporter, can you?"

"But on the night of his murder, he came here specifically to discuss advertising?"

"Kind of – the paper was planning to do a feature on all the real ales produced in the district. A surprising number of micro-breweries have sprung up over the last few years. We always like to have a couple of the local ales on sale in here and they go down especially well with the tourists. Would you care to try one – on the house, of course?"

"Some other time, thank you. We're trying to uncover a story he may have been working on for a while. We have reason to believe he may have been looking for someone. Did he ask about, or mention at all, any missing persons, past or present? Or can you think of anyone in the bar he may have talked to recently?"

"He always sat on the end bar stool, if it was empty. Otherwise, he just stood at the bar. I don't remember him ever sitting at a table and he'd speak to whoever came up to the bar for a drink. And if there was no one there, then he'd talk to me, or whoever was on duty. He was that kind of a bloke, friendly like."

"Do you remember him talking about anything in particular that night?"

"Nothing stands out, but then every topic under the sun gets discussed over that bar. I can't remember anything more that might help you, but I will keep thinking."

"What about women? Did you ever see him with anyone other than his wife?"

"No, not Derek, his family was his life."

"So we keep hearing, but can you be absolutely certain that when he left here he was alone? You didn't get the impression that he'd arranged to meet someone outside, maybe?"

"I was the only one on the bar while he was here and I didn't see anything to suggest that. I put all this in my statement and your officers interviewed the rest of the staff and my customers from that night. No, the newspaper feature was pretty much all we talked about, I'm sure. We went through his complete list of micro-breweries together, those set within in the Peak District, and a few others on the edge of it. Most of them we'd already tried in this bar at one time or another. There was only one I'd not heard of and he agreed he'd only recently come across it himself."

"A new one was it?"

"So I believe, but I'm not sure that I'd fancy trying it in my pub. Have you heard of the hippy commune up at Parsley Hedge?"

"Yes, we've come across it."

"Then you must know that the idea of them ever getting permission from the food standards agency is laughable. They grow all sorts up there. And I don't mean liquorice allsorts. Heaven only knows what they're putting into the brew. Half of them are off their heads, so I've heard anyway."

"They do have a reputation. Did Derek say whether he'd actually been to see this new micro-brewery?"

"Oh yes, he told me they'd showed him around the place a few weeks earlier. And he did say it was a bit of a dump, but that they were asking him to promote their beer, so he'd tried to encourage them to clean up the place a bit, you know. He tried to offer a bit of advice. Derek was that kind of a bloke. From the rumours I've heard, I'm surprised he got out of there with all his teeth intact. Well I told Derek that unless more than one of my regulars specifically asked for it, I wouldn't be selling it from my bar any time soon."

*

Forbes manoeuvred his Mercedes through the busy market town and joined the other vehicles crawling along the A6 out of Bakewell and towards Buxton, followed the route Austen was thought to have taken. Thirty minutes later he was pulling into the car park at Derbyshire Bridge. A small display of fresh flowers had been propped against the dry-stone wall, and someone had placed a length of chicken wire across them, and then secured it in place with coping stones taken from the top of a wall. Two rain-soaked, pink teddy bears had also been propped up – one at each side of the display.

They walked towards them in silence.

Two ducks were as unaffected by the scene now as they had been on the morning of the murder, scrambling up the bank in a frenzy of anticipation. They noisily waddled behind the two men, and as they all reached the floral tributes, the reason for the wire became obvious.

Forbes turned his back on the pink bears and looked out across the moor. The stark, natural beauty of the place was unchanged. "Does this first murder hold the key?" he looked at Adam. "Could you have been right when you suggested something specific had triggered off a killing spree, something we haven't yet discovered? Was it something Austen did, or didn't do, or was it something he discovered in his search for someone?"

"That's too many unanswered questions, sir."

"Then let's drive on."

After a quarter of a mile, the narrow winding road re-joined the main road, guiding them across onto the open and gently rolling hillside where the bracken and heather competed with the course, natural wild grasses. A mosaic of crumbling, dry-stone walls, some of which encircled not much more than an acre of ground, straddled the hillside like a giant jigsaw, and the few isolated trees which had survived the nibbling teeth of rabbits, sheep or deer, looked very emaciated when compared to those a further down the hillside.

"There should be some chocolate in the glove box. Get it out for me, will you? Do you want some?"

"Thank you, sir."

He turned right off the main road and three roe deer bounded back towards a small patch of woodland, as they did at the first sign of human activity, or bad weather. He always felt sorry for the sheep. When the unpredictable weather of these moorlands turned against them they could only take refuge in the natural hollows of the landscape. Two winters earlier, Forbes remembered how dozens of sheep and their spring born lambs had been buried alive on these hills when an unexpectedly heavy snowfall had blanketed the exposed moors.

"That's a newish Land Rover," Forbes said as they pulled into the yard of the brothers' farm. "I thought all these hill farmers were struggling to make ends meet."

"Some of them are better off than they've ever been. I've an uncle in farming and he loved the Single Farm Payment that they were getting. It's been replaced now though by the Basic Payment Scheme which means that thirty per cent of their payments are linked to a new 'greening scheme'. It's all extra paperwork from the bureaucrats in Brussels, and he grumbles about that, but it makes farming a more profitable industry. Some of the larger farms are drawing in six figures from the Ministry."

"But this isn't a large farm, is it, and those tractors look expensive."

"I know that a lot of farmers lease them," Adam explained, "but you're right, they still have to be paid for. What are you thinking? This is about the very last place you'd expect to find a brothel."

He began picking his way towards the farmhouse, thankful that he'd had the foresight to put his dealer boots on before leaving the office, when yet another tractor rumbled across the field into the yard and stopped beside his car. The two brothers looked cheerful, too cheerful perhaps, as they climbed from the tractor, each of them holding up a dead rabbit.

"A good morning's work; one for us and one for the dog," Craig announced, throwing the rabbit over his shoulder and supporting the black and white collie as it gingerly clambered down the metal steps. "We only kill rabbits when they're for the pot. So how can we help you today?"

"We're here to ask whether either of you have remembered anything more about the night Derek Austen was killed. May we go inside for a few minutes?"

Both smiles momentarily slipped and neither of them offered to move.

"We've told you everything we remember. I don't see how we can help." Craig said.

"Your farm looks across the moors and down the valley, and we know that you go out shooting."

He noticed the brothers exchange a glance.

"You'd better come inside then, I suppose. We've told you before, we're all legal."

Craig pulled a wooden chair away from the kitchen table and sat down with his legs outstretched while Tony hung the rabbits in the porch.

Forbes waited until he had both men's full attention. "Well how about the morning of the fire – any new thoughts – and have either of you seen a silver car around here that you didn't recognise, either before or since the fire in your gravel pit?"

"If we had, then we'd have come and told you, wouldn't we? We've been following the news and we don't want a murderer lurking around our place. We never saw anything at the park, and on the morning of the fire, how were we to know the two incidents were connected? It was well ablaze by the time we got anywhere near it." When Craig finally stopped talking he turned to his brother and scowled.

"We're just double checking statements, Mr Havers." Forbes looked around the tired kitchen. Beige and yellow paintwork could have been white at some point in time, but it was hard to be sure. Everything looked decades old, and the skirting boards hid behind layers of dust and dog hairs, as did the corners of some of the work surfaces. Clothes were draped over every chair back, and empty food containers were preventing the lid of the swing bin from closing. "Do either of you have any relationships with the ladies?" If they did, then they either didn't bring them here, or the females in question were lacking any sense of basic hygiene.

Tony spluttered. "What's that got to do with you? We're not queer, if that's what you're implying, we're brothers. Neither of us are poofs."

"That wasn't what I was suggesting, Mr Havers, not that it would mattered if you were. I was just enquiring, along the lines of our investigation, whether either of you have sought out any female company recently."

"We've both had our share of girls in the past, but they're more trouble than they're worth nowadays. If they can't deal with bottle feeding a few orphan lambs in the kitchen for a few weeks of the year, then we can manage without them, can't we Craig?"

"Fair enough," Forbes smiled at them, "I can understand that. Now please don't take offence, we're asking this question of a lot of men. Do either of you ever use the services of a prostitute?"

"Aha," Tony grinned at them, "you're after some phone numbers are you? Well you've come to the wrong place here, mate."

"Just answer the question."

"Do you think that's the only way a couple of hill farmers like us can get a woman? Well I certainly haven't. I can't speak for our Craig."

"Certainly not; why would I pay for something I don't need? I'm with Tony on that one – women are more hassle than they're worth. Does this mean your suspect is a prostitute, like the newspapers are saying?"

"I can't comment on that. But for now, remaining celibate might be your wisest option, gentlemen."

Craig was looking nervous. "But you are certain that the Derbyshire Bridge murder and the burning car in our gravel pit are both connected with what the papers are calling, 'a high heeled assassin', are you?"

"We're working on that possibility."

"And the latest murder down near Hartington...?"

"I can't comment on that yet."

"Bloody hell," Tony slapped his brother on the shoulder. "That means a serial killer really could have been on our land. That's definitely not good."

"Definitely not good," Craig repeated.

He watched prolonged eye contact between the brothers. "If you've been watching the news then you'll be aware that we've found the burnt out remains of the silver car we were looking for in connection with the murders. We know where it's been for the last month, but not where it was kept before that. Do you think you may have seen it anywhere on these moorland lanes, or on a neighbouring property?"

"It's not an uncommon colour, is it?" Tony replied. "We never take much notice of cars. Now a tractor – that's a different matter. Our Craig can identify any type of tractor from the sound of its engine, long before he sees it. He's been able to do that since he was a nipper."

"I don't doubt that." Forbes considered a small white lie might be in order. "We do have one other matter to clear up. We have a witness who claims to have seen your vehicle in the vicinity of Derbyshire Bridge on the night of the murder. Our witness also claims that you occasionally go poaching for venison."

"Then your witness is either mistaken or lying. There are dozens of old Land Rovers in these hills. Every farmer's got at least one, and half the incomers have bought one for fear of getting stuck in the snow. How would he know it was ours?"

Forbes smiled at Adam, and then stared each of the brothers in turn. "Are you saying, sir, that it was yours that he saw?"

"I'm saying... how could he be sure?" Tony spluttered.

"Then you won't mind if we take a look at the treads of your Land Rover tyres, will you? We can compare them to some impressions that we have on file."

Craig looked at his brother. "There's no point in denying it now, after all we did nothing wrong, we just didn't want to get involved. Let's tell them everything."

*

His father had gone out with friends for the day and Alison and Louise had arranged time off together and been shopping with baby Gemma, in Buxton, for most of the afternoon. They'd prepared a casserole together beforehand, leaving it on a low heat, and that was the appetising smell that had drawn him straight from the front door into the kitchen.

"Louise is upstairs with Gemma, and before you ask, yes we've had an excellent day together. Your sister hasn't lost her enquiring mind, or her very active imagination. I'd be happy to see her working in the mortuary with me."

"It's those qualities that have landed her in so much bother over the years." He wanted to explain why he found it so difficult to always believe what his sister said. "She likes to live her life by different rules to the rest of us, and despite her promises, she still seems too eager to leave Gemma with whoever is to hand."

"Don't spoil our day. Your sister's an intelligent girl who needs a focus in life, and a tiny baby isn't always going to be enough for her. It doesn't mean that she doesn't love the child enough, or that she isn't a good mother. Caring for an infant without any support at all would suffocate her – she's been used to her freedom. She needs both of you at the moment, and I know she's really making an effort. You should have more faith in her."

He hadn't expected such a telling off. "I'll try."

"I do believe you'll be pleasantly surprised with how she does in the next year or two."

"I'm pleased she feels she can talk to you. I've always found conversation with her so difficult."

"Have you tried asking her for some details about her new job?"

"Bar work and waitressing, what is there to ask about?"

"There you go again, assuming she's got nothing to tell you." Alison snapped back. "If you don't talk to her about the mundane things, how on earth do you expect her to come to you and discuss the more important issues in her life?"

"I always felt awkward with childish conversations, and I guess I've never improved. You're already more natural with Gemma than I am. You're the same sex so it's easier for you to get through to her."

"Sometimes Michael... you're unbelievable! That cliché deserves to be struck from the English language. It's never been a case of 'getting through to her'. The fact that she's a female has nothing to do with it. Your sister's an adult, so talk to her as an adult. Imagine her working in the mortuary as a fully qualified pathology technician. It could happen if you give her the support and encouragement that she's asking you for at the moment. You'd be forced to drop the baby-sister attitude. Just because she isn't there yet, it doesn't mean that you can't treat her with the respect that she so badly needs to rebuild her confidence. She earned the respect of the wrong sort of people while she was living on the streets because she could drink half a bottle of vodka without blinking, but in our world, your sister is actually struggling."

"Point taken, but right now I'm in the midst of a multiple homicide case and Louise works most evenings. Some days our paths only cross in the hallway. All I really want to say to her is to be extra vigilant, but she'll just think I'm being overbearing."

"Explain to her that it's only because you care. Then you can ask her about the other girls who work there and about any customers that she might not feel comfortable with. Tell her you trust her judgement. Ask for her opinions and offer advice."

"Then she'll think I only want to talk to her to fish for information."

"Give me strength Michael! So what's wrong with that? She's showing an interest in crime solving, for heaven's sake! What better way is there for you to engage her in a conversation?" Alison turned her back on him, picked up the oven gloves, and let out an exaggerated sigh as she took the beef casserole from the oven.

The meal was almost finished before he dared seize the moment. "We haven't had much time for a chat about your work, Louise. Are you enjoying it, and are you getting along alright with the other staff?"

"The place is all legitimate, and as far as I can tell there are no drugs and no prostitution rackets going on behind the closed doors. That's what you really want to know, isn't it? I'm trying to do the right thing here, and unlike many of the other girls, I'll only be there for the summer."

Already she was on the defensive. He looked at Alison for support.

"Michael is very proud of you – we all are. He's trying, in his own clumsy way, to ask you for a little help." She followed up with her low-wattage smile to show she wasn't at all impressed by Louise's attitude.

"You must know your safety is always our main concern, but Alison is right, I was hoping you might be our eyes and ears in the busiest club in town."

"Sorry, I didn't mean to snap." Her expression changed from resentment to mild curiosity. "What is it exactly that you want me to look for?"

It was time for the direct approach. "Anything I tell you has to remain confidential."

"Sure." Her eyes widened and she leaned forward.

"As you know, we're fairly certain now that we're looking for a female killer, possibly either a prostitute or a woman who poses as one. She's slim, youthful in stature and reasonably fit, and so far she selects her victims after dark. We think she's blonde, with manicured, but fairly short fingernails. But we also believe she isn't working alone, and she may have been driving around in stolen cars until she's set them alight. Does any of that sound familiar to you?"

"You're joking, right?"

He smiled. "I just want you to watch for anything unusual, and to listen for any circulating rumours. People get careless with their talk when they're in a relaxed atmosphere and they've had a drink or two. But what I don't want you to do is become too involved with anyone, however friendly they might appear on the surface."

"I think I can manage that," she replied, sarcastically.

"You do know that we all love you, don't you?"

"Don't be so soppy."

Chapter 20

Forbes leaned forward in his chair; had he heard right? "Woodbine Cottage... Long Rake Mine... Youlgreave... are you sure you've got that right? Bloody hell, constable, that's a blast from the past!"

PC Gary Rawlings took a step back under the unexpected force of his boss's outburst.

"Woodbine Cottage... that place gave me nightmares for years... it still does." He closed his eyes and took a deep breath.

"Yes sir, Woodbine Cottage," PC Rawlings repeated. "DS Ross requested that you attend immediately, sir. He's bringing your car around to the front."

He lifted his jacket from the chair. "I was about your age when I last went there, and the file on Mark Brundell remains open. It must be almost thirty years since Mark went missing – but that was before I'd joined the force. And it's about twenty-five years since I rescued a small child from that horror of a place. Are you familiar with the case, PC Rawlings?"

"Vaguely sir, I've read some of the old reports, and I've heard about the child and your part in her rescue, but I'm sure I don't know all the facts."

They walked past the incident room. It was unusually quiet.

A ghost had just entered the building.

Forbes was the only one talking, as much to himself as to the young PC two strides behind him. "Ian and Elizabeth Chester lived there. Ian hanged himself in the woods, and as a direct result of that we found Mark's wife, Katy, and her emaciated daughter. The poor child wasn't far from death. Katy was detained for psychiatric treatment and the little girl went into foster care. Elizabeth Chester went back to Woodbine without any charges being brought against her. Does she still live there?"

"DS Ross has the details, sir."

Adam was waiting in the driving seat with his mobile phone still in his hand.

"Please don't tell me it's the Chester woman again."

"No sir, she apparently passed away last summer." Adam looked at the notes he'd scribbled down. "You're not going to like this, sir."

"You can tell me on the way. Move over – I'm driving."

"Mr and Mrs Markham bought Woodbine eight weeks ago intending to turn it into three luxury flats. While waiting for planning permission they began clearing out and investigating some of the contents of the outbuildings."

"Pass me a square of chocolate, will you. I'm getting a bad feeling already."

"Yes sir, it was when they cleared the floor of the largest barn and peeled up a long length of old lino that they found what they thought was either a cellar or a large inspection pit. When they lifted the wooden boards covering it, they saw something resembling human remains. Mr Markham then fetched a torch, for a better look, and thought there appeared to be more than one, very decomposed body in the hole."

Forbes opened the car window and took a deep lungful of cool air. The first incident, before he'd joined the force, could at a stretch be dismissed as two people being in the wrong place at the wrong time, resulting in a missing person's case that would possibly never be satisfactorily solved. The second wasn't a coincidence, rather a sad case resulting from the poor mental health of three adults who were sharing a house, and who the system had failed. But the third time around, this surely had to throw into question everything they thought they'd known about Woodbine Cottage. Assuming they weren't the remnants of a Halloween party, or animal bones, something far more sinister had been happening at Woodbine than any of them had realised.

"Can we be sure Mrs Chester is dead, and not tucked away in some nursing home somewhere?"

"I don't have any further information, sir. We only have what Mr Markham told us over the phone."

"We'll need to run a check on the death certificate. I want cause of death, date and place, and then we'll find out what happened to Katy Brundell after her treatment finished. But first, let's get over there and see for ourselves what this couple think that they've found."

Most of the seven mile drive from the station was familiar to him, but for the last two decades he'd managed to avoid turning onto the lane which led past Long Rake Mine and the narrow strip of woodland beside it.

For the last twenty-plus years it had been a quiet area where not a lot had happened.

He realised he hadn't been watching his speed. Disappearing into the trees ahead of him he saw a familiar vehicle. Alison must have already been in the area to have responded so quickly. He squeezed gently down on the accelerator and knew that Adam was watching the speedometer.

He recognised a sharp bend which led to a straight stretch of road, along which lay the entrance to Woodbine. It was an uncomfortable experience, changing down the gears and slowly turning his steering wheel. Over the preceding quarter of a century, the entrance seemed to have closed in on itself. Someone had been cutting back the trees nearest the house, but apart from that it all looked just as it always did in his nightmares – until he looked up.

There were no bars, and there was no sunken, doll-like face staring down at him.

The new owners had been busy with the weed killer, around the house and on the gravelled yard, but it didn't appear that they'd touched the fabric of the building. Off-white paintwork was peeling away from the windows and from the huge front door, revealing black paint underneath, and several of the windows looked as if they might have been cracked. It was difficult to be certain because of the accumulations of dirt.

He looked across at the sheds. It must have been decades since the sun had last shone on any of them – their roofs were smothered in moss and tall grasses and even a few small trees sprouted from choked gutters.

He knew from the original reports that the sheds had been searched when Mark and Katy had first gone missing, but he'd seen no mention of a pit or a cellar. Four years on, they'd looked through these same sheds, but Sergeant Walker had seen no reason to do a full search when Katy had turned up alive, and claiming that Mark and herself had been taken miles from Woodbine. The one constant in the two women's stories had been that Mark had left the premises on the day following the storm. If some of the remains turned out to be Mark's, then how and when had he returned, or had he been there all along?

He thought Alison always looked sensual when driving her twenty-six year old, green Toyota Hi-Lux, the vehicle she used for any work beyond the boundaries of the town centre or clean tarmac. She'd already parked up, so he magnanimously waved his hand, offering her the courtesy of being the first to view the scene. As he unfastened his seatbelt and reached for the remainder of the chocolate bar, he watched her slim, trouser covered legs swinging gracefully out of the high vehicle, and her sensible shoes landing onto the mat of dead and dying weeds. As she leaned across to the passenger seat to pick up her bag, a loose fitting navy jacket that would have looked bland and shapeless on many women clung to her curves. Her long, dark hair was secured in its normal, working-day style, a plait straight down the centre of her back. It looked so much better tumbling free over her smooth shoulders.

She acknowledged him with the briefest of nods.

"Shall we take a look, sir?" Adam was watching him.

A convoy of police cars trundled up the driveway behind them, while in front, the door of Woodbine Cottage opened.

As he stepped from his car, Mr and Mrs Markham began walking down worn, stone steps.

Alison took control, ordering the large, corrugated-iron, sliding doors on the front of the shed to be closed and forcing everyone to use the small personnel door on the side of the building. In the few minutes before the natural light was obliterated, they saw why Mr Markham had sounded so certain about his find.

"Have we finally found Mark Brundell?" Forbes muttered into the blackness of the large, oblong hole. "Has the poor sod been here all along?"

"I can't tell you anything until I get this lighting rigged up," Alison answered, "except that the gentleman who called in was correct in thinking there may be more than one cadaver down there. From here, I can see at least two separate sets of remains, and possibly a third in that far corner."

Above their heads, and running along the central beam of the large building, a row of dust covered florescent tubes buzzed and flickered, creating a harsh light. They were evenly spaced along the shed, with the central two tubes directly above what appeared to be a large, old, inspection pit. The oblong hole looked about five or six feet wide, between twenty and twenty-five feet long, and maybe five or six feet deep, but someone had heaped soil and stones along most of its length. Random lumps and mounds suggested it had been used it as a dumping ground, and the whole area looked black and soggy as if ground water had been seeping into it over many years.

The air tasted stale and acidic.

"I've never seen an inspection pit that looked anything like this," Adam stared into the shadows. "It's a huge, ready-made grave."

"That's the detective in you speaking," Forbes answered. He'd thought exactly the same.

Alison seemed happy that the floodlights were exactly where she needed them. "I did see something not too dissimilar once," she shouted across to them from the opposite side of the pit. "An old farmhouse had been demolished and a shed built on the site, and the owner had converted what had once been a cellar into an inspection pit by building up the sides. He didn't make a very good job. I was called out to it after he fell into it, knocked himself out and drowned in six inches of water. That was when ordinary folks could work on their own vehicles, of course, before everything was computerised and the motor industries realised that they could charge whatever they liked just to diagnose a problem. Did I tell you a friend of mine has to go to the garage just to get a brake light bulb changed, and that it takes their trained mechanics two hours to do that simple job?"

What could he say? He knew how chatting helped her cope with some of the more gruesome aspects of her work. And he knew she loved her old Toyota as much as she loved her job. "If this was a cellar, it must have been huge. See that mound there… against the side wall… could that be another body?"

"It looks about the right size and shape, doesn't it?"

"If this hole in the ground…," Adam was saying, "was originally used as a winter store for a family's food or for their winter fuel, and then became an inspection pit, we're talking about going back a long way into this property's history. It doesn't take a forensic anthropologist to see that those remains have been there for a good many years. According to Mr Markham, Mr and Mrs Chester owned Woodbine for about fifty years, but these remains could well predate even their ownership of the place."

"Hopefully I'll soon be able to answer that one for you," Alison wriggled into a white protective oversuit, preparing to be the first one down the extending ladder now being secured into place for her.

She was in her element, they'd seen what they came to see, and three murder cases were live. He turned to leave.

*

Back in his office, Forbes phoned the Chief Constable's office to inform them of the situation before they heard about it from the media. The findings at Woodbine could prove embarrassing enough to the force if they proved to have been there during the earlier investigations. He couldn't risk making things worse.

The original missing person's file was open on his desk as he searched for a good reason why the floors of the sheds had been overlooked. His mobile startled him.

What was it about a phone call that you were expecting that always made you jump, he thought as he flicked the accept icon – especially a call you were not looking forward to. "Alison, how's it going at Woodbine? What have you found?"

"Two dogs, five cats, and seven humans have all been laid to rest in this pit. And I know you're not expecting this, Michael, but they're all female. I'm not sure about the sex of the animals, of course, but I'm sure I can find out if necessary." Alison sounded stressed. He wasn't sure whether she was joking about the animals.

"Are you absolutely sure? All those poor souls and we still haven't found Mark Brundell?"

"Quite sure – I've had my full team working and the soil wasn't terribly deep. We're leaving them exactly how we've uncovered them for now. It's best to try to identify them where they are and we've found nothing to help with that yet. We haven't looked for obvious causes of deaths. I didn't want to call you until we had them all exposed, I was expecting to find Mark here, almost as much as you were."

"Any idea how long they've been there?" He flinched when he heard her draw breath.

"There's a lot of dirt to be sifted through, but let me quickly run through what we know with a reasonable amount of certainty. I can tell you that they were all young women. From what I can determine in these conditions, the medial clavicular epiphysis – the collar bone if you prefer, doesn't appear to have fused on any of them. That would put their ages at between fifteen and thirty two, but probably in the late teens to mid-twenties." She paused to cough. "Sorry, it's the dust. We have to take our masks off sometimes. I know it's psychological but I've been feeling like a dried-up, walked-on rug since I first put the overalls on. I'm in serious need a long hot shower."

"Just give it to me straight – in your opinion, do you think we really screwed up all those years ago?"

"Well the good news is that the odontologist I requested has just arrived. He's quite brilliant. He has his own private database of records of missing people, dating back decades. If anyone can identify them quickly, he can. I came outside to call you and to give him room to work. We'll know more when he's finished, but as they all had some degree of dental work, we might be in luck."

"Stop stalling – how long do you think they've been down there?"

"I'm getting to that. They were all originally covered by having a few shovelfuls of earth thrown over them, maybe even a wheelbarrow full, and the damp has rotted away most of the clothing to the point where I don't hold out much hope of it revealing anything important. The most recent of the cadavers did still have a few ligaments remaining, and a few traces of skin, so DNA analysis should be able to back up dental records as I'm fairly sure she's been there for less than five years. The remainder have been there for longer, but probably spread over decades, rather than years, because the oldest bones we've uncovered are discoloured and beginning to flake. Do you know whether the pit was searched when that couple first went missing?"

"Search and rescue dogs were brought in but no cadaver dogs. They were looking for someone newly deceased or even still alive at the time. I've found nothing in the reports about a pit being searched, so I'm guessing it wasn't uncovered."

"I won't be able to give you too accurate a time frame unless we can identify them and get an idea of when they went missing."

"I'm feeling ashamed, and slightly guilty. I really believed that I'd done something worthwhile after rescuing that little girl all those years ago, but if you're saying there were bodies already lying in that shed...."

"You did do something worthwhile, and don't forget you were a rookie back then. And you weren't even on the force when Mr and Mrs Chester first came to the attention of the police. I realise it's looking less likely now, but it is still a possibility that they weren't involved. Someone else may have been using the sheds and the couple may have been unaware of what was happening on their property."

"But we should have looked more closely. This could turn out to be another Cromwell Street, couldn't it? Fred and Rosemary West killed ten people while living in the suburbs of Gorton, Gloucester. How much easier would it have been for this couple to have committed similar crimes hidden away in these woods? But unlike the Wests' they'll never have to face up to their crimes."

"No, think about it, Mike. Ian Chester has been dead for thirty years, and Katy was removed from Woodbine on that day. One or more of the remains may pre-date that event, but I'm sure that most of them don't. I can't imagine someone of Elizabeth Chester's age and stature lugging dead bodies around, can you? If she's guilty, then it would be my assumption that she must have had help. She only died last year, so if I'm right then someone out there knows exactly what's been happening here."

PC Gary Rawlings stood in front of the desk, waiting for the call to end. "I've got a copy of Mrs Chester's death certificate here, sir, and I've spoken to her GP. She died from a massive cerebral haemorrhage in August of last year, just as Mr Markham said. Her doctor told me that until then she'd been a fit and active lady. She'd been to see him just a fortnight earlier and he remembered telling her that she was the fittest seventy-five year old he'd ever come across. She wasn't on any medications at all, and he'd been genuinely surprised by her sudden death."

"Where did she die?"

"She died in Calow Hospital, the day after her admission, and without regaining consciousness."

"But where did she collapse – who found her?"

"She was found in the hallway of Woodbine. A woman called the emergency services at eight-thirty on the morning of the twelfth, a Tuesday, but without leaving a name. That person never came forward and her GP said he had no idea who it might have been. I've asked for a transcript of the call, sir. The hospital doctors thought she'd probably been on the hall floor for at least twenty-four hours before she was admitted."

He felt his stomach tightening. Had Mrs Chester become another victim, and if so, how were they ever going to prove it unless someone confessed? "Check the electoral register, the names on all the household bills, and check back into the Poll Tax Records. Then we'll start another house-to-house enquiry. Check for milk deliveries, grocery deliveries, and so on, and find out who their postman was. Someone may know if Woodbine had a regular visitor."

"The village of Youlgreave would have been where she did her shopping," Gary Rawlings obliged. "I think I remember seeing her there."

"I'd forgotten you originated from there, Rawlings."

"Yes sir, and my sister still lives there with her husband, and their two girls both attend the local school. It has a population of about a thousand, a couple of small village shops, one of which houses the post office, three public houses and a British Legion, and a village school which takes the local children up to the age of eleven. The businesses rely quite heavily on the tourist trade. The quiet roads are popular with the children for bike riding so it could be worth having a gentle word with them as well as everyone else."

"Then what are you still doing here? Start asking around."

He watched his office door close, put his elbows on the desk and covered his eyes with the palms of his hands. As a young, naive police officer, he'd been convinced that Mrs Chester hadn't given them a true account of what had happened at that property. But he'd been selfish, basking in the belief that his actions had saved the life of a child, and lapping up praise from his fellow officers and then from the local press. He'd been too ready to forget his concerns that Mrs Chester hadn't been fully investigated, let alone charged with anything. He remembered how those thoughts had initially made him feel uncomfortable. Now they were a rapidly growing knot in the pit of his stomach. At least seven women had died because of someone at that property, and now he was in charge of an investigation which could prove extremely embarrassing for the local force.

On top of that, they had three recent murders, three burnt-out cars, and no clue as to motive or suspects. The only evidence had come from Derek Austin's car, in the form of DNA and hair strands, but without anyone to compare them to they were only useful for elimination purposes. If only Mark's remains had been uncovered today, at least one case would have been well on the way to being solved.

But as the Senior Investigating Officer, he didn't intend letting those women down now. He picked up his phone and after three rings, Mr Markham answered.

"I need the name of the solicitors who handled the sale of Woodbine for Mrs Chester's estate," he said. "Was it a local firm?"

"Yes, I have it here somewhere."

He listened to papers being shuffled.

"It was Johnson, Johnson and Watson, on the High Street of Buxton. Their Mrs Tyler handled everything as far as I know. Would you like their number?"

"Thank you; did the sale go through smoothly? Were there any problems or any other interested parties that you were aware of?"

"Not that we knew of – we offered a thousand over the asking price and it was accepted the following day. I think we were the only serious purchasers and we had the money in place, ready to go. The whole process took about ten weeks."

Johnson, Johnson and Watson promised to get back to him as soon as they had the information he'd requested.

Next he called Mrs Chester's GP. "We need the name of her next of kin. Who was she closest to after the death of her husband?"

Chapter 21

"I'm telling you all... I've been there." Anna stared at the small television screen Brian had kindly fastened to the living room wall of the flat for them. "I've been to that place. I took the car from the commune and I drove out there a few months ago. Then I took the car back for Verona. There was a sold sign at the bottom of the driveway and the house was empty. I walked around the gardens but they were all overgrown, and then I looked inside some of those sheds and banged on the windows of the house. I even tried the door handles and looked for an open window, but it was all locked up tight."

There was a long silence while the four girls stood listening to the television announcer struggling to make her voice heard above the background clamour of television news crews and newspaper reporters.

Carol shifted uncomfortably from one foot to the other, and then back. "What are you on about... why would you go there? I don't understand. Did you know there were bodies there?"

"Of course not, I was… I was curious."

"Curious about what… tell us." Maisie demanded.

"I needed to take a look at the place, and I was hoping the old lady would still be living there. I wanted to ask her something. I wanted to tell you all, but Verona wouldn't have understood, and you two were still grieving for your lost family. I wanted to find out a few things and to see the place for myself before I said anything. But, as it turned out… there was nothing to tell."

"What are you prattling on about… what did you want to find out?" Carol persisted.

"It's a long story. You might want to sit down."

"We're sitting, get on with it."

"Well, do you remember at the commune, when that local reporter came snooping around, saying he was planning to write an article on the micro-brewery the commune had just set up?"

Maisie smiled. "Sure… we all thought he fancied you. You didn't…"

"No, it's nothing like that you idiot. I didn't tell you then because I didn't want to worry you, but he'd been at the hospital while we were there. He'd been covering Verona's story and when he saw us in the vegetable gardens he recognised us. He kept coming back, wanting an interview, so I offered to sneak out one night to meet him, and tell him our stories, but only as long as he promised to leave Verona alone. You must remember how fragile she was."

"But… that reporter… he was the one murdered!"

"Shut up and listen or I won't tell you anymore."

She watched the twins exchange a glance. She had them in the palm of her hand – all she had to do now was keep them there.

"We're listening," Carol placed her hand on Anna's arm. "Take your time and tell us everything. Whatever it is, we're all in it together, remember?"

"OK, but just remember, what I did, I did for us. I walked up to the main road one night, just before midnight as I'd arranged with him, and he was waiting in his car. He said he was still slightly interested in Verona, but that her story was old news now. He asked how she was and then said that he didn't want to cause her any more stress in case she lost the baby, because then he'd feel responsible. He sounded genuine. He said it was my story that he was really interested in. He called it a 'human interest' story, and claimed he'd be able to sell it to the national newspapers. He even offered me a share of the money if I'd come forward and have my photograph taken with someone."

*

Mrs Chester's GP was the first to return a call. Forbes listened with growing interest. "Since the death of Mr Chester, Mrs Chester's next of kin had been a Miss Catherine Rowland. The Chester couple were childless and I was led to understand that Miss Rowland was a niece, slightly younger than Elizabeth, and residing in Greater Manchester. I have her phone number if you'd like it."

The solicitor's return call came only a few minutes later. While he waited for a secretary to put him through to their Mrs Tyler, he wondered whether the firm might be having a quiet morning.

A softly spoken voice came onto the line. "Mrs Elizabeth Chester left a quite straightforward will, Chief Inspector Forbes. We acted as sole executors. The house and contents were sold and the proceeds added to the not inconsiderable sum Mr Chester had left invested in the stock market. After costs and taxes, the monies were divided equally between three nieces."

Several seconds of silence followed.

"Could you give me their names and details?"

"Certainly; Mrs Tara Chambers, residing in London, and Miss Catherine Rowland, residing in Manchester, are the daughters of Elizabeth's late sister. Mrs Mary Ghent, residing in Aberdeen, is the daughter of Ian Chester's late brother."

"Do you happen to know whether any of them have any children?"

"I'm afraid we don't. We distributed the estate through their solicitors without having the pleasure of meeting any of them."

"So you wouldn't happen to know whether any of them had lived with the Chester family at Woodbine, at any time in the past."

"Sadly no; but they're family so you expect they would have visited from time to time, wouldn't you? And coming from London or Aberdeen, they may well have stayed over, but that's all supposition and you're searching for facts, aren't you, not the ramblings of an old spinster. I'll e-mail their details over to you."

"Thank you that would be helpful." He slowly replaced the phone. Three nieces; Katy Brundell had originally claimed to be a niece of Mrs Chester – another co-incidence perhaps?

*

PC Gary Rawlings had struggled to concentrate on work during the last hour. He'd been raised on the outskirts of Youlgreave, albeit on the opposite side of the village from Woodbine Cottage, but he'd always known the property. He had three sisters and they'd all enjoyed the outdoors. It could so easily have been a member of his family being uncovered in that pit, after years of being a missing person.

Katy Brundell's placement in a high-security psychiatric unit was on police record. It was the first thing that he'd checked after the confirmation of human remains at Woodbine. What wasn't on record, and few people seemed to be aware of until he'd made a phone call, was that Katy had once again gone missing. She'd completed the mandatory part of the sentence that the courts had imposed upon her and had been the subject of a discretionary supervision order. The doctors hadn't considered her to be a risk to the general public and therefore not reported her disappearance.

But now he had to really concentrate. He had ambitions to become a detective, following on a long family tradition, and for the first time was addressing the incident room, with DCI Forbes and DS Ross standing at his side. "Reading between the lines, Katy had been public enemy number one at the time she was first arrested, and when she failed to return from her first day-release, the hospital wanted to avoid any bad publicity." He looked at DS Ross and saw a slight nod. "The hospital staff I spoke to were very reluctant to admit they'd no idea where she might be. I've also been speaking to social services about Katy's daughter. She recovered quite well, but couldn't be legally adopted without her birth mother's consent and so remained in long term foster care until she turned sixteen. Social services were adamant that Katy had never contacted them, and they have no idea where the grown-up daughter might be now. Katy's parents have both passed away. I've been phoning around some of her known relatives but none of them admitted to knowing where either Katy or her daughter might be. But the story gets worse. The child recovered physically, but had some mental problems."

DCI Forbes interrupted. "So Katy Brundell has vanished again, only this time no one has bothered to look for her, and her daughter, also off the radar, has problems. She'll be in her late twenties now. With the internet and other social networking sites, I suppose it's possible that they may have found each other. Did social services tell you the name that Katy's daughter was given?"

"She was fostered by Mr and Mrs Jenkins and she was known as Rose Jenkins, although they did put Brundell on her birth certificate. I was about to start on an internet search for both names."

"Thank you, PC Rawlings. I'll let you get on with that."

"There's more, sir," Rawlings looked at his notebook. "It seems Rose Jenkins was an uncontrollable child. When she'd just turned twelve, she gave birth to a daughter. Mr and Mrs Jenkins helped look after the child, but when Rose left at the age of sixteen, she took the four-year old girl with her. The foster parents had no legal rights over the young child and social services have no idea where either might be now."

"Rose will be twenty-nine, so her daughter must be sixteen. Do you have a name for her?"

"Not yet sir, I'm waiting for someone to phone back."

"Chase them up, and Rawlings, good work."

Forbes shuffled papers on the desk, picked one out, and began to write on the board. "I now have three new names from the solicitor who handled Mrs Chester's estate, and at the moment these are the only known blood relatives of either Mr or Mrs Chester. They were equal beneficiaries in Mrs Chester's will. Check the police computer for their names and then we'll need to speak to each of them to establish whether they've been visiting Woodbine over the years, and whether they, or their partners, have had any children. And establish how long they've been at their present addresses."

"They live at opposite ends of the country," Adam said. "Do you want formal interviews?"

"Until we know differently, they're potential suspects. DS Green can go down to London. He's got family down there I believe, so he's more familiar with the smoke. I'll find Catherine Rowland in Manchester, and Adam, you can pay a flying visit to the Granite City."

*

Alison Ransom's name flashed onto the screen of his mobile. "It's good news so far, Michael, for us at least. The odontologist has identified the first two victims I asked him to look at. We're working in what I think is chronological order, beginning with the most recent cadaver. The first is Jane Evans, aged seventeen when she was reported missing in June, six years ago. The second is Amy Jacks, also seventeen when she went missing in April, eight years ago. You should have available files on them. Both girls came from the Stockport area. I'll let you get to work on them and just hope we have as much luck with the others. I'll call you as soon as I know any more."

A familiar face flooded his computer screen. The Evans family were even now still sticking posters to lamp posts and fences, and anywhere people either walked or drove slowly. It had seemed as if they'd covered half of the Midlands at one point, and their reward for information had steadily risen from one thousand to twenty thousand pounds. Their daughter, Jane, had been a quiet, ordinary schoolgirl in the first year of her 'A' level studies, when she'd vanished on her way to school. Her family were about to receive the worst possible news.

After a slight hesitation, he clicked on the file for Amy Jacks. Hers was another familiar face, last seen walking away from school at four fifteen in the afternoon, but she hadn't been reported missing for two more days. Her home life was very unsettled with her parents in the process of separating and she'd regularly stayed with one of three school friends without letting either of her parents know where she was. It was rumoured she was drifting into prostitution. There were two unconfirmed sightings of her heading in the general direction of London, and one of her walking the streets of Manchester. For a while it was thought she was just another runaway, but when her mobile phone and one of her shoes were found together in a ditch a fortnight later, she was upgraded to a potential murder victim.

Both cases had stalled.

The events of the day were accelerating. Fastening pictures of the two girls back onto the board and briefing those left in the incident room had been difficult. Everyone there remembered both fruitless searches, and he couldn't help dwelling on the fact that there were more to come. Stockport officers would have been notifying the bereaved relatives at about the time that his phone flashed again.

"Tragic as it is, Michael," Alison began, "you can now finally offer closure to seven families. I guess it's lucky for us they were all young British girls, with dental records on the database and all officially listed as missing. Are you ready for the list?"

"Let's hear it. He picked up a pen."

"The third girl was Rachael Carr, aged nineteen when she went missing in Sheffield in February, twelve years ago. The forth was Jennifer Baxter, aged seventeen when she disappeared in Buxton in May, twenty years ago. The fifth was

Harriet Flowers, aged eighteen when she also disappeared in Buxton in October, twenty-eight years ago. The sixth was younger than the others and I remember my parents telling me about the search for her that they'd taken part in. She was Alice Carter, aged fifteen when she went missing in Bakewell in January, thirty-eight years ago. The seventh and oldest remains are Belinda Coates, aged twenty when she vanished from Ashbourne in December, forty-one years ago."

He stared down at the list.

"Did you get all of that, Mike? I'll e-mail them through to you."

"That's all right, I've got them. A part of me was expecting Katy Brundell to turn up again. They're all relatively local, but the killings span a thirty-five year period. Three of those young women were already in that pit when Mr Chester killed himself and we took Katy and her daughter away."

"We're going back more than forty years, Mike, and Mark and Katy may yet turn up elsewhere on the property. It's a huge garden, about an acre apparently, and search teams will be arriving at first light with Ground Penetrating Radar. But I think that's enough for one day, don't you?"

"I think that's an understatement, Miss Ransom. We'll put out a statement for the press as soon as we've notified the families. If any of the press mobs you on your way from Woodbine, you can tell them that."

"I'll try not to drive over any of their toes," she laughed.

"You've had quite a day, and I appreciate your call. Do you want to come round for supper?"

"I thought you'd never ask. What are we having?"

Talking about the normal everyday stuff was still helping her cope. "I'll call Dad and ask him to defrost some lasagne. Will that be all right?"

"You mad impetuous fool," she laughed. "You sure know how to spoil a girl."

"We can walk to the Dog and Duck for a drink afterwards, if you really want me to spoil you."

"I may be too tired."

He heard the teasing note in her voice. "Now who's being impetuous? We'll have tea at about seven. I'll try not to be late."

He looked back at list. Forty-one, thirty-eight and thirty-three years ago; the files for those missing girls might not have been transferred to the computers. Anything prior to nineteen eighty-eight usually involved paper records, although some had been transferred before the money had run out.

He looked up to see a uniformed PC standing before him.

*

Alison switched off her phone and returned to the fetid atmosphere of the shed. The scene was barely recognisable from that of a few hours ago, when the rodents and the invertebrates had had the cosy, but gruesome ecosystem to themselves. The SOCOs looked to be working with less urgency now that all the victims had been identified, but the row of evidence bags was already well over two metres long and still being added to as she stood in silence and watched.

The mounds of dusty bones didn't seem much to offer up to seven families.

*

"Sir, the first of the door-to-door enquiries has produced a positive sighting – actually, two sightings, sir."

Forbes stared at PC Philip Coates. "Well….?"

"You'll find this hard to believe, sir… I know I did," his thin face was trying to disguise his excitement, "but the closest neighbours to Woodbine, Mr and Mrs Nott, were both adamant about who they'd seen. I'll read from my notebook, sir, if that's all right. These are Mr Nott's words. 'About two months after Mrs Chester died, a reporter from the Buxton Advertiser called saying he'd been to Woodbine and seen the For Sale board, but that it wasn't the house itself he was interested in, but a woman who may have been living there. He said he was researching a 'human interest' story for his newspaper, and asked whether we knew where she'd gone. He showed us a very old photograph of Katy Brundell, but we told him we only knew her face from the newspapers when she first went missing, and from when they took her and her child away. We hadn't seen any signs of her since, and we'd no idea where he might be able to find her. We told him how Mrs Chester had always kept to herself and that we couldn't help him. Exactly one week after that, we saw that same reporter's face on the local news when he'd been murdered, but we didn't come forward because we couldn't see how his visit could have had anything to do with his death. Then the Sold sign went up on Woodbine and we began looking for the new owners. One afternoon, we were driving past and saw a silver car on the driveway, and thinking it was the new owners, we went to introduce ourselves, but the house was locked up and we couldn't see anyone. This alarmed us, being such a secluded spot, so we drove onto the road and parked up. We were about to call the estate agents when the silver car came tearing down the drive and almost went into the ditch. It turned away from us but we both thought it was a young blonde woman who was driving. I memorised part of the number plate and wrote it down. When the new owners arrived, a few days later, we mentioned the incident, but they didn't know who it might have been.'"

PC Coates looked up from his notebook. "I came straight back with this report, sir. I thought you'd want to know immediately." He had the expression of someone who'd saved the best piece of news till last. "Sir, the partial plate matches the one on the burnt out car that you called in last weekend. And with the description they gave me of the driver, I think it could be the girl we're looking for. But I can't figure out what she might have been doing at Woodbine."

Chapter 22

When he entered the living room, Louise and Alison were both leaning over a table completely covered by textbooks and random sheets of printed paper. He was undecided whether they were deliberately ignoring him or so engrossed in their subject that they couldn't raise their heads to acknowledge him. He stood watching them. It was a long time since he'd last looked at his sister with anything resembling pride, and perhaps it was the result of an over-emotional day, but he realised he was now regarding the two women with their backs to him, with equal amounts of affection.

"Are you ready to eat?" his father's voice jolted him. "I've been keeping it warm so we can all eat together."

"Dish it out, please Dad. I'm sorry I'm a bit late; it's been a hectic day. I'll get a quick wash while the girls clear the table." He left the room without risking looking back at them.

*

Finding a quiet corner in the Dog and Duck on a weeknight was never a problem, unless the darts team was at home. "Tomorrow is darts night, if you're interested," the landlord informed them, hopefully.

"Thank you, we'll just take a seat in the corner and enjoy your log fire." Too many conflicting scenarios still whirled around his brain. The food had relaxed him but he needed a couple of pints of real ale to slow his brain cells down a little. He needed to isolate his thoughts and study them in some kind of chronological order. Half way down his first pint he began with the incident freshest in his mind, and he watched Alison's face open up with surprise.

"So… you're trying to convince me now that the dusty bones I've worked on for most of the day might be connected to your knife attacks of the last few months. The last I knew you were looking for one or two young women in connection with those."

"I don't know how, not yet, but I just know that they are. It's a complex puzzle, but those two separate sightings at Woodbine couldn't both be coincidences."

"The couple who gave this information, are you sure that they aren't mistaken, or attention seeking?"

"They were both adamant. They live about five hundred metres along the road from Woodbine, but with the trees stretch between them they've never been able to see the place from their property. They were neighbours of a similar age to Mr and Mrs Chester, and they'd lived there over forty years, yet they'd only seen the couple on a handful of occasions. Don't you think that's odd?"

"Not really, some people prefer the life of a recluse."

"And some hide away for a very good reason. When they realised what they may have witnessed, they were shaken. We've advised them, to avoid the press coming to their door, to pack a bag and move in with relatives in the village for a few days."

"If that was me, I think I'd be inclined to do something similar. It's a gruesome thought – young women being murdered and dumped, right next door."

"If we assume that the three recent murders, and the two Brundell incidents of twenty-nine and twenty-five years ago, and now the bodies at Woodbine are all linked, then I think we have to look again at what happened when Mark and Katy first disappeared. I've contacted Police Scotland, Glasgow Division, and they've confirmed that Mark remains a missing person and has been declared legally dead. That leaves us with his wife, Katy. Was she really afraid of an abusive husband and a vengeful gangland family? The officer I spoke to in Glasgow told me that as far as they were aware, none of Mark's family had committed anything more serious than a few minor traffic offences."

"It's a long time since the neighbours last saw the official pictures of Katy; it must have been when she was taken into custody. Have you shown them the old photographs that you have on file to be certain that it was Katy who Derek Austen was looking for?"

"We have, and they are, but we still don't know where she is, or even if she's still alive."

"Austen believed she was alive. If he was right, she must be into her fifties by now."

"But the oldest two cadavers at Woodbine predated Mark and Katy's disappearance, so let's assume that Mr and Mrs Chester were predatory killers. The young couple stumbled into their lair during the storm – they all agreed on that. Then they killed Mark – maybe because he realised what they were. Most couples who kill have a sexual as well as a sadistic love of what they do, and the bodies in the pit were all female, so for obvious reasons, they kept Katy alive. They may have kept the others alive for a time; we'll probably never know that for sure."

"I won't be able to narrow down the dates of the women's deaths. So... what was different about Katy that they didn't kill her?"

"For a start, she was pregnant. Did her account of how the swell of her body turned them on, actually have a ring of truth to it? During her pregnancy did they manage to brainwash her? Or did Katy already have the killer instinct in her and the three of them began to work together? Harriet Flowers disappeared twenty-eight years ago when Katy's baby would have been about six months old. Was she involved in that? Was she perhaps proving herself to them?" He reached for his glass.

"Wow... and I thought I had dark thoughts. Did you consider the idea that Katy may not have known about the killing?"

"Not for more than a few seconds. Not after I remembered the look in her eyes when she sat in that interview room all those years ago. The GP told us that Mrs Chester was fit for her age, but I find it hard to believe that she kept on killing and then dumping the bodies of her victims, years after the death of her husband."

"So you're thinking that when Katy walked out of the psychiatric hospital, that she actually went back to Woodbine."

"I think it has to be a possibility, and if so, it might be what Derek Austen discovered. In which case, I think it may then have somehow led to his murder."

"Then there's your link. But it's a girl people have been reporting in the car, and a girl on your CCTV footage, and even the child that you rescued must be almost thirty by now."

"OK... so let's assume that Mr and Mrs Chester groomed Katy, and that she actually enjoyed what she did. Is it too much of a leap to think that with Mrs Chester gone, Katy might have wanted to groom her own protégé to work with her?"

"How would she possibly find someone – put an ad in the local paper? No, I think that's one step beyond, Mike, even for you. But have you considered a prostitution ring? Katy would have needed money from somewhere just to live, and there isn't usually a shortage of willing young women. Was there ever any suggestion that they were involved in prostitution at Woodbine? Do you think that could be a motive of some kind? I'm grasping at straws now."

"No, I think we'd have heard by now if Woodbine was being used as an out of town brothel. Everything so far points to the three of them wanting to remain isolated from the outside world. But once out of Woodbine... who knows."

As usual she was reading his thoughts. "I think you need to find Rose Jenkins. If we're right in thinking that her mother is the link between the crime scenes, then Rose could be in danger."

"I'd not forgotten about her." He hadn't forgotten about Rose's daughter either, who was about sixteen now.

"And you'd really like to meet her again, wouldn't you?" She reached for his hand.

*

DC Harry Green left for London at 3 a.m. to beat the worst of the traffic, and to allow himself a full day to locate and interview Mrs Tara Chambers and her husband. Neither of them had any kind of police record and they were on the electoral register at the address the solicitors had provided. Asking for a DNA sample shouldn't cause a problem if they'd nothing to do with the homicides, but he couldn't force them to provide one.

"It's purely for comparison, to rule them out." DS Ross had told him to say.

The row of terraces he'd been sent to find were all smartly painted, and with either net curtains or blinds to provide privacy from a pavement which ran directly across their front doorsteps. He found the right number, waited for an elderly couple to walk past, and then rapped on the door. After a few moments, footsteps directly behind him made him turn, and suddenly he was face-to-face with a middle-aged woman carrying a folded newspaper.

"We don't need anything... whatever it is, we don't want it," she said, brushing past him and unlocking the door, all in one fluid movement. Instinctively, Harry placed his polished left boot into the doorway while he reached for his ID. She stared at his card for a second and then studied his face. "My husband's a security guard on the London Underground. He works nights and he'll only just have got off to sleep. Can't this wait?"

He hoped he'd hidden his surprise. Most people, when faced with a policeman on their doorstep first thing in the morning, want to know the reason for the visit. Harry was certain that no one had ever demanded that he return at a more convenient time without first asking what the visit was about.

"Mrs Chambers, I'm sorry to disturb you both, but I only need to ask you a few questions. Did you watch the late evening news yesterday?"

"The news... no I didn't. If it's important, then I suppose you'd better come in. Come through to the living room. My husband never has the news on – he says it's too depressing. We have a newspaper most days, but as you can see I haven't opened it yet."

"Then perhaps you'd better sit down."

He watched the colour drain from her face. If she was faking shock, then she was very good. "Could you tell me, to the best of your memory, how often and when, you or your husband visited Woodbine over the last forty years?"

"Forty years... I can only hazard a guess. My husband, Simon, he works nights, I told you that, and I work part time in the grocery store on the corner. Mostly we've been too busy. I wish now that we'd gone more often. Maybe we could have stopped whoever it was from using Elizabeth's barn like that. We used to go up and see her every Christmas and then perhaps two or three weekends throughout the summer. She was a lovely old lady." She hesitated. "You can't be suggesting that aunty and uncle were involved in anything so dreadful, surely."

"I'll need a word with your husband while I'm here."

"I'll see if he's awake. If he's heard you, he'll want to know what it's all about and he won't be able to get back to sleep until I've explained."

Harry listened to her footsteps on the stairs. There were no family photos in the room, but that meant nothing, his mother never displayed family pictures, either.

Mr Chambers was wide awake but had the unmistakable appearance of a man who'd just been roused from his bed. His blue pyjamas were only partially covered by a grey towelling bathrobe and his feet had been hastily shoved into a shapeless pair of navy moccasins. He was struggling to keep them on his feet as he entered the room. Of the few strands of his remaining hair, at least half of them sat at right angles to his peeling scalp.

"Aunt Lizzie's place was sold weeks ago. Seven bodies did you say – all young women? But what's all that got to do with us?" The muscular frame folded into the centre of the two-seater sofa, almost filling it. Without being invited, Harry sat on the armchair opposite and leaned forward. It was time for some tactful questioning.

*

DS Adam Ross landed at Dyce airport, just outside Aberdeen, and was met by an extremely attractive redheaded taxi driver by the name of Sharon. He was no great expert on women's perfumes, but she smelled seductively expensive in the unexpected heat.

"*It's always cold and wet up there,*" everyone had warned him. "*Take a thick coat. No, take your thermals.*"

And if they were right then he must have arrived on Aberdeen's one day of early summer sunshine. He felt conspicuous carrying his bulky overcoat when all around vast expanses of white flesh were on show. His small overnight bag landed on the back seat of the taxi and his heavy coat landed unceremoniously on top of it.

A refreshing pint of real ale in the golf club bar beckoned.

Mrs Mary Ghent had married a Scotsman she'd met while on holiday with friends in Aberdeen. After her husband's death, six years earlier, she'd decided to remain as manager of the bar they'd run together for most of their married life. It was a vital cog of the prestigious golf club, and she looked every inch the middle-aged pub landlady. Adam ordered a pint of their finest cask ale and settled down to observe her. She conversed easily with the separate groups of customers, while still quite obviously the lady in charge of the room. Adam knew that the first twenty years of her life had been spent in Derbyshire, but there was absolutely no trace of a Midlands accent. Unless they were told, no one would have suspected that Mrs Mary Ghent was not a born and bred Aberdonian, albeit with a slightly upper-class accent.

She flashed her welcoming smile at him as she headed towards his table. Nothing about her expression changed when he showed her the ID that he'd been holding under the table in his left hand. "Could I have a word with you in private, Mrs Ghent?"

"I've seen the news," she replied softly. "I've been expecting someone to contact me. Come on through to the living quarters."

Several customers were watching as he eased himself off the leather couch and he quickly stuffed the ID wallet back into his jacket pocket.

"Would you care to bring your drink with you? It will get cleared away if you leave it there for more than a few minutes, and it's far too good to waste."

This is a lady that his DCI would approve of, he thought. He picked up his glass and returned her warm smile. "There are just a few questions that we need to ask you, Mrs Ghent."

"Call me Mary, please. Only the accountant calls me Mrs Ghent."

The room was small but expensively furnished. He sat on a two-seater, cream leather couch which matched those in the bar. "Mary, I need you to tell me when, and how regularly, you and your husband visited Woodbine Cottage, and whether you were aware of anyone else ever visiting or staying there. We're taking the investigation back a full forty years so take your time remembering."

"It's not difficult. Before Elizabeth's death I'd only set foot in the place twice. I went down for the old girl's funeral a few months ago and as far as I was aware the place was empty. I never heard of anyone else living there with her after that dreadful Katy woman was taken away, and I wasn't in regular contact with any of her family. I was alone for Aunt Elizabeth's funeral of course – I'd lost my Cyril by then. I was fifteen years his junior, but his death still came as a terrible shock. We'd just begun making plans for our retirement, and yet here I am."

"Do you have other relatives down in England?"

"I have no blood relatives at all now. My parents never approved of Cyril, they had a thing about the Scots, and they both thought he was too old for me. They practically disowned me when we became engaged. We both went to their funerals twenty years ago, and we saw Aunt Elizabeth on both occasions. And five years before that, we both went to Woodbine for Uncle Ian's funeral, of course. It does sound a depressing story, doesn't it? I honestly never expected to be in Elizabeth's will. Her two nieces from her elder sister were always closer to her than we were and it's not as if we kept in touch regularly. As for the bodies; I really had no idea. I had a real shock when I saw it on the news."

"How familiar were you with her nieces, Tara and Catherine?"

"It's the same sad story. I only remember meeting them at family funerals. I'm afraid I'm not a family orientated type of person. The regulars here have become my family, especially since I lost Cyril."

"This visit is just a routine, but as you seem to be the only living relative of Mr Chester, we'd like a statement from you and also a DNA sample. The results of the sample will be destroyed when the investigation is closed."

"I'd be grateful if you can do all that now, while we're quiet. At Elizabeth's funeral, people were saying some very odd things about her stroke and about the way the ambulance was called. And I can guess at why you want a DNA sample from me – I always thought that hiding that poor baby away like that was highly suspicious, and Cyril and I wondered if she may have been Uncle Ian's child. If you come across her during this investigation, would you do a favour for me and let me know? She could be my cousin and I don't have any blood relatives left. A part of me hopes that Cyril and I were right."

*

Katy's blood group was on record, but her disappearance predated routine DNA testing. Forbes had checked. Only Elizabeth Chester's DNA was on file, and that was merely because someone in the mortuary had felt suspicious enough about the way she'd died to request a sample. He studied the twenty-five year old picture of Katy, the distinctive blue eyes and the sharp bone structure. He needed to see the niece who'd remained in the Midlands.

"Katy Brundell was a striking-looking young woman," he handed the picture to PC Coates. "And I think we should assume that Derek Austen was on her trail."

"Do you think she could still be alive, sir?"

"Until we find a body, I think it's safe to presume that she is. Her features are quite distinctive. If she's now living as Catherine Rowland, I'm sure I'll recognise her."

"But why would she?"

"Oh come on PC Coates... one of the two oldest incentives in the world – money. Mr and Mrs Chester had been living off the income from inherited monies and when Woodbine was sold and Elizabeth's estate wrapped up, three women were looking at a very nice share of over one million pounds. If Katy is the killer, she may have taken the real Catherine's life. Or it may be that a third niece never existed and Katy and the Chester couple invented her."

"But the other two nieces wouldn't want to share that inheritance with a bogus relative... not unless they were in on everything."

"Families get split up, siblings get separated, and at the moment I'm not ruling anything out. My father has an old friend who he calls Uncle Pete, and to this day I'm not sure whether he's a blood relative or not. I don't even think my dad's that sure any more. Start a new action. Put someone onto a search for the birth certificates of all three nieces. Even in the fifties and the so-called enlightened sixties, children born out of wedlock were occasionally brought up by a different family member."

"We've only got their words for it that Mark and Katy Brundell and Mr and Mrs Chester never met before the night of the storm, sir."

"You're quite right, PC Coates. Did we have the wool well-and-truly pulled over our eyes all those years ago?"

*

Louise slung her bag and her jacket over her shoulder and reached for the front door before her father could change his mind about looking after Gemma for a few hours. "A quick look around the shops and a coffee with my new friends – I won't be long Dad, I promise." She hadn't been able to get the new girl at the club, the dark-haired foreign girl who went by the name of Verona, out of her mind. She was hoping there might be more opportunities to talk to her alone while they were in town. She just needed to separate the girl from Anna and the twins for a few minutes.

The thoughts that had rattled around her head for most of the night would never have formed if she hadn't seen that single tear on Verona's cheek. And now she felt bad. She'd been boasting about the one thing in her life that the other girls didn't have – a beautiful child, but then turned and seen Verona's face.

The seed had been planted, and it wouldn't wither. During the early hours her memory had reeled off the February news reports and TV appeals, over and over again.

Did the others know? They must do. It hadn't made the media headlines the previous October, but three other girls had disappeared from the same hospital ward at exactly the same time, and two of them were identical twins. Alison had told her about them when they'd been discussing the advances in DNA profiling. The girls had been almost sixteen at the time and not actually ill, so their disappearances had only warranted a few lines in the local newspapers. And as far as she was aware, no one had tried very hard to find them. They were runaways – just three out of the hundreds who disappeared of their own free will every year.

One abused and pregnant girl from Moldova had made the national headlines for a couple of days. But she'd never been found. And from what she could remember from the media reports, and allowing for the fact that that the girl's face could have filled out over the last few months, it could be her. Was that why Anna and the others were so protective of her? It must be. But she needed to be certain before she said anything to her DCI brother.

Chapter 23

Gorton looked no different from any of the other suburbs of Manchester, and there was no reason why it should, Forbes thought, not knowing what he was really expecting to find that might single it out, apart from its one major landmark, the Gorton Monastery; the magnificent Franciscan, nineteenth century, high Victorian Gothic monastery which dominated the skyline as he drove past it. The take-away restaurants were thriving, judging by the familiar printing on the pavement litter, while most of the traditional corner shops were either boarded up with For Sale signs attached to them or already converted into flats. Most of the properties were depressing tones of grey and red brick.

Two teenagers rode alongside him, trying to peer into his car. They looked about fourteen and presumably should have been in school. The tallest of them pedalled hard and swerved his bike from side to side down the centre of the road.

He wasn't interested in rising to the boy's challenge. He gave him a friendly wave and drove on.

The door opened. "Miss Rowland… Miss Catherine Rowland?" She wasn't at all what he'd braced himself for – a good six inches shorter than he remembered Katy to have been, and with a round face and figure to match, the only thing that he recognised in Catherine was a strong resemblance to Mrs Elizabeth Chester.

"I've been expecting someone to call round with some questions. Ever since I saw the dreadful news I haven't been able to think of anything else," she beamed at him as if she'd been looking forward to some involvement. "Come on through to the kitchen. Please will you have a coffee with me?"

"Thank you, I'll have one if you're making one for yourself. The electoral register produced two names for this address. Do you share the house?"

"I have a partner, Susan Roberts," she was still smiling at him. "At first I thought it must be a different Woodbine Cottage. I couldn't believe it when I recognised Auntie's home on the television news. I'll do anything I can to help clear Lizzy's name. She was a lovely old lady. What is it you want to know?"

"Anything you can tell us at this stage, as far back as you can remember. You don't live too far away, so did you visit Woodbine often?"

"Aunt Lizzy always scared me when I was a small child, and when she met Uncle Ian I remember I wasn't too impressed with him, but maybe it was just the scale and the isolation of the property which spooked me at the time. I absolutely hated going there. Auntie was sixteen years older than me, but I remember how the age gap seemed far greater at the time. I suppose it does when you're young. I remember their wedding day, I must have been about eleven or twelve, and it was the first time I'd been a bridesmaid. I was so excited. But my clearest memories of that day are of the poor photographer trying to persuade me to smile when all I could focus on was Uncle Ian's hand on my backside."

"Did you never voice your concerns to anyone?"

"I was too afraid of the pair of them to speak out... it was as simple as that."

"Has Susan, or have any of your previous partners, ever been there?"

"There's only ever been Susan. No, the formidable Elizabeth would never have approved, and I know I'd never have been able to stand up to her scrutiny if we'd gone there as friends. I'm certain I'd have been cut out of her will the very next day."

"We're just gathering background information at this stage. I'll need to speak to Susan, and do either of you have any children."

"No, there's only Tara down in London who's keeping the blood line from dying out. She has a son and a daughter."

"Going right back to your teenage years, can you tell me how often you've visited Woodbine?"

"Very infrequently for many years – it was my parents who dragged me there on their monthly visits until I was about eighteen or nineteen and I left home." She shook her head. "I knew nothing about that poor baby girl because I didn't go there at all in those days. And as for that young man's disappearance, well I still don't know what to think. On the afternoon of Ian's funeral I found some courage from somewhere and I accompanied the other mourners back to Woodbine after the service. But that was most definitely a day to forget. Auntie did her best, I suppose, and she did put out a few plates of dried-up cheese sandwiches and some jam rolls, but the whole thing was a pretty miserable affair. Talk about the elephant in the room! What with the recent business of that poor baby and the supposedly missing girl turning up there and getting arrested, not to mention that missing husband of hers never having being found, no one knew what to say! Is that coffee all right for you?"

"It's just perfect... Woodbine... you were saying?"

"Yes, it was a very sombre day. I know funerals often are, what with people facing their own mortality and all that, at least until the alcohol starts flowing, but there was no alcohol to take the edge off the proceedings that day. Anyway, what with the police presence, and Ian's illness and suicide, much to my surprise, let me add, I found myself beginning to feel sorry for the old dragon. That's when I began vising once a month, just as my parents had done when they were alive. It felt like the right thing to do."

"Did you ever get the impression that anyone else was visiting her on a regular basis, or living there with her?"

"No, never, and she never spoke of anyone else, only of her late husband, it was as if she couldn't move on. Mind you, if she'd wanted to keep someone hidden from me it wouldn't have been difficult. She knew when to expect me because I always phoned before setting off. I still can't quite believe what you've found there."

"Did you ever go into any of the sheds or garages?"

"Crikey, no, some of them looked decidedly unsafe, and I told Aunt Lizzy so in no uncertain terms, but I never saw her going into any of them. Anyway, I've got a thing about spiders – arachnowotsit," she shuddered, "especially those huge cardinal spiders. I always do... I always did some cleaning for her and one or more of those monsters were always lurking in the back porch underneath a box or a plant pot. I thought the sheds must be full of them."

"Actually I have some camping in my greenhouse." He watched her face wrinkle. "They're one of the most harmless spiders you can find, but they are very large, and very fast. I have a plastic tub especially for the job of catching them and I release them a few hundred yards down the road, but I wouldn't be at all surprised if a few of them didn't find their own way back."

He watched her shudder again. "Susan should be finishing work about now, so you won't have much longer to wait. Would you like another drink?"

"No thanks, I would like to wait for her though." He was there to check them out, both of them, and there was still a slim chance that it might be Katy who was about to walk through the front door. Besides, he didn't want to give the women the opportunity to talk. He leaned back into the wooden kitchen chair. "Have a think would you, Miss Rowland. Is there anything at all that's ever struck you as out of the ordinary at Woodbine, any small detail, anything at all?"

"Well there was one puzzle. I don't suppose it relates to your enquiry at all, and I wasn't going to mention it, but a painting went missing."

"How do you mean... missing... when?"

"Elizabeth left her money equally between the three of us, as nieces, but because I was the only one who'd ever bothered to visit regularly, she told me to help myself to a painting from her bedroom, but only after her death. She said it was quite valuable and that her other nieces knew nothing about it, but so that no one could ever contest my ownership she gave me a letter together with a signed photograph of the picture saying that it was her special thank you gift to me. Would you like to see it?"

"Please… "

"She was very fond of the picture. I think she'd known the artist."

It wasn't a photograph of a large, heavily framed oil painting as he'd expected. Instead she handed him one of a plainly framed work that appeared to be about the size of his sister's new tablet. It made him sit up straight.

"I know what you're thinking, but unless it was hidden under the frame, it didn't appear to be signed. She always said that to have it valued would ruin it for her. She'd been good friends with the artist before he was well-known and she just wanted those strange looking matchstick men to be the last thing she looked at every night. Beyond that, she wouldn't discuss it at all."

"When did you last see the picture?"

"I know it was there on my last visit, three weeks before she died, because I always changed her bed sheets and I would have noticed if it had been moved."

"And when did you realise that it was missing?"

"Her doctor's receptionist phoned me to say that she'd been found in a critical condition and rushed to Callow Hospital, and that things didn't look good. I know this may sound callous, but it only meant a very short detour on my route to the hospital, so I went to Woodbine first. I went to make sure that the house was secured and that nothing electrical had been left on and I went into her bedroom. The picture wasn't on the wall. I did a very quick search of her room but I wanted to be with Elizabeth in case she woke up, so I locked up and drove to the hospital. Aunt Lizzy never regained consciousness, and although I never expected to, I do actually miss the old girl. After her death I had a good search for the picture, but it had gone."

"You didn't call the police?"

"I didn't know exactly when it had disappeared, and I didn't think the police would take me seriously. I had my share of the estate and that was very welcome, and I couldn't be certain that it was a genuine Lowry. It might have only been worth a few pounds. But I'm not totally naïve. I've been regularly checking the internet and the on-line auction rooms up and down the country. An unknown Lowry should produce a few ripples in the art world, wouldn't you think? I won't give up. It may yet turn up."

"With this paperwork, it isn't too late to report it and to get an incident number from your local police. Would you mind if I took the photo and the letter away with me? I'll make copies and some enquiries and I'll deliver it straight back to you. If the picture does surface, an incident number will help immensely with your claim of ownership."

"That's exactly what that poor reporter from the Buxton Advertiser, Derek Austen, told me when I showed him that photograph. He even took a photo of my photo and said he'd make enquiries for me. I've seen you on the TV appealing for information, haven't I? Are you any closer to finding his killer, or aren't you allowed to divulge that kind of information."

His coffee mug clattered over. "Sorry...?"

"It's all right, it was empty."

"No... no, I meant pardon, would you explain what you just said?"

"That reporter, Derek Austen, the one killed near the reservoirs, I'd been telling him about the missing picture just a few days before his murder. He came here asking about Katy Brundell. Apparently he was researching an article about the lack of support in the community for the mentally ill once they'd been released back into society. He was a good man, it's such a shame."

Before he could phrase his next question, he heard the front door.

"Here's Susan now. We're in the kitchen, love."

He could see why Aunt Lizzy might have asked questions.

Susan definitely wasn't Katy. For a moment he wondered if his coffee might have been spiked. Derek Austen had landed into the conversation as if it was a normal everyday occurrence, and now Susan, with a huge toothy smile and the most predominant Adam's apple he'd ever seen on a woman, was offering out her, or his, muscular arm and long, slim, manicured fingers in the obvious expectation of a handshake.

*

Finally he had a trail to follow. He felt a physical spring in his step as he marched into the incident room and he actually smiled at PC Philip Coates, who'd just looked up as if he'd been awaiting his return.

"Has anyone found any links between the Woodbine seven and the Chester household? No... nothing... anyone? Right then, gather round. I want you all to take a good look at this photograph and tell me what springs to mind." He held it out at arm's length for everyone to see and then placed it in the centre of the whiteboard.

"Is that a picture of a forged Lowry? I have a cousin who specialises in art forgery detection – digital image forensics he calls it." Newly promoted DC Robert Bell, who had been first on the scene at two of the murders, spoke up. He'd worked in most of the Midlands forces during his career. If any courses were on offer, then there was a good chance that he'd either done them or had applied to do them, or had a relative who'd successfully completed them. Most of his family had worked in law enforcement of some sort, giving him his impressive number of useful contacts. If any police information needed to be extracted from outside of the Derbyshire Constabulary Forces, then DC Robert Bell usually knew the right person to contact in order to obtain it in the shortest possible time.

"I think there's a good chance that it's genuine," Forbes replied. "But it's also been stolen." He ran through what he'd learned in Manchester. "We need to make contact with Lowry experts and auction houses, starting in the UK and if necessary spreading out to America and Europe. Something like this is only worth stealing if you're a collector or if you intend to sell it."

"My cousin will have a list of names and numbers."

"Thank you, Robert, I thought he might."

*

"Louise, we're well impressed," sugar from the jam doughnut trickled off Maisie's lips. "You're going to be studying forensic science, and dead people and stuff. That's so cool!"

"I've got to get five decent 'O' levels first. That's what I'm saving up for – that and a little car. Driving lessons don't come cheap and I don't want to borrow more from my family than I have to."

"But you must be interested in all that stuff already," Anna leaned onto the table and looked into her eyes. "Tell me something, Louise tell me honestly, do you believe that people are ever born to be bad?"

"No, I don't. I think we're born to be different, and we all have to deal with some shitty stuff sometimes. Life affects people differently, and some have more ability to cope with bad stuff than others do, that's all. But it's the science behind finding the clues that help to catch the criminals that fascinates me."

"Sure," Anna persisted, "but that involves DNA and stuff, doesn't it. So do you think there is such a thing as a bad gene?"

Louise shrugged and looked at the others. Verona looked puzzled. "I suppose it's possible. We're all programed differently, aren't we? If you're thinking of the *nature versus nurture* debate, there is no real answer, and probably never will be."

Anna wasn't being put off. "For instance – let's say you had a close family member and you knew they'd done something really, really bad – something really evil and you were given a choice. What would you do, Louise? Would you maybe shop them to the police and let them take what was coming to them? Or would you try to get them some help from somewhere, maybe from the doctors or from the church? Or would you perhaps say, to hell with it, let's have some fun together. Would you join in with something that you knew was really bad?"

"That's a stupid question. It would depend on what it was, but I suppose I'd try and get help for them, and I think most people would do the same for a family member. Drink your coffee."

To her relief, three young mothers with pushchairs and toddlers jostled the seats behind Anna, forcing Anna and Carol to adjust the positions of their chairs.

Louise stared into her coffee and calculated. Verona's family may as well be on another planet for all the chance she had of ever seeing them again. The twins had absolutely no family left – that's if they'd been telling the truth. So Anna was talking about herself – she had to be. And judging by the uncomfortable expressions on the faces of Maisie and Carol when Anna had begun quizzing her, they knew what she was talking about. She felt a sudden chill. Had they seen her pocket the strands of hair that she'd brushed from Verona's back when they'd entered the café? Did they think she was conspiring against them?

They settled back into their chairs but were watching her. She decided to try to call their bluff. "Every one of us at this table has had terrible things happen to them, but we're dealing with them. What I mean is… even if there is such a thing, there's nobody here who's really evil. We're friends now, aren't we, and whatever problems we have we should be able to help each other through them."

"Listen to you," Carol tugged nervously at her fringe, "you've got a family to pick you up if things go spectacularly wrong for you."

"But isn't that what we're all doing here today, we're all picking ourselves up? Sometimes life gets tough and that's when having good friends can help." She looked down into her coffee mug. "All I'm saying is that no one here is actually evil."

Anna leaned towards her again. "But Louise… sweet Louise… how can you be so sure that no one here is truly evil when you've only known us for a couple of weeks?"

"This is a rubbish conversation," Maisie chimed in. "We're going back to the flat for our tea. Anna's gran is visiting and she's a very good cook. She's offered to cook for us every day this week."

"Really... " Louise was unsure what to say.

"Oh dear," Anna was holding her position, leaning onto the table. "We've got our lovely Louise all freaked out. We're messing with your head, college girl. You know you really should learn how to take a joke. Come back with us for some tea. It'll be a squeeze, but it'll be fun." She leaned back into her chair and laughed.

"I left Gemma with Dad and told him I wouldn't be long. I don't want to push my luck. Maybe I could come to the flat tomorrow, if the offer's still open. I'd like to meet your gran, really I would."

"Dinner tomorrow then, that's settled. I'll tell gran to cook for one more."

*

It was another one of those days when however hard he tried not to, he kept visualising a hollow face behind a barred window. He knew why it was. After years of deliberately pushing her to the back of his mind, he felt he was within touching distance of discovering how her life had unfolded. He hoped the knock on his office door would bring a distraction.

"I'm sorry, sir, I know this isn't the news you wanted," PC Gary Rawlings looked as if he'd been volunteered. "Rose Jenkins, as she was known from the time she was placed into a foster home, committed suicide three months ago. Apparently her drinking had spiralled out of control and she'd actually been in hospital on the dates of both Austen's and Deakin's murders. I spoke to the council – they'd organised the cremation. Two of their staff attended, but despite putting a death notice in the papers, there were no other mourners. And I do have some more slightly disturbing news, sir."

"Let's hear it."

"We know from social services that she'd had a daughter when she was barely thirteen, so I contacted her GP. Apparently there'd been problems with the pregnancy which had possibly caused long term damage to the baby. The child has been in and out of hospitals and psychiatric units for most of her young life, receiving treatments for various emotional and mental disorders. According to their last GP, none of the treatments seemed to work long term and he considers the teenager to be 'unstable at best, and very likely to deteriorate'. She should be on daily medication. Her mother, Rose, kicked her out of the family home after a particularly violent episode, and the girl hasn't been seen since she walked out of a hospital ward last October, a few months before her sixteenth birthday."

"Does this girl have a name?"

"Yes, sorry sir, she's called Anna Jenkins."

"So Katy Brundell's daughter is dead, but her granddaughter is out on the streets somewhere, possibly in an unstable state of mind. I don't suppose you've got any pictures of Anna Jenkins."

"Not yet, sir, but I'll get onto that next. There must be some school photos somewhere."

"Make it your priority.

Chapter 24

DS Adam Ross and DC Harry Green both arrived home with more baggage than useful information, Adam's holdall weighted down by the two bottles of rare malt whisky that Mary Ghent had offered him in exchange for any news on her possible one remaining blood relative, and Harry's crammed with woollen socks and jumpers that his mother had been convinced he'd need to survive the harsh Peak District winters that she'd seen on the television. Before the morning's briefing, Forbes gratefully stuffed a carefully wrapped bottle alongside the pair of thick woollen socks in the bottom drawer of his desk.

Without any real evidence, they had a new name at the top of the board in the incident room, and his educated guess would be that Derek Austen had been unlucky enough to find not only the mother and daughter that he'd been searching for, but the granddaughter as well.

Before the morning's briefing could begin, DC Robert Bell walked into the incident room looking even more smug than usual. "Sir, my cousin e-mailed back late last night. He can't find anyone who recognises the Lowry picture but he says that previously unknown originals do still come onto the market occasionally. One turned up only a few years ago, apparently. The owner had it stashed away in a suitcase on top of his wardrobe because of its value. That one was fourteen inches by ten inches and was valued at between three-hundred and five-hundred thousand pounds. He can't tell from our photo of course, but if it is an original then it's probably worth upwards of a quarter of a million pounds, and if not an original then it could be worth anything from three pounds in a charity shop, to thirty-thousand pounds if a known artist from the Lowry School of Art painted it. First thing this morning we both began e-mailing the picture to the trade and I got lucky. It was local, sir, and I've got it locked in the boot of my car. I hadn't got an evidence bag with me."

Here were some actual crumbs on the trail. "Share your news with the rest of the team, DC Bell."

"Fine Arts Emporium, on Leaburn High Street, was offered the picture about eight months ago and the owner bought it for his collection for three-thousand pounds in cash. He hoped one day he might be able to prove it was a genuine Lowry and he put it away until he'd time to research it. A few weeks later, Derek Austen walked into his shop and showed him a picture that he had on his phone. The art dealer recognised it as the artwork that he'd recently purchased. It was the same picture as ours. Austen was looking for the vendor of the picture, and as the dealer had known the Buxton Advertiser reporter for many years, he obliged, and gave him this address."

Forbes read the entry in his DC's notebook. "Well you'd better read it out. I'm sure everyone else in this room is dying to know what's in there."

"Kat Blood, Church Street, Bakewell... K B, sir, Katy Brundell, it has to be. She knew the picture was valuable but she realised she couldn't offer it for sale on the open market, not without a lot of people asking questions about its origin, so she had to take what she could get for it."

"Nice work, Robert. Get the picture along to forensics. The rest of you... we have to assume that Katy could be both desperate and dangerous. We'll need to mobilise the Local Support Team before we go to Bakewell."

*

"I'll only be a couple of hours, Dad," when Louise heard his fake sigh, she knew she could win him round. "I promised a friend from work that I'd meet her gran. She's cooking dinner especially, but it's such a tiny flat that I can't really take Gemma. I'll be two hours tops, guaranteed."

It worked. She kissed her daughter on the head and her father on the cheek, slung a jacket over her shoulder and grabbed her bag from the hallway. Two hours of freedom, she'd better make most of it. It might not be a good idea to ask Dad to babysit again during the day; not for a while.

*

He'd felt so confident, and more than a little apprehensive when the convoy had driven away from the station. But his mood had taken a distinct nosedive now that he was accelerating away from the empty terraced house on Church Street which had been professionally cleaned in readiness for its next tenant. The property rental agency had been given false references, and no one had bothered to check. They'd already returned the woman's deposit in cash, and the forwarding address that K.B. had provided them with had turned out to be false. The most frustrating part of the morning was that the woman who both the neighbours and the agency had described to them, fitted with what little they knew about Katy.

"SOCOs may still find some hair samples to compare with those from Austen's car," he said to Adam who was sitting beside of him, looking as despondent as they both felt. "The best professional cleaners are never as good as our officers."

There was considerable heat in the late spring sunshine when Forbes suddenly pulled off the road and into a layby. He opened a window and then reached for the bar of milk chocolate in his glove box. "Let's talk this through for a few minutes, Adam. We know that Austen liked to be known as an investigative journalist. None of his colleagues were able to help us very much, but if Mr and Mrs Nott, the Woodbine neighbours, are right, then he was working on something that his colleagues were unaware of, and something he had described as a 'human interest' story. The disappearance of the Brundell couple in the middle of a storm, and the subsequent reappearance of Katy and her baby on the day that Mr Chester killed himself, are almost folklore in this area. Anything to do with them still sells newspapers today. Let's suppose that he'd been looking for Katy and her adult daughter for a while, for his article. Through Mrs Chester's will, he located the niece in Manchester, and then we know that from there he learned of the painting. He was on the same trail as us and we found it easily enough. From there he located Kat Blood or Katy Brundell as we now presume. We can only guess that he'd already found Katy's daughter and granddaughter. Maybe he had contacts in the social services departments. It's possible that someone working there gave him the name of Rose Jenkins and Anna Jenkins. Maybe he offered to arrange a family reunion. Could that have been his 'human interest' story?"

"Sir, we also know that he covered the story of the rescued girl who originated from Moldova. PC Rawlings has just discovered that Anna Jenkins had been placed into the same hospital ward as her. That was where they absconded from together, along with twins Carol and Maisie Evans. None of them have been seen since, but they're all on file as runaways so no one has been actively looking for them. Derek Austen could have recognised Anna, or seen her name, while he was at the hospital. It does fit, sir."

"So let's assume for a moment that Derek was planning a public family reunion, for a newspaper story. When he visited the Woodbine neighbours, Mr and Mrs Nott, he told them that he was doing a feature on people who'd been let down by the system which cared for those recovering from mental illnesses, didn't he? All three women were let down in some way, and their particular story was guaranteed to make local, maybe even national headlines."

"The night he was killed he must have picked up Katy after he left the pub because the landlord maintained he had no one with him. Maybe she let him think that she wanted to meet her long lost family, but actually there was no way she could risk any kind of publicity. Woodbine was on the market and it was only a matter of time before those bodies were uncovered. She would have had to silence him, and if you're right about her involvement with Mr and Mrs Chester, then she wouldn't have found it difficult. It's a chilling theory."

"It does make sense of a few things. And she'd never bothered about her own blood relatives before, so why start now? She had far more to lose than to gain. But if Katy killed Austen, and we know Rose was in the hospital during that particular night, then it must have been her granddaughter, Anna, who picked her up from the end of the road down to Derbyshire Bridge. Did Derek Austen make the mistake of giving them each other's contact details? The witnesses from both vehicles said they saw someone of a slight build. The Katy I remember was a slightly built woman. We've been looking for a girl because of the CCTV footage, and the descriptions from the other murder scenes and the fires. But if we're right, Austen's killer was actually a grandmother."

"And she's well enough to be aware that if a reporter could follow the trail of the Lowry picture, then so could the police. That could be why she moved out. So where is she now? If those two generations have joined forces, it doesn't bear thinking about, sir."

"If all of that is correct, then we've linked a lot of the dots, and we have some additional information. We know that Anna Jenkins left that hospital ward in the company of a young, pregnant, foreign girl, and a set of identical twins. None of them have been brought to the attention of the authorities since, and that would indicate that they've remained together. And they could have a baby with them by now. Contact all the maternity units in the area. As a group, they shouldn't be so difficult to find, should they?"

"I wouldn't have thought so."

"This chocolate's melting – want a piece?"

Chapter 25

His sister, Louise, had trusted Alison more than she'd trusted him, her big brother, and he was only now learning about it through a phone call. It felt like a slap in the face.

"Michael, she gave those hair samples to me because that's a part of my job, and because she was concerned about a motherless baby. She didn't tell you in case she was wrong. In her eyes you're still the mega-successful detective who she thinks she'll never live up to, but there isn't the time to massage your ego. Just listen." Alison was sounding more frantic with each sentence. "She gave me six hairs which had all been shed naturally and I told the laboratory technicians I needed the results as a matter of urgency. Without an attached hair follicle, we couldn't run a complete DNA check – hair itself doesn't contain any nuclear DNA, so we did the only reliable test available – the Mitochondrial DNA test which is used to determine whether two people share the same maternal line. One of the hairs was from a different person to the other five, but both samples produced a positive result. I ran both sets of results through the Familial DNA Database. Louise was right about that abandoned baby... she's found a close relative, most probably the mother. But the single hair turned up something which scared me. I had to call you right away. It's a familial match to the hairs found in Derek Austen's car. You're looking for a young girl, aren't you? I believe Louise works alongside both of these girls at the club."

"Can you be absolutely certain?" He hoped she was going to say the test wasn't one hundred per cent reliable.

"Yes, Michael, and we've asked her to snoop around and to ask questions. You must stop her from going back there."

"Louise doesn't start work till seven tonight; that gives us six hours. I'll call you as soon as I know that she's safe."

*

Louise stepped inside the flat and was met by a sickly sweet odour which caught in the back of her throat. She guessed a cheap air freshener had been opened in her honour, but instead of masking the cooking smells from the chip shop below, it mingled with them and thickened the atmosphere. The room felt claustrophobic. How did four girls live in this space, even without the added burden of two visitors? She'd seen larger drug dealing dens in the days when she'd regularly accompanied her junkie pals to buy what they needed to keep themselves functioning – and one or two of those hadn't smelled as bad as this, either.

Verona was sitting on a large cushion on the floor, and smiling at everyone. The scene looked wrong. If Alison confirmed her suspicions, then this fragile-looking girl should be in a comfy armchair now, feeding her baby boy, or gently rocking him to sleep.

She'd convinced herself she was right, so much so that she'd been dreaming up ways to help the girl. She could be the one to reunite them. Dad's house was way too large – Verona and the baby could have the two empty bedrooms at the back of the house, and they'd have Dad's massive garden to relax in throughout the summer. She'd even imagined her dad telling people how pleased he was that his daughter was finally thinking of others, he'd called her selfish so often over the years, and he'd been right, she had been. It wouldn't be a permanent arrangement of course, but Verona was so sweet, and Gemma might eventually have a playmate. Yes, it could work. She took a step into the room and held out the bottle of Cava.

"Come in, take a seat," Anna directed her to the empty sofa. "Gran's been dying to meet you."

Before she could sit, the twins appeared from the next room, each clutching a pair of pillows.

"Welcome to our humble abode," Maisie dropped her bundle against the wall and then hugged her.

"We haven't room for chairs," Carol explained before copying her twin's actions.

"Hullo Louise," a slim, fair haired woman turned her back on the stove, smiled, and offered out her hand. "I hope these girls didn't promise you a gourmet meal because there are limits to what anyone could cook on this tiny gas stove. I'm Kat, by the way, as my granddaughter seems too rude to introduce us properly."

Her resemblance to Anna was striking. She would have been a stunning looking woman when she was younger, and in fact still was, with cheekbones to die for and the deepest of deep blue eyes. "I'm Louise... hullo, I'm pleased to meet you. They've all been telling me how much they've been enjoying your cooking."

"We all eat off our knees, as you can see. I hope you don't mind. There's no room for a table but we're having fun, aren't we girls? Anna, would you give me a hand dishing out the meal?"

Her nostrils must have quickly grown accustomed to the atmosphere because she tasted and enjoyed every forkful of the sweet and sour pork casserole, and the mashed potatoes and mixed green vegetables. "Anna was right to praise your cooking, Kat. That was delicious, thank you."

"You're welcome my dear."

Kat looked directly into her eyes.

"My Anna tells me you're starting college in September, and that you're hoping for a career in the mortuary, working on dead people. I'm genuinely interested. Whatever made you choose that?"

Louise felt her pulse quicken. "I'm hoping to become an anatomical laboratory technician. I've always been interested in science, and from what I already know about forensic science, I think it would be a good career choice. My brother's friend works in that field and she's been encouraging me."

"Louise, humour an old lady for a moment, will you? Anna told me your surname and I felt sure that I knew it from somewhere, but I've forgotten it now. It comes with old age, you know, this forgetfulness. Would you tell me your brother's full name, just as a matter of interest, and I'll see if I can narrow it down to somewhere or something."

"Michael… his name's Michael, but he's a lot older than me. He was eighteen when I was born. Our mother died suddenly when I was just a few weeks old and my dad and my brother raised me. I don't think they did too bad a job, do you?" She smiled at them, trying to relieve the tension that she sensed the others were feeling almost as much as she was. The last thing she wanted to do was to let any of them realise that he was a DCI. She began to wish she could turn back the clock and refuse the offer of a free lunch. Nothing was worth this discomfort. All eyes were on her.

"That isn't his surname though, is it? I've lived in this area most of my life so I might know him. Does he have a surname?"

"I wouldn't think so, he doesn't socialise much."

"You mean you wouldn't think he has a surname. That can't be right." She was smiling but the gesture didn't go any further than the corners of her mouth.

Louise had to look away from the blue eyes that quizzed her without any further need for words. "I meant I wouldn't think that you'd know him." Her face was burning.

"You see my Anna can be a trifle nosey at times, and she uncovered your brother's name by fiddling about with your phone. You really ought to have kept it secured it with a password. That was very careless of you, Louise."

She raised her chin and stared into the woman's eyes. Discomfort was becoming fear. Maybe it was time to let them know her brother's occupation. "His name is Michael Forbes."

"And would that be Michael Forbes, the plodding policeman?" The woman angled her head slightly.

"If you know all this, why are you asking?" Her insides felt ice-cold. "He's a Detective Chief Inspector now, and he knows I'm here."

"Ah... but I'll bet you any money you like that he doesn't know who you're with, because if that was the case, trust me, you wouldn't be here at all."

"What do you mean? These girls are my friends, and I don't know you. Why wouldn't I be here?" She felt her self-control slipping. Her tongue was sticking to the roof of her mouth.

"You wouldn't be here because he won't have forgotten who I am, just like I could never forget him. When Anna told me your name, do you know what I did? I cheered. Then I began searching the good old internet. I know all about your little family."

"Whatever he does at work is nothing to do with me... I don't..."

"You see," she continued, "I once had a baby girl, only I never got to take care of her properly. I was young and I was unwell... mentally unwell... and when your brother found us, what did he do? He took my baby away. And now she's dead and I never got to say how sorry I was. Can you even imagine my pain?"

"Is... is your name Katy... Katy Brundell? I know that he's been looking for you. He wants to help you. I know he feels guilty about..."

"So... you are a bright girl, after all. What exactly has your plodding policeman brother been telling you about me?"

"That you were being treated in hospital but that you walked out. There was plenty of help for you if you'd just stayed there. Things could have turned out differently."

"They weren't helping me. This is twenty plus years ago that you're talking about. All those so called doctors knew how to do was to stuff me full of drugs. Some days I hardly knew where I was, but I knew I was too ill to look after a child without help and support. I was sane enough to recognise that fact, but they never offered me practical help. And now it's too late... now my baby's dead and I've found a beautiful granddaughter who I never knew existed. I was so gutted when I realised that she'd been in and out of mental hospitals for most of her young life. If I'd only known about her, I could have helped. We were all denied that chance. That reporter was spot on. The system failed all three of us, and it began with your brother. What do you say to that?"

"You're wrong... you're so wrong, he saved your daughter's life by taking her out of the attic room that day. He was doing his job, and he only ever wanted to do the right thing. He loves children." She glanced at Verona. It was an instinctive eye movement, but it was the wrong one.

"So you think you've worked out the story of Verona and her baby, do you? How clever of you. Well let me tell you something that you won't know. That girl is no angel. And how do I know that? I know that because she'll do anything to be a part of this little family, anything at all, and she has absolutely no conscience. But who could blame her after everything she's been through?"

"Verona's a victim. She needs counselling, professional counselling. Things are different now. It's not the same as it was when you were sick."

"You really have no idea, do you? For what she's done they won't give her counselling. They'll lock her up and throw away the key. And the irony of it is that she was only ever trying to impress my Anna."

Louise looked at the twins. They were huddled together on the floor, holding hands, their faces several shades paler than when she'd last looked. Just an arm's length away, Anna was on the floor, cradling Verona.

"It's no use looking at them," Katy leaned closer and whispered. "The twins are never going to shop their friends. If they do, they know that we'll tell everyone they were both involved. We can so easily take them down with us. They've got no one else to turn to, you see. Those girls will keep our sordid little secrets."

Words were forming in her brain but she couldn't get them out. Those terrible things – she thought she knew what they might be. She didn't want to hear her thoughts out loud. She took a deep breath and pictured her daughter sleeping in her cot. "I'll have to go now. If I'm not home for Gemma's bath time, Dad will come looking for me."

"Will he now? That's a shame. I was hoping it might be your brother who came looking for you. Of course, if he leaves it much later, there won't be any trace of you left in this flat."

"I have to go," she leaned forward but was pushed back into the sofa. She felt the anger surging through Kate's hands into both of her shoulders.

"What do you want? Let me go! I've done nothing to you!"

"It's your brother that I intend to hurt. Don't you get it yet? I've been doing my research, and I know that you are the closest thing he has to a child. He took away my child, so I'm going to return the favour."

"He was only doing his job, he..."

"Doing his job..." her voice rose to a screech. "Doing his job cost me what small bit of sanity I had left. The only home I could remember by the time I got out of that nuthouse was Woodbine Cottage, and the only people I remembered were Mr and Mrs Chester. I didn't even remember that Ian had killed himself. What could I do except crawl back to that house of sexual depravity and death? I knew of nothing else. I couldn't even remember where my parents were. Your so-called experts had trashed what was left of my brain. It was months before I felt any better."

"But you're better now. You don't have to make things worse for yourself... and what about Anna? You can't want to ruin her life."

"Things can't get any worse for either of us. Don't you want to hear the rest of my story?"

"I don't need to know. Just let me go."

"Not going to happen... just sit there and listen. The old pervert, Ian, he was dead but he'd left Mrs Chester nicely provided for. She welcomed me back as her skivvy and when I was feeling stronger she sometimes allowed me to take the van into town. I worked the occasional nights on the streets, just for the odd bit of excitement, and to get a few pounds of my own. But when it came to money, I didn't need much.

Elizabeth was generous enough when the mood took her. She rewarded me handsomely when I brought a girl back with me to Woodbine. We had our fun with them for a week or two, sometimes even a month or two, just like in the days before Mr Chester fell sick, and then it was my job to dump the bodies. Am I shocking you, Louise? We didn't do it all that often."

"They've found them... they're looking for you... they're..."

"They've found the bodies, yes, that was inevitable, and that's why I had to kill that reporter. He'd found us, you see. He wanted a grand family reunion for his newspaper. He wanted to make money out of our tragic story. He was even taking me to a hotel that night. I was to stay there so that the next day he could come along and set it all up. Can you imagine it, me in the papers, grinning like a Cheshire cat at a wonderful family reunion? Some joke... eh?"

Louise sensed movement on the sofa beside her.

"That's where I came in," Anna was saying.

She listened, her eyes refusing to focus on anything and her heart pounding.

"Gran only killed that reporter to protect us. We would have been freaks as far as everyone else was concerned. He'd already given us each other's phone numbers – that was clever of Gran to persuade him to do that. She told him she needed to talk to me first, as proof that I existed. I was expecting her call that night, and I picked her up from the moors. That was the first time we'd met. It was a beautiful night. Poor Gran, she saw me looking at the blood on her clothing and thought I'd be shocked when she described what she'd done, and how she'd made it look like a sexual killing. But nothing she did could ever shock me. I assured her it was all right. I told her I understood. I told her how I'd fantasised about taking revenge on the men who'd wormed their way into my mother's bed. And then it just hit me – if we both killed in the same way, I'd have some kind of revenge and there would be a bond between the two of us that no one could ever break. So out I went, onto the dark street corners of Leaburn. I'd never done anything like that before, but Carl Deakin was only too willing. He was pathetic – he was so easy to kill. I left him on the pavement, drowning in his own blood, but not before I'd wrapped his tie around one of his wrists, just as Gran had done with that reporter. I liked that touch."

"Verona...?" She shook her head – it was a feeble attempt at defiance. When she stopped, everything in the room was still blurred. Tears trickled down her face.

"Verona won't help you," Anna tilted her head towards the girl and smiled. "She's in this every bit as deeply as we are. She overheard us discussing how we'd made the murders look so similar. It's remarkable how her English has come along, don't you think? The poor girl wanted so much to belong to a family that she sneaked out one night while we were at work, did the deed, and the next morning proudly showed us a blood-stained knife. She'd taken the knife that we'd both used, and she'd actually killed that bloke – Peter Stansfield. We were gobsmacked, weren't we Gran? Way to go Verona!"

They were all looking at the girl on the floor.

The sound of traffic from the road below roared in her ears.

There were only two doors in the flat – one to the bedroom – no good, and one to the corridor. Had they locked that behind her? She hadn't noticed.

The full-length window overlooking the street was her only escape route. She forced herself not to look and tried to picture it from memory.

It had been partly open... hadn't it?

Beyond it were bars, but only about four foot high.

She could clear those, if she had an uninterrupted run at them. She'd fall... but... what was she thinking... Anna was a prankster, she'd proved that. What if this was nothing more than a sick joke they'd cooked up between them?

But Anna's grandmother...? Everything she'd said fitted with the murders... and she knew about Michael... and the look in her eyes...

Her vision cleared enough to focus on what Anna's grandmother held in her right hand. A four-inch long blade glinted in the rays of sun streaming through the window.

"What... what are you doing?"

"You're a bright girl. You'll work it out."

She turned to Anna. "This isn't funny... your gran's scaring me. Tell her to stop."

"She scares me sometimes, but then that's a family trait of our, isn't it gran. And I'm sorry, Louise, really I am, but this is no joking matter. One way or another, you're going to die here today."

Chapter 26

"Dad, I'm outside the Club. Where's Louise? She's not answering her phone and I need to talk to her, urgently?" His knuckles were white against his steering wheel and Adam had put his phone onto speaker.

"We agreed not to hassle her. She should be home in the next half an hour. What's...?"

"Dad, this could be a matter of life and death – Louise's. Now think, did she tell you where she was going?"

"She's with her new friends – the ones from the club. Someone's grandmother is cooking dinner for them, I think she said. I don't have the address."

He turned to Adam. "Get in there and pray they've got an address for those girls."

"Dad, listen, it's vital that you phone me straight away if you hear from Louise. I'm going to try to find her, but don't let Gemma out of your sight, and don't answer the door to anyone."

It took ten frustrating minutes to reach the Tasty Fryer, twice the time it should have taken because of an accident blocking the main road.

He could see nothing beyond the small group of people on the pavement in front of the chip shop. At least one of them was kneeling over something. His legs almost buckled as he jumped from the car, leaving the engine running and the car door bouncing on its hinges.

Sirens screamed somewhere in the distance. It was all he heard before he fell onto his knees and recognised the dark stain spreading across his sister's blouse.

She was breathing.

That was good.

"We've called for an ambulance," a woman said. "She just jumped. There was a lot of screaming from the room she jumped from. I don't know what's happened up there."

"No one's left the building," a man added.

If only he could breathe for her.

Anything to keep her alive while the sirens grew louder.

"Stand back please." Adam's voice sounded distant.

He was the Senior Investigating Officer - this was his case and he was meant to be in charge.

None of his officers even paused to acknowledge him as they rushed past him into the shop and clattered up the stairs.

The ambulance arrived and he stepped back, willing the paramedics to perform their magic. He tried to take stock of the situation. From the flat where Louise had either jumped or been pushed, female voices were alternately sobbing and screaming.

"We need paramedics up here... now," Adam shouted down through the open window.

"Can you manage the scene?" he shouted up to him.

"Yes, sir, you go with Louise." Adam held his hand out level, a signal they'd developed between them to signify a fatality. "I'll call you."

Chapter 27

At eight o'clock in the evening he finally arrived back at the station and saw from the car park that none of his team had gone home. A violent death had that effect on them. They wanted justice for the victim, whatever that victim had been guilty of before that final day.

That was what made his reception all the more surprising.

He couldn't remember, at any other time in his career, ever being greeted with a round of applause. Everyone in the incident room was on their feet.

"Louise is going to make a full recovery, isn't she, sir?" PC Gary Rawlings spoke first.

"She's going to be just fine, thank you. I don't think any of us appreciated just how tough my little sister is. She has a fractured pelvis and a slight concussion from a fall which would have killed some people, and a flesh wound to her abdomen from a knife which had already killed three grown men. But believe me – she knows how lucky she is. What's the news on the other three girls?"

"The twins will most probably be given bail," DS Adam Ross had just switched off his phone. "The sister of their deceased foster mother has been in contact with the courts and offered them a home. Apparently she'd known the twins for most of their lives and felt she'd be letting her late sister down if she didn't offer to help the girls. Their solicitor is arguing that they'd been influenced by peer pressure. They'd been too afraid of Anna Jenkins to speak out, or to walk away, and of course their flat came with their jobs and they needed both. Louise's initial statement has backed up their story."

"A tragic outcome, all the same," DC Robert Bell added his thoughts. "When Katy Brundell lunged forward with that knife, she couldn't have expected Anna to move so quickly. From what we've heard, Anna Jenkins saved Louise's life by losing her own."

Forbes felt unexpectedly emotional. "But it wasn't a selfless action. We think she was trying to grab hold of Louise to prevent her from escaping from them when she took the full force of her grandmother's forward lunge, resulting in a single stab wound to her heart. That allowed Louise the time to stumble to the open window, from where she was in such a state of panic that she jumped to the pavement. If she hadn't, she'd almost certainly be dead now. As it is, we have one more body to add to this tragic case."

DS Ross stepped forward. "I don't know if you've heard, sir, Katy Brundell has been charged with the murder of her own granddaughter while we sort out how many of the deaths she was responsible for at Woodbine."

"It was a harrowing scene when we opened the door to the flat, sir." PC Gary Rawlings added. "Katy was cradling Anna in her arms, but the girl was obviously already dead. The window to the street was wide open but the other three girls were huddled together on a single bed in the other room, all sobbing their hearts out."

"Has anyone any news on Verona?" PC Vivien Harrison spoke up from the side of the room.

"The abandoned baby was hers and she admitted to leaving him," DC Robert Bell had been in touch with the social services. "For now he'll have to remain in foster care. She's been charged with the murder of Peter Stansfield, but she needs psychiatric assessment before anything further can be done. I can't see that she'll ever get custody of the child, even if she wanted it, which she says she doesn't. He was the result of her long-term abuse."

"A tragic case all round," someone added.

Forbes walked to the nearest desk and perched himself on its corner. His legs had suddenly felt weak. "So here we go again..." he said quietly, "with an unstable young woman who wants nothing more to do with her own child. Wasn't that the pivotal point of this case all those years ago?"

He hadn't noticed Alison walking into the room.

"But this time we'll make sure that the outcome is different," she said, taking his right hand between both of hers and squeezing it.

The gesture embarrassed him. He looked down at a picture of Verona on the desk and tried to pull his hand away, but Alison was holding on tight.

She continued speaking to the whole room and she had everyone's full attention. "I intend to take a personal interest in both Verona and her infant son. They've been victims for most of their young lives, and I'm hoping that this department will help to make sure that the system provides them with all the help that they need – in the short term and in the long term, whatever form that help may take."

DCI Forbes had never shed a tear in front of his colleagues before, but it had been one hell of a day. He squeezed her hand back. Every word that this woman was saying was making him love her even more. He couldn't hold back any longer.

Another round of applause erupted when Alison kissed his wet cheek.

It was going to be months before he lived this down.

ENDS

Serene Valley Kill

Sylvia Marsden

The body of a young woman who has recently given birth is found in a ditch. Her identity and the whereabouts of her child remain a mystery.

College boys are being run down and left for dead and a small rural community closes ranks and points a finger at a particular group of women.

A female officer on DCI Forbes's team is drawn deeper into the investigation until her life becomes in danger, and DCI Forbes comes to an uncomfortable realisation in a case which extends to neighbouring counties and a distant decade.

Mine To Kill

Sylvia Marsden

Is the abduction of a teenager linked to a deceased serial killer, or are other dark forces at work in the limestone hills of Derbyshire?

Old cases return to haunt DCI Forbes and shadow his attempts to find Debbie. He is acting on instinct, unaware of the race against time that he and his team are in.

Debbie is also acting on instinct, but for her it's a matter of survival – she knows how many days she has left in her terrifying, underground world.

Mary Stone is a city girl, becoming increasingly uncomfortable after moving from the environment she's always known. Is she being paranoid or has she allowed herself and her young daughters to be placed in danger? And if so, is that danger very close to home, or not?

Kill For Luck

Sylvia Marsden

How far would *you* go to change your luck?
For DCI Forbes, the discovery of body parts on a moor produces a worrying link to his station. He becomes concerned that his colleagues and their families have become targets.

When the financially compromised, little butcher's assistant with the unfortunate nickname of *Beetle,* is handed an opportunity to become a *killer for hire,* he hopes it might be just what he needs to change his luck and his fortunes.

His first attempt at murder goes disastrously wrong, leaving him afraid for his own life and with two bodies to dispose of.

Then fate lends a hand and his victims seem to be falling over themselves to die for him. His luck has finally changed for the better and he begins to believe that maybe, just maybe, the one thing he wants above all else is finally within his reach.

But someone is watching.

47805911R00151

Made in the USA
Middletown, DE
14 June 2019